SOULLESS FURY

NECROMUNDA®

SOULLESS FURY

WILL McDERMOTT

ENJOY THE CHASE

Will McDermott

BLACK LIBRARY

A BLACK LIBRARY PUBLICATION

First published in Great Britain in 2020 by
Black Library,
Games Workshop Ltd.,
Willow Road,
Nottingham, NG7 2WS, UK.

10 9 8 7 6 5 4 3 2 1

Produced by Games Workshop in Nottingham.
Cover illustration by Neil Roberts.

ISBN 13: 978-1-78999-083-6

See Black Library on the internet at

blacklibrary.com

Find out more about Games Workshop
and the world of Warhammer 40,000 at

games-workshop.com

Printed and bound by CPI Group (UK) Ltd, Croydon, CR0 4YY

---

*To my editor, William Moss, who brought me back in after years of
wandering the White Wastes. His invaluable guidance helped me imbed
this story more firmly into the deep foundations of Hive Primus and freed
me to give voice to two truly remarkable characters.*

In order to even begin to understand the blasted world of Necromunda you must first understand the hive cities. These man-made mountains of plasteel, ceramite and rockrete have accreted over centuries to protect their inhabitants from a hostile environment, so very much like the termite mounds they resemble. The Necromundan hive cities have populations in the billions and are intensely industrialised, each one commanding the manufacturing potential of an entire planet or colony system compacted into a few hundred square kilometres.

The internal stratification of the hive cities is also illuminating to observe. The entire hive structure replicates the social status of its inhabitants in a vertical plane. At the top are the nobility, below them are the workers, and below the workers are the dregs of society, the outcasts. Hive Primus, seat of the planetary governor Lord Helmawr of Necromunda, illustrates this in the starkest terms. The nobles – Houses Helmawr, Cattalus, Ty, Ulanti, Greim, Ran Lo and Ko'Iron – live in the 'Spire', and seldom set foot below the 'Wall' that exists between themselves and the great forges and hab zones of the hive city proper.

Below the hive city is the 'Underhive', foundation layers of habitation domes, industrial zones and tunnels which have been abandoned in prior generations, only to be re-occupied by those with nowhere else to go.

But... humans are not insects. They do not hive together well. Necessity may force it, but the hive cities of Necromunda remain internally divided to the point of brutalisation and outright violence being an everyday fact of life. The Underhive, meanwhile, is a thoroughly lawless place, beset by gangs and renegades, where only the strongest or the most cunning survive. The Goliaths, who believe firmly that might is right; the matriarchal, man-hating Escher; the industrial Orlocks; the technologically minded Van Saar; the Delaque, whose very existence depends on their espionage network; the fiery zealots of the Cawdor. All striving for the advantage that will elevate them, no matter how briefly, above the other houses and gangs of the Underhive.

Most fascinating of all is when individuals attempt to cross the monumental physical and social divides of the hive to start new lives. Given social conditions, ascension through the hive is nigh on impossible, but descent is an altogether easier, albeit altogether less appealing, possibility.

– excerpted from Xonariarius the Younger's
Nobilite Pax Imperator – the Triumph
of Aristocracy over Democracy.

CHAPTER 1

SLUDGE TOWN

Kordon Brann surveyed the dingy little town he'd built in one of the underhive's deepest holes and mused about his lot in life. *If there is one constant in the universe*, he thought, *it is this: crap runs downhill.*

Brann, a young businessman with big plans, knew that for every ruler sitting on a throne, living in luxury under sparkling stars at the top of the world, there must be uncountable serfs and peasants living in squalor, hip-deep in the murky runoff that collects at the bottom of the heap.

This was never more true than within Hive Primus, the largest and most impressive (and most oppressive) hive city on Necromunda. The glittering spire reaching to the heavens kilometres above was just the tiny tip of an immense, grubby iceberg. Filled with fat, wealthy, clean nobles, it sat above the nightmarish rioting masses of Hive City, and the vast wasteland of a planet stripped clean of natural resources.

The wealth of the entire world had been syphoned off

over the centuries to feed the gluttonous desires of those few noble houses, while the common people toiled their lives away at the bottom, amidst the accumulated muck, dust and effluvia of the vast complex.

And yet for some, like Kordon Brann, there was still a glimmer of hope for a better life. While most denizens of the underhive's numerous settlements were content to lie low and make a meagre living outside the oppressive conditions of Hive City, some ventured forth into the depths to seek their fortunes.

The heartiest and foolhardiest hunted the sump-spiders in the toxic lake at Hive Bottom. The adventurous searched for hidden pockets of long-lost archeotech that remained as yet uncrushed by centuries of settling domes. Others simply scavenged whatever they could sell. Plasteel piping, rockcrete fittings, copper wiring and clean water all brought handsome sums of scrip to the right buyers. Even humans, when they had been deemed waste in the eyes of the law, could be sold, making bounty-hunting a growth industry in the underhive.

There was an old saying in the underhive that Kordon Brann had taken to heart: one man's waste is another man's profit.

Wherever waste products formed in the underhive – whether they trickled down or bubbled up – some guilder would come along and find a way to make a profit from that waste. Take corpse-starch, for example. The dead were not done working for the hive. Without that proteyn, every hive on Necromunda would starve. When some new use for a waste product was found, someone always got rich; normally the first guilder to recognise the potential of that waste.

Thus was Sludge Town born.

Residents of Dust Falls, the border settlement lying between the edge of Hive City and the underhive, knew of the sludge pits burrowed deep into the White Wastes beyond their borders. Within the layers of ancient domes crushed together beneath those cliffs lay a vast manufactoria labyrinth that stretched for kilometres underground. The level below the manufactoria was filled with thousands upon thousands of vats' worth of sludge, the accumulated toxic runoff from a dozen decades of industry.

No sane soul had ventured into those levels since the manufactoria had closed more than two generations past. Rats had ruled the floor, while creatures more foul had lived in and slithered among the vats. That all changed a decade ago when an enterprising (and too-trusting) archeochemist named Scoot Hunder devised a process for safely extracting and storing promethium – the liquid fuel upon which all of Hive Primus runs – from the sludge.

This new fuel source would have made Scoot rich beyond his wildest dreams if he hadn't had an unfortunate accident in the sludge pits shortly after demonstrating his process to a young and industrious guilder looking to prove himself and make his fortune. With the initial backing of the guild, Kordon Brann began building the infrastructure to collect and refine the sludge into promethium.

Within a year, Sludge Town, housed on the manufactoria floor above the pits, was bustling with residents. People came where credits were, after all. The shells of behemoth machines that once formed plasteel pilings or the giant rockcrete slabs used in dome construction, their internal workings long ago stripped clean, were converted into buildings to house the gamut of establishments required by a boom town: markets, supply stores, saloons, gambling dens and pleasure houses.

Windows and doors were cut into sheet-metal housings and holes bored through the tops to allow for ventilation. Long-dead machines that once produced the walls, doors and roofs of manufactured buildings had unironically been converted into tract housing for workers. Power for the entire settlement was supplied by the first sludge convertors to be brought online.

Unfortunately for Kordon Brann, the sludge pits were only just starting to turn a profit. In addition to the enormous investment needed to bring the sludge convertors online and transport promethium off the side of a cliff, cost overruns, bribes and gang-related damage had kept Brann's books in the red, forcing him to plead for more time and more funds from his nominal superiors. Brann's visions of rising above this squalor and finding his place amongst the Spire-born were quickly fading. If things didn't turn around soon, Brann knew he would be replaced as plant director – permanently.

'This is your year, Kordon,' Brann told himself as he stood on the balcony outside his office and surveyed the early morning shift change. Below him, sufficiently rested and lubricated workers stumbled out of their cramped sheet-metal homes, where they lived with dozens of others, and shambled towards the ramps that would take them to the pits. They barely nodded at the wearier crews heading towards off-shift activities before crashing for a few hours of rest until the cycle started all over again.

What Kordon called a balcony was, in reality, the roof of a control room that jutted off the side of the ancient two-storey-tall machine, which had been turned into the main offices of the Mercator Pyros sludge operation. He had insisted his office have access to this roof so he could better monitor the town and his workers. To be honest, it was the only bit of status Kordon Brann had been able to wrangle out of this cursed enterprise. At least some crap could still run downhill, past him.

As the streets started to clear, Kordon allowed himself a moment to imagine a brighter future for himself. If production continued to ramp up as he knew it could, and he became responsible for a lucrative new source of promethium, there was no telling what heights he could reach in the guild. Who could deny him his rightful place within the upper echelons? How much of the smell of this place could he finally get out of his skin?

Kordon considered reaching out to his Mercator Nautica contact about a bathtub, but he knew the guilder would inflate the costs of the tub and the supply of water it would need. It would negatively impact his bottom line.

'Not to mention that excessive bathing is seen as sinful in the eyes of the redeemer,' Kordon chuckled. 'But then, what isn't?'

Brann glanced down the main street towards the large building at the other end of Sludge Town, which House Cawdor had claimed for its own. It was by far the largest of the converted machines that made up the town. Rumour had it that the three-storey-tall manufactorum had once produced battleship plating for some off-world noble house's fleet.

The machine had been deemed perfect as a meeting place for the numerous Cawdor workers that Brann had been forced to hire early on. Brann hadn't minded. The Cawdor worked hard, cheaply, and were easy to manipulate with a little theatre. As a house with little to no industry of their own, their most valuable assets were the lives of their people.

So, the director gave House Cawdor the flagship building at the edge of town while he worked in a much smaller converted machine. He looked the other way when the Cawdor workers stole small trinkets they had found in the sludge vats.

They all thought they were being so sly, but Brann knew exactly what was going on. Most Cawdor were devout Redemptionists who spent their lives scavenging through the refuse of the Hive, hoping to unearth blessed relics from the past. The sludge pits and the Cawdor were a natural match that Kordon had no problem profiting from... at least while he was forced to do so.

But then the religious services had started. House Cawdor had turned the main floor of their building into a church and held regular services inside that all workers were required to attend. In fact, the heat stack rising up into the dome above from one end of the half-kilometre long machine had been turned into a church steeple, complete with the mark of the Cult of the Redemption.

Brann understood the power of the church better than most. A good dose of religious fervour helped keep the masses in line. A strong sermon helped make workers pliable to obeying orders that often went against a more rebellious mind's sense of self-preservation. And the occasional burning of a heretic kept the worst of those minds in check, while offering a nice spectacle for everyone else.

As Brann watched, the more zealous stragglers among the overnight shift shuffled past the drinking holes, brothels and gambling dens towards the Cawdor shrine. All of these distractions were of equal value to Brann. Anything these workers could latch on to to make their off-hours pass without incident and that re-energised them for their next shift was good for the guild.

Of course, Brann was open with his faith. All Promethium Guilders abased themselves before the God-Emperor in his aspect as the Eternal Flame, and no aspirant to the upper echelons of the guild could afford to be seen as less than entirely devout. He could recite the prayers and devotions to the letter. But truth be told, Brann's pragmatic nature had never allowed him to cross the line from flourished recitation to fanaticism. He'd never seen the profit in believing too deeply. To Brann, it was one tool amongst many.

As the last score of stragglers from the overnight shift milled around the various distractions that Main Street provided, Brann heard shouting coming from the ramps behind him. His first thought was that another vat had broken open, spilling a tidal wave of sludge that would drown his workers and eat into his profits. He'd lost more money and employees that way than he ever had to gang violence.

But then the sharp retort of gunfire echoed through the cavern, immediately followed by the bloodcurdling screams of valuable employees dying.

'Damnit,' hissed Brann. 'Another scavving gang attack?' He ran to the other side of the balcony to get a better look. 'They always attack at shift change. My venators know that. Where are they?'

Brann got his answer as soon as he reached the edge of the balcony. Six members of the venator gang he'd hired to guard the vats lined the sides of a tunnel cut into the floor of the cavern. As Brann watched, they fired autoguns and stub pistols into the tunnel that led down to the vat level.

More screams emanated from down the ramp followed by a great gout of blood and gore and, Brann swore, a severed head that flew up into view before falling back down through the hole in the floor.

To their credit, the venators kept firing while they backed away from the entrance, the lead one shouting at the others.

'They're scavving unstoppable! What the hell is–'

His exclamation was cut short by a crack of thunder as a superheated stream of plasma vaporised the venator's chest, dissolving him into a pink sludge. The rest of the venators retreated from the edge of the tunnel hole, but not before a second peal of thunder echoed through the cavern and another dissolved from a second plasma bolt.

Brann's feet and legs felt like lumps of lead, rooting him to the spot despite the obvious danger to him if the four remaining venators broke ranks and ran. They weren't the best, but they were what he could afford, and were more loyal than Brann deserved. The four survivors moved back and formed a line facing the tunnel opening.

What emerged was like nothing Brann had ever seen before. The monstrous beast stood at least two metres tall and its barrel-shaped chest was nearly a metre across. Its legs and arms were as big around as the torsos of the vena-tors facing it. What looked like conspicuously well-made albeit worn armour plates were strapped across its shoul-ders and centre-mass. It carried a shield as big as a door in one hand and a metal club the size of a normal man's leg in the other.

The venators opened fire as soon as the beast's metal-plated face appeared, but their autoguns and stub-pistol shots bounced off the creature. Once it cleared the hole, the beast roared and slammed its massive club against its shield as if in challenge. The venators dropped their projectile weapons and drew long fighting knives, axes and flails. But none were brave, or dumb, enough to be the first to advance.

Brann wasn't sure what the beast was waiting for. From his vantage point, it could easily take out the venators with a single sweep of that gigantic club. Behind him, Brann heard another squad of his venators rushing down Main Street to join the battle. Perhaps this fight could still swing in his favour.

That's when he heard it. The grating, metallic sound of grinding gears and whining motors echoed through the caverns as a chainsword thrummed to life. Behind the beast, another figure climbed the ramp and strode into view.

Although standing nearly as tall as the beast, any similarities ended there. Instead of metal plates and heavy, textile clothing, the second attacker, a well-toned and muscular woman, wore a string of pearls around her neck and a black leather corset adorned with raven feathers atop an ebony lace skirt that fluttered in the air venting up from promethium refineries down on the pit level.

Flat black boots pounded the floor as she strode forward, her chainsword swinging in a dangerous arc around a powdered wig adorned with stained ornaments atop her head. She would have radiated an air of dangerous elegance if the fabric hadn't been so tattered, the feathers cracked and bare in spots, and the wig not streaked with soot and dirt.

'What are you waiting for, Dog?' growled the woman at her companion. 'Attack!'

The beast and the woman charged. The air filled with the reverberating whine of the chainsword and the screams of venators. One was cut nearly clean through from her left shoulder to her right hip with a mighty swing of the thrumming blade. Another venator dropped to the ground missing both arms.

The terror and ferocity of the attack and a deep dread of the attacker – the most recognisable and feared lunatic in the underhive – finally freed Brann's feet from the imagined cement that had rooted him to the roof. He ran to the town side of the balcony and yelled at the oncoming reinforcements.

'Protect my office,' he cried. 'Inside. Now! Do not engage! It's Mad Donna!'

CHAPTER 2

SCRUTINATOR PRIMUS

Lord Gerontius Helmawr, planetary governor of Necromunda, sat in his office atop Hive Primus behind a giant oak desk he had imported from a world he had forgotten the name of at a cost that would have fed most of a large underhive settlement for a decade. Helmawr was at once the most feared and the most hated man in all Necromunda because of the vast powers he wielded to maintain control of the general populace below the Spire and punish political rivals within it.

Despite this, Helmawr was not an imposing figure of a man. His balding head sat atop a round, pudgy body that he kept covered by the raiment of state in court. His impressive attire – long, embroidered cloak, high-collared linen shirts, wide, curtain-like epaulets, an ornamental breastplate – made him look much more statuesque and much less like a pear.

In the privacy of his office, though, Helmawr eschewed all that frippery for a simple, silk tunic belted below his prodigious waist by a strap made from real leather, and soft, satin leggings. Despite being descended from generations of lazy, decadent rulers, Gerontius Helmawr knew the value of hard work. He demanded it from every inhabitant of the world, including himself.

Without the labour of every downtrodden resident of Hive City and the underhive, the royal coffers would not over-flow, and the Imperial Tithe would not be met. Without his own diligence, the noble houses would rebel, against him or one another, more often than they already did. His duty was eternal.

Helmawr pored over reports on everything from underhive gang activity levels – which he was happy to see at a healthy high frequency, giving the people a pastime that helped to keep resource consumption down – to promethium and corpse-starch production, which both lagged enough to keep the populace hungry and pliable without dropping to the point where they were forced to action. Riots damaged quotas.

Helmawr couldn't take an active role in every problem faced by the millions of residents of the Spire, but he did like to keep apprised of leading indicators that affected the peace of the hive. One such report had caught his eye this morning and he had called for his lord chamberlain. The overly officious man entered Helmawr's office and bowed so low his combed-back hair almost flopped forward onto the marble floor.

'You summoned me, my lord,' said the man, after rising. Helmawr hadn't yet found the need to remember the name of his current chamberlain, the latest in a long line of offi-cials to hold the post since he had lost his long-time servant, Stiv Harper.

'Have you seen the damage reports from Mad D'onne's

latest rampage through the underhive?' asked the lord, waving a vellum report in the air.

'I have, my lord,' replied the chamberlain. 'Taken together with other gang-related destruction, the costs remain within acceptable limits. Her recent activity should not affect the quarterly bottom line one iota.'

'This is damage from one woman!' shouted Helmawr. 'A woman of noble birth no less. It sets a dangerous precedent. What are we doing about this?'

'We dispatched the scrutinator primus to track down and capture D'onne, my lord,' replied the chamberlain.

Helmawr sat back in his padded chair and steepled his pudgy fingers in front of his face. 'The pariah woman,' he said, thoughtfully. 'Gave me a stomach ache being in the same room with her when she was presented with my royal seal.' He shuddered slightly at the memory.

'Servalen, yes,' said the chamberlain. 'She is uniquely qualified for the job, my lord. Your seal gives her the power to follow her prey anywhere, and as a null, witnesses may be more afraid of her than they are of Sylvanus Ulanti's crazy daughter.'

Helmawr nodded, but then his face clouded over. 'That house,' he murmured. 'They have been effective, albeit unpredictable. Have Mad D'onne brought to me when she is captured. She may prove to be the insurance we need.'

Scrutinator Primus Servalen stepped into the small, dark room and eyed her suspect, a brutish Goliath ganger with more scars than muscles. The dimly lit room served Servalen's purposes perfectly. From the stains splashed across the rockcrete walls and floor to the numerous, forehead-shaped dents in the plasteel table where the Goliath sat, it was obvious this room had been the site of many interrogations in the past. The type where questions were asked with fists and answers given in blood.

This would not be that type of interrogation, but that had nothing to do with the size difference between the suspect and the scrutinator. As soon as Servalen, a senior member of the special investigative arm of the palanite enforcers, locked eyes with the hulking brute, there was no question who was in charge. The Goliath shivered under her gaze and instantly dropped his eyes to the floor.

People hated being in the same room as Servalen, and the feeling went far beyond the effect of her stern demeanour. No. It was that prolonged periods in her presence made most people squirm as if some multi-limbed underhive bugs had got into their clothing and started crawling around. Worse yet, if she stared, it began to feel like those bugs were burrowing through your flesh looking for suitable spots to lay their eggs. Or so people whispered when they thought the scrutinator wasn't listening.

Servalen's gaze didn't so much burrow into a recidivist's soul as worm its way into the deepest, darkest recesses of their fears and anxieties and begin playing out every unimaginable horror their subconscious had ever dredged up to splash across their worst nightmares. Her blank stare was the most effective interrogation tactic ever devised.

'Nice room, isn't it?' said Servalen as she slipped into the chair opposite the Goliath.

The brute lunged, straining at the chains that held his legs and arms locked into plasteel rings bolted to the floor. A metal mastiff, previously silent by the door, growled a raspy warning at the ganger.

'Sit, KB-88,' Servalen commanded, still staring at the

Goliath. She hadn't flinched. 'Everything is fine.' The cyber-mastiff sat with a clank on the rockcrete floor next to her as she looked into the ganger's large, scarred face and smiled. 'Isn't that right, scarhead?'

'Grengor,' replied the Goliath. He tried to sit up straight and puff out his chest, but the chains kept him in a permanent crouch. 'Grengor the Terrible! I ain't got nothing to say to you.'

'That's fine, scarboy,' said Servalen. 'I'll talk.' Without removing her gaze from Grengor's face, Servalen waved her arms in an arc in front of her. 'You see this room?' she asked. 'I find it interesting that we find ourselves in such a place in your gang's hideout.'

'Why?' asked Grengor. His right eye, which was crossed by not one but three different scars, twitched as if he couldn't keep himself from responding.

Servalen smiled. 'This room does not scream "Goliath", does it?' she said. 'Your kind are not big on back-room torture. You're more the "rip arms off enemies until someone talks" type, right?'

Grengor had no response to that. Servalen paused, noticing that both the Goliath's eyes were twitching. His plasteel chair squeaked against the rockcrete floor as the Goliath squirmed in his seat.

'If I had to guess – which I don't,' continued Servalen, 'this room and the attached warehouse where your gang has been living are owned by House Delaque.'

'So?' hissed the Goliath, his normally booming voice reduced to a whisper. Grengor's eyes were red with worry, and sweat was beading up on his bald head and dripping down his face, following the paths of his many scars.

'This is where I offer you a lifeline,' said Servalen. 'I don't give a plague-rat's ass about you or your oversized scarboy gang. Why would I care about the pitiful lives and gruesome deaths of scum like you in some random underhive hole? I want the monster who's running weapons into Hive City without Iron Guild approval – guns that are being used by recidivists to disrupt legal business operations and interfere with the flow of house trade.'

'I can't–' said Grengor, his bravado deflated. Every ounce of strength seemed to have vacated his giant body and his head dropped onto the table. 'I won't.'

'You will,' said Servalen. She reached out and laid a palm on the Goliath's bald head. Grengor cringed and gasped at the touch as if her hand burned. 'Give me the name and you're free to go. You'll never see me again.'

'Never?' asked Grengor, a spark of hope tinging his voice.

'I promise,' said Servalen, patting his head for emphasis.

'Kev'n,' said Grengor, the name sounding more like a grunt than a response. 'Kev'n Askal.'

'See? That wasn't so hard, was it?' said Servalen. She stood and walked towards the door, stopping to pat the mastiff's metal head on her way out. KB-88 sniffed at Grengor and then, reassured the Goliath was no threat to anyone, padded out of the room behind its master.

Servalen and KB-88 made their way through the grubby, battle-scarred offices back to the warehouse where a squad of enforcers were guarding and cataloguing the haul of weapons they'd confiscated.

The lead enforcer, a sergeant, looked up and saluted. 'Orders, ma'am?' he said, the same look of dread in his eyes that Servalen had seen in the Goliath's scarred orbs during the interrogation.

Servalen hardly noticed the sergeant's reaction. It wasn't

his fault, she knew. It happened to her everywhere she went. 'Impound the illegal ordnance and escort Grengor's gang down to Hive Bottom and drop them in the deepest, darkest hole you can find. I want them as far from Hive City as humanly possible.'

'Understood, ma'am,' said the sergeant, producing a smirk despite his discomfort. He turned to his men to continue his work, but then snapped his fingers as Servalen walked away.

'Ma'am?' he called to her from behind. 'A message came in over the vox for you. There's been another D'onne attack.'

Servalen stopped dead in her tracks and turned on the sergeant, giving him the full force of her gaze. 'When did the call come in, sergeant?' she asked. KB-88 growled at its master's stern tone.

The sergeant shrank back but rallied quickly. He was a palanite enforcer after all. 'Fifteen minutes ago, ma'am,' he replied.

'Give me that vox,' she snapped. 'You should have pulled me out of the interrogation. A caryatid could have broken that scar-faced buffoon.'

The sergeant handed over the vox without comment and turned back to his task, studiously avoiding making eye contact with her.

Servalen thumbed on the vox and spoke into it. 'Scrutinator Primus Servalen checking in,' she said. 'Repeat recent report on activity involving D'onne Astride Ge'Sylvanus of House Ulanti, also known as Mad D'onne.'

Servalen listened to the report, which was sketchy at best. A frantic call had come in from Sludge Town that two attackers matching the descriptions of D'onne and her ogryn bodyguard were seen fighting a local gang at the edge of town. Contact with the caller was cut off before they could get further details. The call came in a half-hour earlier, so D'onne could still be there.

'Sergeant,' called Servalen. She tossed the vox back to him when he turned to face her. 'New orders!'

'Yes, ma'am?' replied the sergeant, coming to attention.

'Assign a detail to transport the contraband to the nearest precinct-fortress,' she said. 'You and your squad are with me. We move out in five.'

'What about the prisoners?' asked the sergeant. 'You still want them escorted to Hive Bottom?'

'What prisoners?' asked Servalen.

'The Goliath gangers, ma'am.'

'Listen to me closely, sergeant,' Servalen said, her words punctuated like a staccato beat meant to slap the man in the face. 'We took no prisoners. There are no prisoners. Execute them – and do it quickly. Is that understood?'

The sergeant nodded, keeping his eyes lowered to avoid Servalen's gaze.

'Five minutes,' said Servalen. 'Outside.'

With that, Scrutinator Primus Servalen turned on her heels and marched out of the warehouse, followed closely by KB-88. She stepped into the haze of the dust rain and instantly regretted leaving the warehouse. An acidic stench from the detritus mist coated the town each morning and permeated the air. Most who lived in Dust Falls stayed inside until the air recyclers kicked on and cleared the haze.

Servalen didn't want to think about what the haze was doing to her lungs, but she had noticed that the rockcrete buildings were pocked with corrosion and that every resident of Dust Falls spoke in a raspy voice, like they had smoked five packs of sticks every day for decades.

None of that mattered now. This was the first break she'd

had in the Mad D'onne case. Never before had any enforcers been this close to an attack site. The former princess of House Ulanti had stormed through town after town, leaving nothing but blood, bodies and questions in her wake. Perhaps this time, they could catch up to her and get some answers.

She kept popping up in remote sections of the underhive, seemingly with no rhyme or reason to her targets and no way for the enforcers to catch up to her before she blew out of town. Moving through the underhive was never easy; not like in Hive City, where there was transportation and, more importantly, roadways you could rely on not to end in blank walls, sheer cliffs or huge sink holes. In the underhive, the shortest distance between two points was never a straight line.

But now. Now, D'onne was practically right below Servalen's feet. Dust Falls sprawled around the Abyss, a gaping hole that dropped all the way down to Hive Bottom and the Sump Lake. Not far outside the settlement, though, lay the White Wastes, an interior sea of dust collected in a giant bowl of sunken hive layers by the currents of air recyclers over the course of millennia.

Sludge Town sat deep inside the cliffs overlooking the White Wastes, levels that stretched all the way beneath where Servalen now stood. A few years ago, the trip from Dust Falls to the sludge pits would have been torturously long and complicated. But the promise of profits always found a way to shorten supply routes and now there was a lift of sorts – little more than a cage and a crane outside town – that she could commandeer to take her to Sludge Town.

'Sergeant!' Servalen yelled through the door into the warehouse. 'Time!'

CHAPTER 3

BLOODY REDEMPTION

Mad D'onne had burned every bridge she had ever crossed and slammed shut every door that had ever opened to her. The former daughter of House Ulanti, and betrothed to a prince of House Ko'Iron, she had ended both of those relationships when she had stabbed her intended in the eye with a fork during a formal dinner.

She had found herself houseless once again when she had left her mentor to die on the Sump Lake docks to seek vengeance against yet another Ko'Iron prince.

As a former hired gun for the Orlocks, she had led a score of gangers to their deaths in search of archeotech deep in the underhive. She had returned alone, no richer than when she left, and with one less door open to her.

Some might look on Mad D'onne's life and see a series of exciting adventures, or a cursed woman trying to survive against spire-sized odds. All D'onne saw was the fight in front of her. Life was nothing but series of battles. All that mattered was getting through them alive. If that meant she needed to sink her teeth into the neck of someone trying to kill her – or get in her way – so be it.

Shoot first and cut the other guys down before they cut her down. That was life in the underhive. There was no hope of something better, no desire to improve her situation, no expectation of finding salvation or even acceptance. Just keep moving.

But then, D'onne had heard a rumour, one of the many myths that worm their way through the underhive. The big score that can set you up for life. They were rarely true, and even then, the score was more likely to kill you than reward you. But the rumour stuck in her mind, offering more than riches. D'onne had known wealth, and it did not call to her. This was more – something like closure.

Now, D'onne had a mission, a goal beyond self-preservation to drive her forward each day. And as ever, once she had a goal in mind, she was like a dog with a bone: nothing could break her vice-like grip on it. She followed it with a zeal and passion and single-mindedness that went well beyond her normal, everyday homicidal madness.

D'onne stepped over the broken and bloody remains of the venators, taking care not to slip on their entrails or trip over their severed limbs. 'Come on, Dog,' she said to her bodyguard, who dropped the bloody arm he'd been gnawing on and followed his master.

D'onne thumbed her chainsword off. 'There will be more meat for you later, Countless,' she purred to the weapon as she sheathed its massive blade. 'Time for Dog to earn his keep.'

She repositioned her wig, which had slipped down past her forehead into her eyeline, and scanned the way forward.

One large machine-husk building stood between her and the main street. Exhaust-fan ports had been turned into windows, through which she could see the glint of drawn weapons as well as a few more venators who weren't as good at hiding as they ought to be.

No door cut into the rear or side of the building, so D'onne expected the gangers to attack as soon she passed by the building. 'No reason to keep them waiting,' she said. 'Dog, move your fat ass. Forward. Go.' She kicked him in the back-side to punctuate the command.

Dog grunted but complied and loped round the side of the hulking, plasteel-sheet building towards the front. D'onne kept an eye on the gangers behind the windows while making a big show of hustling forward to keep up with Dog.

At the front corner of the building, D'onne stopped and pulled out her plasma gun, which she lovingly called Pig, and waited. As Dog ran down the street, his huge feet slapping the rockcrete with the force of pillars, the door to the large building opened and several venators, wearing the same armour as the ones D'onne had painted blood-red, poured out through the door and opened fire on Dog.

Idiots, thought D'onne. 'Can't you scum count to two?' she yelled. Almost as one, the group turned their autoguns and stub pistols towards D'onne, but it was too late for them. She pulled Pig's trigger, sending a wide beam of plasma at the too-bunched-up-for-their-own-good group of fighters. The supercharged plasma blasted a hole through the first venator's chest, caught a short one behind her in the neck and clipped the arms of the third and fourth, burning them off above the elbow.

All four fell to the ground – two dead and two down and screaming in pain. Unluckily for the two venators left alive,

Dog, enraged at being shot in the back, turned and charged. On his way through the door, the ogryn behemoth stepped on both downed fighters, crushing one's skull and the other's chest, ending their screams and spraying blood across the front of the building.

By the time D'onne reached the door, the inside of the building looked much like the front. Dead venators lay in pieces and the walls were covered in blood. No one else was in the room, just desks, chairs and cabinets, many of which had been overturned or tossed aside during Dog's homicidal charge.

As Dog huffed and puffed and pawed at the wounds in his back, D'onne thought she heard a sound coming from upstairs. She sheathed Pig and drew Countless, preparing to cut the survivor in half with her chainsword, but then realised the sound was nothing more than pitiful whimpering – and male at that. Whoever was hiding above wasn't worth the time it would take Countless to slice him in half. Besides, she had a date with House Cawdor, and she was already late.

'Come, Dog,' called D'onne. She sheathed her chainsword and turned to exit the building. When Dog didn't follow immediately, D'onne looked back to see what was wrong with the ogryn. He pointed at the bullet holes in his back, which had mostly hit the fleshy bits around his hulking torso.

'Coward,' said D'onne. 'Rub some dirt in it and come on. I'll sew it up later.'

With that, D'onne strode down the main street towards the huge building with the makeshift steeple at the other end, followed closely by her injured bodyguard. Amazingly, after all the plasma shots and screaming, townspeople still milled about on the street. At the sight of Mad D'onne and her dog, everyone scurried inside.

D'onne ignored the townsfolk. Those wretches were dead already, they just didn't know it yet. No one escaped the sludge pits. Of course, this was the case for the underhive in general, but she kept up her momentum. To slow down, to put down roots, was to beckon the end. D'onne would outlive these sludge mongers.

No, they were of no concern to her. The Cawdor in the big machine-house, on the other hand, were a major concern. This time it wasn't because of the crap the true believers spewed to rile up the rest of the Cawdor masses, turning their fears and anxiety into anger and hatred. Sure, they all deserved to die in vats of sludge. But at the moment D'onne's gripe with them was specific. This gang had information she needed.

She stopped in front of the large, ornate doors. The Cawdor had spared little expense installing brand new, four-metre-tall plasteel doors that shone in comparison to the dingy, patina-covered walls of the huge machine. Intricate carvings depicted some famous scene of redemption, D'onne supposed, showing tall warriors illuminated by bright, heavenly rays, casting down a large crowd of shadowy sinners into a fiery chasm. Saccharine filth.

'Knock and announce my presence, Dog,' D'onne commanded to her bodyguard. She stepped aside and smiled, as Dog strode forward, raised massive, plasteel-gauntleted hands over his head and slammed them into the middle of the double doors.

A thunderous boom echoed throughout the cavern and the top hinges on both doors snapped loudly as they ripped free from the thin metal of the church wall.

'Again,' said D'onne. Her smile widened.

The ogryn slammed his fists into the doors again. One of the huge panels tore free of its frame and slid into the building, scraping a curved line clean through the sheet-metal floor of the sanctuary inside. As it toppled over, its weight pulled the second door free of its hinges and it crashed to the floor with a deafening clang.

Dog grabbed his giant shield and club and entered the building ahead of D'onne. She followed close behind, using his massive bulk as her own shield. Once inside, he drew a massive breath and roared, announcing D'onne's presence as requested. It was answered with a smattering of haphazard autogun fire. Any shots that came close to hitting the ogryn clanged harmlessly off his shield. Most of them hit the plasteel walls around them and a few went through the cavernous opening left by the broken doors.

D'onne scanned the room. A dais, pews, and a smattering of so-called artefacts. Little more than bits of bone and broken pieces of tools, all reverentially displayed in nooks under sparking lumens. A few terrified-looking robed fools fired blind over upturned furniture.

Just Cawdor scum down here it seems, she thought. *No real gangers left to defend their sanctuary. Good.*

As Dog and D'onne moved forward under fire, D'onne called out to the shooters. 'Look,' she yelled. 'You don't want to die, and I don't want to take the time to kill you – not all of you anyway. Answer my questions and some of you – one, maybe two – may live!'

It wasn't a great incentive, D'onne knew, but in life-and-death situations, the truth could be effective. Especially when they were particularly bloody, gruesome truths.

'We don't believe you,' replied one of the holy gunners. The autogun fire continued but several shots were now coming from wider positions as the Cawdor tried to flank her and Dog. 'Mad D'onne doesn't bargain. She destroys.'

They got me there, thought D'onne. But she only needed one alive and there seemed to be plenty of Cawdor. *Time to change tactics.*

As Dog continued to stalk forward down the centre aisle with D'onne at his back, she kept her eyes on the pews to either side and waited for a lull in the firing. For a brief moment, the autogun fire nearly stopped as the Cawdor's weapons ran dry and they hunkered down to reload. D'onne crouched low and dived in between the pews.

Once clear of Dog and hidden by the pews, D'onne ordered the ogryn to charge. He roared again and stormed towards the dais at the far end of the sanctuary, his footfalls booming on the metal floor and shaking the painted windows.

All of the ensuing autogun fire concentrated on the charging ogryn. Meanwhile, D'onne scuttled down the pew to the edge of the sanctuary. As she suspected, several Cawdor had started making their way down the side of the pews to get a shot at D'onne from behind. Sadly for them they were now focused solely on Dog. D'onne drew Pig from its holster.

Taking careful aim with the plasma pistol, which was like trying to direct a waterfall, she squeezed off a single shot. Her plan was mostly successful. She aimed low, hoping to wound and not kill. The plasma beam ripped a trough into the metal flooring on its way to the targets before melting feet, shins and calves off the three Cawdor.

Their shrieks of pain mingled with the screams of the gangers on the dais who hadn't been quick enough to evade the onrushing ogryn. It seemed that nobody had noticed that D'onne had peeled off from the main attack – nobody but the three Cawdor she had shot. Two of them had the presence of mind to pull themselves behind the pews and return fire at D'onne. The third, a female Cawdor who had lost both feet, lay on the ground screaming in pain.

Not willing to risk another plasma shot, D'onne holstered Pig, stood, and drew Countless. She dashed forward under fire, weaving as she sprinted. The Cawdor were terrible shots – worse than most juves, luckily – and D'onne closed the gap quickly. She vaulted over the last pew, triggering the chain mid-air, and swung in a downward arc as she landed.

The spinning blade sliced through the Cawdor's upraised forearm, down through his skull and into his chest, spraying blood, bone and brains across the pew and the other Cawdor, who took one look at D'onne standing above him, her boots slick with his friend's blood, and dropped his weapon. 'I'm ready to talk,' he said.

D'onne smiled and pulled on Countless to free the chainsword from the dead man's chest, but the blade was stuck in the man's ribs and wouldn't budge. D'onne swore and revved the weapon to cut through the bone, but Countless caught on the Cawdor's sternum and kicked back. D'onne fought to keep control of the weapon and maintain her balance on the blood-slicked pew, but lost that battle and tumbled to the floor, flinging the chainsword away to avoid hacking off one of her own limbs, or worse.

Pulling herself back to a kneeling position behind the pews, D'onne checked on the rest of the battle and smiled to see Dog pursuing the remaining Cawdor through a door in the back of the sanctuary. She turned towards her willing informant to find him lying in a widening pool of blood and gore, Countless sticking straight up out of what remained of the man's face.

D'onne grabbed the chainsword and moved to stand over the last Cawdor. She had stopped screaming, but now lay in the foetal position, whimpering, her hands clamped around her legs above the stumps where her feet had been.

'Looks like this is your lucky day,' D'onne said as she pressed the gore-covered chainsword against the woman's neck.

CHAPTER 4

QUESTIONS

'I'm sorry, lady,' said the grubby lift operator, his voice quivering as he spoke, 'but this transport is for official Promethium Guild business only.'

Scrutinator Servalen could tell that the small man regretted his decision to stand his ground in front of her and the imposing enforcer squad backing her up. He was malnourished, skin and bones under tattered clothing, and was shaking so hard that the dust from the White Wastes covering him fluttered off his clothes and short-cropped hair, creating a cloud around his body.

The lift operator could have been a skinny kid or a grizzled old man under all the dirt. It was impossible to tell. But something – or someone – had him scared enough to face off against a scrutinator and an entire squad of enforcers. Even so, it took a strong will not to wither under her gaze.

Interesting, thought Servalen. It never ceased to astound her how the smallest crumb of genuine authority could bestow the lowest wretch with confidence beyond their ability. She fought the urge to order the sergeant to introduce the operator to a shock baton.

Instead, Servalen reached inside her jacket to produce a folded, real-leather wallet, the only extravagance she allowed herself. She flipped it open and pulled out the personal seal of Lord Helmawr, awarded to her for meritorious service. The seal allowed Servalen unfettered access to the entire hive. No request could be denied, nor any door barred, to someone bearing the seal of the Lord of Necromunda.

'Here!' said Servalen as she shoved the seal under the lift operator's nose. 'Now, take us down to Sludge Town.'

'Pretty picture. Does it look like I can read, lady?' asked the scrawny man. His voice still quivered, but he and his cloud of dust did not budge.

Servalen sighed and looked at the sergeant, who successfully squelched the smirk that had been forming on his lips. The scrutinator nodded at the lift operator and motioned with her thumb towards the side of the lift.

Without hesitation, the sergeant grabbed the man at the shoulder and waist and tossed him over the side as easily – both physically and morally – as if he'd been emptying a bucket out of a window. Servalen noted with some interest that the lift operator didn't scream on his way down the cliff side. It was if the man had always known he would die this way and simply accepted it when it happened.

She stepped over to the lift controls, KB-88 on her heels. She absent-mindedly patted the cyber-mastiff's metal head as the squad positioned themselves around the platform. She stared at the dog, which was really nothing more than a collection of electronic commands controlling a plasteel body. It was her only constant companion, the closest thing she had to a friend, and yet it had no soul.

Perhaps I shouldn't have had the lift operator killed, she thought. For some reason the action had sent her mind on a strange tangent. She mentally pushed the encroaching web of distractions behind a locked door in her brain and concentrated on the task at hand. The lift controls were a simple mechanism on a cable with three large buttons. She pushed the bottom button. The lift lurched and began descending.

The platform swayed in the stiff, regulated breeze that blew down towards the White Wastes. The wind and dust stung Servalen's face as they descended, and her legs began to tense from the strain of maintaining her balance. But it was the tinny whistle that followed them down the cliff side that gave her pause.

At first, she thought it was the whine of the crane engine above her, but the sound never abated. By the time they reached the level of Sludge Town, she had figured it out. It was the harmonics of the wind whistling past the thick, metal cable, abrading the rough iron fibres with the same dust that stung her face.

One day it would fail, and when it did people would die. This was a constant of the underhive, as it was in Hive City. It might be the only constant that connected everything and everyone below the noble upper spire. Servalen clenched her fists, using the pain of her fingernails digging into her palms to help focus her thoughts again and close the morbid doors that kept opening inside her head.

Was she tired? No. She never got tired. Not when on a job. Servalen's constant drive and lack of distracting emotion was what had brought her so high in the job. *It must be something else*, she thought. Something was trying to influence her. She decided to file it away for now and diagnose it later once she had more data.

After several minutes riding the swaying lift and listening to the whistling wind, Servalen saw a tunnel wide enough for cargo transports come into view. She jabbed the stop button as they drew near and the lift lurched to a standstill half a metre above a platform that extended from the tunnel.

As the squad jogged towards Sludge Town down the meandering tunnel, Servalen focused on the strange patterns covering the walls and ceiling of the tunnel. She looked closer and realised the patterns were formed by the severed ends of old power cables, gas lines and waste tubes. The tunnel had been cut through the old utility lines that ran from the manufactorum floor to the cliff wall. Where they had gone from there was anyone's guess.

Progress is always cut from the dusty and bloody remains of the past, thought Servalen as the squad neared the town. *And D'onne always leaves a bloody and gory trail to follow*, she added as they stepped into the manufactorum cavern.

Ahead of her she could see the devastation left from the mad noblewoman's latest rampage. Parts of dead bodies littered the bloodstained ground. Rats scurried about searching for entrails to feast upon or drag back to their holes. Clean-up wasn't Servalen's problem, though. She needed to find someone in charge.

'Who runs this town, sergeant?' she asked as she slowed to a walk. She peered at the various machines turned into shacks for the workers as they made their way towards the gory remains of the recent battle.

The sergeant tapped at a panel embedded in the yellow plasteel gauntlet on his left arm. 'Kordon Brann,' replied the sergeant after a moment. 'A low-level Promethium Guilder. His office is ahead – in the middle of all of D'onne's carnage.'

Kordon Brann dived under his desk when he heard the metal-on-metal stomping of an armoured squad entering the lower offices. The sounds of weapons fire and screams coming from the Cawdor sanctuary had only stopped echoing through the caverns fifteen or twenty minutes earlier. Whatever was happening now, he wanted no part of it.

But his luck was never that good. Barely a minute later, two pairs of black-gloved hands pulled him from under his desk by his feet. He instinctively curled into the foetal position to protect his vital organs and wrapped his arms over his face. Taking a quick peek between his fingers, Kordon saw the intruders were wearing the distinctive blue and yellow armour of the palanite enforcers.

He relaxed a bit. They certainly looked imposing in their bulky head-to-toe armour, and on any other day the glowing eye sockets of their full-face helmets – not to mention the weapons dangling at their hips – would have struck terror into Kordon's heart. But he was overjoyed that it was the authorities and not Mad Donna and her ogryn returning to finish the job.

Brann smiled and scrambled to his feet, adding a bow once standing, to show his respect for the rule of law. 'Thank you, gentlemen,' he said during the bow. 'You are a sight for weary eyes on this rough morn–'

Before he finished bowing or speaking, two enforcers grabbed Brann by the arms and lifted him off the ground. 'The scrutinator primus wants to talk to you, Mr Brann,' said one. 'Now.'

Kordon tried to explain that he was more than willing

to comply and could follow under his own power, but the enforcers were done listening or explaining. They half carried, half dragged him down the stairs and dropped him in a chair in the middle of the destroyed first-floor office. His fine linen trousers squelched in a sticky puddle on the seat.

Brann felt sick. And not from the thought of what he was sitting in. This was his first look at the devastation left in Donna's wake. He'd been too scared to leave his office after the short, brutal battle. Blood spray had painted the grey metal walls with vivid streaks of red.

The desk next to him held the torso of one of his venators – just the torso and the crushed remains of a woman's head, her blonde hair matted with blood and bits of brain. Her arms and legs were nowhere to be seen. No, that wasn't quite true. Brann found the bloody stumps sticking out from under another desk down the line.

Everywhere he looked, Kordon Brann saw gore. He tried to lean to the side to throw up, but the enforcers held Kordon still, not letting him move from the spot, so he vomited on himself instead.

After wiping the half-digested remains of breakfast from his mouth and best shirt, Kordon said, 'We could have done this upstairs in my office, you know?'

The stern woman sitting across from Kordon looked up from a tablet she had been studying and said, 'No. This is fine, Mr Brann. We won't take much of your time.'

Brann stared at the woman. Her face showed no emotion whatsoever. Sitting amidst this horror show would make the strongest soul quail in revulsion. He was certain of that. For all the impassive bravado of the faceless helmets worn by the enforcers surrounding him, he could see their heads moving to avoid looking at the worst of the gore, and their feet shifting as if they were ready to leave. He knew he wanted nothing more than to go home and shower and then leave town and never return.

But this woman showed no sign that the horrific sights and the horrible stench – which had assaulted him as soon as he was dragged downstairs and had now coated every millimetre of his nostrils, throat and lungs – affected her in the least.

'I have one question for you, Mr Brann,' said the strange, detached woman. 'Answer it and I'll be done with you.'

The woman paused to let the gravity of her implied threat settle, and then, finally, asked her question. 'Where did Mad D'onne go after she attacked your office?'

Kordon tried to look into the woman's eyes to get a read on her. He had a knack for determining what a person was thinking. It was the secret to his success in business, such as it was. But this woman's eyes were as blank as the impassive expression on her mouth. They were practically black from the pupils out to her eyelids.

To say her eyes were vacant would be a mistake, though. There was a definite burning strength and intelligence behind those black orbs, and her gaze pierced Brann's soul. But there was nothing else. No emotion, no empathy, no compassion. Her eyes were nearly as robotic as those of the mastiff that sat behind her, which he now noticed was also staring intently at him.

'Mr Brann?' said the woman. 'Answer the question. Now.'

'Right,' said Kordon. 'Sorry. I didn't exactly see where Donna went after...' he trailed off as his gaze fell on the gory remains of his venators.

'Because you were hiding under your desk,' said the woman, again with no emotion. Brann could tell the remark was intended to make him feel small, but it almost felt practised and robotic. There was no emotional derision. 'It is a pity you cannot be of any help,' she added.

The coldness of this entire exchange and the woman's detached demeanour made Kordon feel so uncomfortable that he began to squirm in his seat, which pressed the bloody entrails on the chair further into the crevices of his pants.

He tried to rally and regain some small measure of his self-respect. 'I didn't see where she went,' he said. 'But I did hear the sounds of battle coming from the Cawdor shrine down the street a few minutes after she left.'

At that information, the female interrogator snapped her attention from Kordon and glared at one of the enforcers, a sergeant, Brann thought, from the extra markings on his armour. The sergeant visibly withered under her gaze before frantically typing on the panel attached to his forearm. Kordon was glad he wasn't the only one affected by the woman's intense attention. After a moment, the sergeant looked back up and shrugged, pointing out the door towards the other end of town.

The woman stood and motioned the squad towards the exit and it seemed like they all jumped when she did. The enforcers jogged out, with the woman and her mastiff following behind. She stopped briefly at the door. 'Thank you, Mr Brann,' she said. 'I will leave you to... the rest of your day.'

Kordon glanced at the blood, guts and body parts covering nearly every surface of the first floor of his offices and vomited again.

CHAPTER 5

SANCTUARY, BLOODY SANCTUARY

D'onne kneeled over the lone surviving Cawdor in the sanctuary. The woman had lost both feet up to the calves from the plasma pistol shot, so D'onne had ripped strips of cloth off the vestments of a dead Cawdor and used them as tourniquets to keep her hostage from bleeding out before she could question her.

'Comfy?' asked D'onne, nodding her head at the Cawdor, as if to indicate the proper response.

The woman hesitated a second before nodding in response. She managed to squeak out a weak, 'Great.'

'Fantastic,' D'onne said, clapping her hands together several times. 'This won't take long if you keep cooperating.'

'What do you want?' asked the Cawdor, her question raspy from the shock and her hard breathing. This kind of frantic panic was common in people D'onne had captured. From juves to gang leaders, they all reacted much the same way.

'Just a bit of information,' replied D'onne. She reached up

under her powdered wig and pulled out a dataslate. It was already keyed to a pic pulled from a servo-skull of a thin young man being dragged into a Sludge Town building by a group of Cawdor. The grey metal walls and intricately carved doors of this sanctuary were unmistakable.

'How did you get that?' asked the Cawdor with a cough.

'It's astounding what people will give you when the alternative is losing a limb,' D'onne said, twisting one of the tourniquets to punctuate her point. 'Now, tell me where you took the kid.'

She tapped an image on the dataslate with her finger and zoomed in on the face of the young man. The pict was grainy, but he looked gaunt and emaciated from malnutrition, little more than a boy. His eyes were vacant, though, as if he'd already begun shuttering himself from the world around him.

'I... I don't know,' replied the Cawdor. 'I've never seen him.'

D'onne zoomed out on the image. 'This is your sanctuary,' she said. Then, noticing another detail, she zoomed in on a different face. 'And this is you. Let's try this again. Where is the boy?'

The Cawdor swallowed hard and bit her lip. D'onne twisted the tourniquet again and the woman yelped in pain. 'I can't tell you,' she said. 'The house elders will kill me – slowly.'

D'onne smiled, seeing her opening finally. 'If you tell me, I will kill you quickly – and mostly painlessly. Otherwise you get to choose between a slow death from me, or from your elders.'

The Cawdor still hesitated, so D'onne grabbed one of the hairpins holding her wig in place and jammed it through the tourniquet into the bare bone sticking out of the woman's calf.

The woman screamed and her eyes fluttered before closing for several long moments. D'onne feared she had pushed the pain past the point the woman could handle. But then the Cawdor moaned and opened her eyes.

'He's... not... here,' she said between gasping breaths. Before D'onne could ask the next question, the Cawdor continued. 'The elders... took him to... the Deep Pyre.'

Before D'onne could ask what in the scavving hell the Deep Pyre might be, the sound of metal-booted feet doing military double-time echoed down the street and through the broken doors of the church.

'Love to talk more,' D'onne said, 'but it's time to leave.'

'Kill me,' pleaded the Cawdor, a look of true terror in her eyes.

'Sorry,' said D'onne, as she started pushing herself off the floor, bringing her face close to the terrified Cawdor. 'No time.'

'You promised,' hissed the Cawdor. She grabbed D'onne by the wrist. 'You have no idea what they'll do to me.'

D'onne smacked the woman across the face with the dataslate, which clattered to the floor and skidded under a pew. 'I hope it's more horrible than you even imagine,' she said, using her now empty hand to pull back and break two of the woman's fingers and escape her grip.

With that, D'onne stood and ran through the door at the back of the sanctuary, the profanity-laden screams of the Cawdor echoing around her as she followed Dog's path of destruction. Past the door, D'onne found a maze of twisting and turning metal passages made by the pathways that conveyor belts once took through the giant machine. She could see remnants of the belt housing attached to the walls.

Bloody body parts swaddled in Cawdor robes strewn

through the halls and red, Dog-sized handprints on the walls made following her pet easy enough. The real question was how quickly could she escape this maze once she found Dog? Taking on venators – especially that poorly trained and geared group – was one thing, but handling a squad of enforcers was another.

As she ran, D'onne drew Pig from its holster and checked the plasma pistol's power gauge. Less than a third of a charge. Not nearly enough. Escape was really the only option. But first she had to find Dog.

The enforcer squad slowed to a halt outside the broken doors to the Cawdor sanctuary as fresh screams erupted inside, causing Servalen to run into the back of the sergeant. He turned to see the scrutinator and her cyber-mastiff glaring at him with identical infuriated looks in their eyes. Servalen waved her hands forward several times to indicate they should keep moving.

The sergeant took a deep breath. He knew better than to talk back to his superiors, despite (and especially) when he was sure they were wrong. With any other scrutinator, a sarcastic retort would get him a reprimand. With her – well, Sergeant Nox didn't want to think what might happen, especially with KB-88 at her side. So, with a resigned nod, he turned and spoke to his men instead.

'Enter hot and fan out,' he ordered, pointing at two groups of three and indicating directions with a quick flick of both hands.

The groups rushed through the breach in the wall in pairs, the lead two enforcers spraying the room with autogun fire as they entered. The first two continued firing as they sidled down the wall in opposite directions, allowing the next two to enter firing. By the time the third pair had entered, the screaming had ceased, followed by the squad's autogun fire.

The sergeant followed the rest of the squad through the door and surveyed the room, which appeared empty except for the carnage around the dais at the other end of the sanctuary. He nodded in satisfaction at the squad's efficiency.

'Standard search,' he called. 'Look for survivors to question but stay on alert for hostiles.'

The squad split up and began stalking down the aisles, holding their weapons at the ready as they scanned each pew. Content with their progress and the safety of the scene, the sergeant stepped back through the doorway.

'All clear, ma'am,' he said. 'From the scattered remains of the Cawdor inside, Mad D'onne was here, but she's gone now. Unless one of the gangers took her down, and she's mixed up in all this gore...'

'An unlikely scenario,' replied Servalen. 'Any survivors to question?'

'The squad is searching now, ma'am, but I wouldn't hold your breath.'

'I never do,' replied Servalen. She pushed her way past the sergeant and entered the sanctuary. The cyber-mastiff trotted off towards the left side, seemed to sniff the air and then ran towards the other end of the church.

Sergeant Nox followed Servalen, weapon in hand to keep her safe from harm, despite his flight instincts triggering every muscle in his body to flee from the maddening woman.

'Over here, sarge!' yelled a member of the squad from the front corner of the room. 'The mastiff found a survivor. Hurry! She looks bad.'

Nox ran down the centre aisle as fast as he could, but Servalen easily outpaced him. By the time he arrived, Servalen was leaning over the survivor, a Cawdor with both legs bound in bloody linen and several freshly bleeding bullet wounds in her chest. The woman was barely conscious but Servalen jammed a stimm into her arm.

'Still with us?' asked Servalen when the Cawdor's eyes fluttered open. The scrutinator leaned over to bring herself face to face with her captive.

'What did D'onne want?' Servalen continued in a hushed but fervent tone. 'Quickly. The stimms won't keep you alive long.'

'She promised...' replied the woman, with a wheeze. Her breathing became fast and shallow. 'It hurts!'

The dying Cawdor lifted her hands and grabbed Servalen by the arms. Every enforcer weapon around the scene was immediately raised and aimed. 'Kill me...' she whispered.

'Stand down,' Servalen said.

Sergeant Nox raised his hand to hold their fire.

'Tell me what D'onne wanted and your pain will end,' said Servalen.

'The boy,' said the Cawdor. 'She wants to find... the boy.'

'Who is that?' asked Servalen. 'What boy?'

'She just missed him,' muttered the Cawdor before slipping back into unconsciousness. At that moment, a large clang reverberated through the building and KB-88 howled in response. To their credit, none of Nox's squad jumped, although the sergeant felt his heart skip a beat.

'What the scav was that?' Nox asked. He snapped his weapon up and scanned the room with the barrel.

Servalen stood and regarded her bloodied greaves with irritation. 'That,' she said, 'was something large crashing into a thin sheet of plasteel above us.'

'D'onne is still here?' asked Nox, allowing his incredulity to get the better of him.

'Obviously,' said Servalen, drawing her lasgun in one fluid movement and using it to point at the rear door to the sanctuary. 'Clear the exits, sweep the streets around the shrine. I want eyes on the rooftops.'

Nox tapped a few keys on his wrist monitor and brought up a schematic of the machine-turned-shrine. It had multiple levels, but everything was connected to the corridor behind that lone door. He began assigning floors to the squad in groups of three.

'I want the medic to stay here and keep this woman alive,' said Servalen before the squad ran off. 'I want to question her further.'

Nox looked at the unconscious Cawdor, her ashen face showing she had one foot in the furnace already. He wanted to argue that if they were going to fight Mad D'onne and her ogryn, they might want their medic by their side, but he knew it would be a pointless waste of time.

'Barker,' he called, pointing at his medic. 'Stay with the survivor and keep her alive.' Nox then led the rest of the squad towards the back of the sanctuary. 'Everyone else, you have your orders!'

'Dog!' hissed Mad D'onne as loud as she dared. From the brief eruption of automatic weapon fire below her, she determined she must be directly above the first-floor sanctuary, which appeared to now be swarming with enforcers. 'Heel, you mangy cur!'

She hadn't yet found her ogryn bodyguard or any possible way out of this massive plasteel-sheeted holy prison. The trail of blood and body parts had petered out and she hadn't heard any screams on the upper floors of the church since the enforcers had entered below her.

D'onne tapped the butt of her plasma pistol in its holster. 'You may get your chance yet, Pig,' she muttered. 'I can always count on you for an emergency exit.'

That way out would definitely alert the enforcers, though, which D'onne was currently trying to avoid. She hated to leave Dog behind, although she had – and would again – if the alternative was death. Still, he had his uses and was annoyingly loyal.

That last bit was the real reason D'onne had to find her ogryn bodyguard. She knew if he got left behind, Dog would find her trail and follow it to Hive Bottom and beyond, with no care for his own safety or awareness of any enforcers he might lead straight to her.

'Dog!' she hissed again and then listened for anything to break the silence. The ogryn was rarely this quiet unless sleeping or unconscious. There should be a lot of clanging as he charged about inside the metal box, not to mention the screams of his victims. But nothing.

D'onne glanced around the large room she had entered. It seemed to be a common area with chairs and tables strewn about. Along each wall stood what looked like holding pens that had been turned into workspaces. Bits of bone and broken pieces of plasteel, some covered in foul-smelling black ooze, lay on most of the workbenches.

A path bordered by rivet holes in the sooty, blackened floor ran from each workspace to a wide, floor-to-ceiling cylinder made from large plasteel panels that stood in the middle of the room.

Another foul odour, tangier and older than the sludge, lingered in the air, and the silhouettes of what looked like rails and tracks were visible in the soot. D'onne surmised this had been a waste disposal room. The cylinder must have been a smokestack for the great machine. It had survived the renovations to become the steeple for the Cawdor sanctuary below her.

If she was right, there would have been some way to feed waste into the stack, which would have been heated by a furnace below in what was now the sanctuary. The thought of the Cawdor preaching in a place that once housed a hellish fire brought D'onne some amusement. More importantly, if she could get inside the stack, she might be able to escape.

D'onne crept around the two-metre-diameter cylinder looking for a hatch or opening of some sort. As she did, D'onne heard noises coming from inside the stack. It sounded like a large animal scratching and whimpering.

'Dog?' called D'onne as she leaned closer to the cylinder.

The response was immediate and booming. A deafening clang reverberated through the cylinder and D'onne's skull. Everything around her went fuzzy and her head felt like it was being squeezed by a giant vice while simultaneously being immersed in a bucket of water. She shook her head to clear the feeling, but that only made it worse and she ended up sitting on the floor.

As D'onne's vision cleared, she noticed a handle visible at the bottom of the lowest panel of the cylinder. It had been hidden by a thick layer of soot. D'onne grabbed it and pulled. The panel slid up, creating an opening large enough for her to crawl through.

Unfortunately, Dog's muscular back was right behind the panel. Surprised by the sight, D'onne fell backwards again, but recovered quickly. She closed the panel and went around to the other side. She found a corresponding handle and slid the waste chute panel open. Inside, plastered to the back of the cylinder, was Dog, holding himself in place inside the smokestack with his arms and legs, his shield and club hanging precariously from his belt.

D'onne peeked her head inside and looked around. She could see a sliver of light coming from overhead and surmised Dog must have been tricked into the cylinder by some Cawdor on an upper level and had then slid down to this level while trying to bash his way out.

Typical, she thought, smiling a bit at the image of Dog sliding down the cylinder, terror wrenching his face into a contorted parody of itself.

D'onne's amusement came to a quick end, though, when she heard a commanding voice shout from below: 'Barker, stay with the survivor and keep her alive. Everyone else, you have your orders!'

This was followed by metal-soled boots clanging against the floor in double time. She looked down and saw the sanctuary nearly ten metres below Dog's enormous feet. 'Well done, Dog,' muttered D'onne. 'You got us good and trapped.'

She turned over and looked up. The cylinder continued well past the thin light of a now-closed, larger opening above Dog. Eventually, the light faded to black at the edge of her sight. It would be a tough climb for D'onne – and Dog would struggle – but it was doable.

It would be noisy, though, and D'onne could already hear the squad's boots reverberating on the stairs leading up to this level. It wouldn't be long before their search brought them to the waste storage room. There was no way D'onne and Dog could reach the top of the cylinder in time. They needed a diversion.

Dropping back into the sanctuary might work, she thought, but a ten-metre drop was bone-crushing in the best of circumstances, and the rows of pews made a perfect landing a one-in-a-million shot.

They had no good options and their time was running out. *That's it!* thought D'onne. *What we need is more time.*

D'onne lay flat on the floor of the waste storage room, hooked her lower legs around the opening and dangled her torso down the cylinder. She craned her neck to see the back corner of the sanctuary, where she had left the Cawdor. Sure enough, a lone enforcer was there tending to her wounds.

Down the hall from the waste storage room, D'onne heard the shuffling of metal boots and the clanging of doors being shoved open. This was going to be tight. D'onne reached back to her holster, grabbed Pig by the grip and pulled it free. She slipped down a bit further to get a clear shot, holding onto the cylinder with her ankles, aimed and fired the plasma pistol.

The beam of charged plasma incinerated the enforcer's forearm and tore a hole through the Cawdor's chest. D'onne then turned and pressed Pig's trigger again, this time holding it down and guiding the barrel about in several tight circles.

When she was done, there was a large, escape-sized hole in the plasteel-plate siding of the sanctuary. D'onne holstered Pig and slipped the rest of the way into the smokestack, pulling the panel down as best she could with her foot. She then wedged her arms and legs against the side of the cylinder to hold her body in place, upside down, and waited.

CHAPTER 6

MISTAKEN PURSUIT

'What is that?' exclaimed Nox as a low, crackling sound emanated from somewhere in the Cawdor building. The sergeant was about to lead the squad into a large room on the second level. Another emanation was accompanied by the walls and floors reverberating around them.

'That, sergeant,' Servalen answered, 'was the sound of a plasma pistol firing twice, the second shot removing a large section of a supporting wall.'

'Sarge, this is Barker,' called a voice through the vox attached to Nox's utility belt.

Sergeant Nox detached the vox from his belt and raised it to his face, but Servalen strode forward and snatched the device from her subordinate's hand. 'Report, enforcer,' she commanded. 'Did Mad D'onne double back to you?'

'I believe so, ma'am,' said Barker, his voice strained. 'I think she escaped.'

'What do you mean, "you think"?' demanded Servalen.

'She blasted me and the Cawdor with a plasma weapon and I blacked out for a moment,' Barker explained. 'When I came to, there was a big hole melted into the side of the sanctuary and no sign of D'onne.'

Sergeant Nox and the enforcers had gathered around Servalen, although they gave her and KB-88 at her side a metre of space – and looked uncomfortable standing that close.

'Are you certain she escaped?' asked Servalen through the vox.

'Are you badly hurt, Barker?' asked Sergeant Nox at the same time. Servalen stared at the man with deeply furrowed eyebrows, forcing him to look away.

'I never saw her, ma'am,' replied Barker, who was apparently smart enough to know who to answer. 'But she must have run out that hole. Why else burn through so much charge?'

Servalen tossed the vox back to the sergeant. 'Get your squad down there, Nox,' she commanded. 'Fan out from the hole and find her. Take KB-88 with you. There must be a trail. She's not a subtle woman.'

As Nox and the squad double-timed back down the hall, Servalen commanded the cyber-mastiff to follow the squad and obey the sergeant. The metal dog made a grating sound that Servalen knew to be the equivalent of a whine. It hadn't moved from its last position, facing away from the retreating squad.

'Stop complaining!' said Servalen. 'I know you don't like him, but I need your eyes and ears out there now.'

KB-88 refused to budge until Servalen snapped her fingers. She pointed down the hall. 'Do as I command or I will melt you down.' The mastiff turned and moved slowly down the hall, looking back towards its master several times before turning the corner.

Servalen sighed and strode down the hall. She hated being mean to KB-88. But this was important.

As she walked back towards the stairs, Servalen took time to consider what they had found so far. D'onne had questioned the Cawdor, so now they knew she was looking for someone – a boy, for some reason – and not mindlessly wreaking havoc on the underhive. That was more than they had known before. The squad had arrived shortly after D'onne had left the sanctuary through the rear, but she had somehow found a way back, shot Barker and then melted a hole in the wall.

How did she outmanoeuvre us? wondered Servalen. *And why did she blast a hole in the side of the church when the front doors had been ripped off their hinges?* It was all a bit odd. D'onne was known for slipping away, but not for leaving survivors who could point out where she'd gone. The scrutinator had the nagging feeling she was missing something.

Back in the sanctuary, Servalen took stock of the scene, which was more or less exactly as Barker had described. Another member of the squad was tending to Barker, who had lost his arm below the elbow. The Cawdor, though, was dead. Half her chest had been melted through by the blast. *Looks like D'onne kept her promise in the end*, thought Servalen.

The rest of the squad had gone through the hole in the side wall of the sanctuary. Nox had sent them out in pairs to search the worker housing surrounding the town. Servalen moved to the hole and watched their progress, but knew they weren't going to find her. The cavern was enormous and filled with old, rusting machines big enough to house entire families. Plenty of places to hide. And beyond the town the entire cavern was pitch-black.

The scrutinator listened for indications of fighting anywhere out in the darkness. Mad D'onne was a force of nature. Anything that got in the way of her flight would be eliminated in a noisy, bloody clash.

But Servalen heard nothing, not even the regular rabble of bar fights and drunken arguments one would expect from a mining town. Everyone must have scurried for the nearest hole when D'onne came crashing through town. She heard KB-88 barking at something in the distance and some dull scrabbling noises that sounded like rats in the machines, but nothing else at all.

How do people live like this? wondered Servalen as she strode back through the hole to see if the Cawdor could be of any more help. Yes, the woman was dead, but that was no excuse for not helping. The dead often had secrets to share, if you knew where to look.

'I'm missing something,' Servalen said to herself again as she moved towards the dead woman. 'What is it?'

She stood above the dead Cawdor and surveyed the scene, looking for anything she might have missed before or any new information she might elicit from the woman's dead body that could help them track D'onne. Barker sat next to the woman, his wound being well tended by another enforcer.

There really was nothing to see here except a cauterised hole where the woman's chest had been. D'onne's shot had obliterated the gunshots the Cawdor had suffered when Nox's men breached the building. *Less paperwork, I guess*, thought Servalen.

She glanced at Barker again. Following the medic's instructions, the enforcer had cleaned the foam from the wound and was stitching it closed. 'Good work, enforcer,' said Servalen. 'Should take a prosthetic nicely.'

'Thank you, ma'am,' said the enforcer.

Servalen studied the pair. Nox's patrol were more capable than most, but Servalen was used to having to keep those sent to accompany her on a short leash.

Servalen turned her attention back to the Cawdor's smouldering corpse, and felt that gnawing doubt creep back into her mind. Something about this scene was wrong. She stepped over the body and looked straight down at the woman's blasted chest and studied the wound.

There it is, she thought. Servalen leaned over, being careful not to move the body, and peered beneath the Cawdor's head and shoulders. 'Interesting,' she said before straightening up.

'Barker!' she commanded. The man practically jumped. 'Has this body been moved?' Servalen asked, already surmising the answer.

'No, ma'am,' said Barker. 'I mean, she fell backwards when we got shot, but other than that, no.'

'You were holding her in a sitting position,' said Servalen, noticing the blackened fingertips of the enforcer's right glove.

'Yes, ma'am,' replied Barker. 'How did you know?'

'Doesn't matter,' replied Servalen, getting excited now. 'Come here.'

Barker looked at the enforcer stitching his arm. 'That's an order,' Servalen barked. 'Damnit, man. This is important. I need your help.'

Barker scrambled off the floor, wincing and leaving a blood stain on the floor when he pushed off with his stump. Servalen stepped to the side as Barker moved over the Cawdor.

'Position your body and hers as you were when the shot

came,' ordered Servalen. It took some doing and Barker needed help from the other enforcer to lift the dead weight of the Cawdor and hold her corpse in place.

As Servalen suspected, Barker's right hand was behind her back, his fingertips barely reaching the hole left from the plasma beam. Meanwhile, his left arm, which had been severed, was raised above her body. He had been spraying wound foam at the time, she guessed.

None of that was important, though. Servalen moved to stand at the Cawdor's feet and peered through the hole in her chest. She then moved around the body towards Barker an inch at a time, and then finally inched her way forward over the dead woman's legs.

'What are you doing, ma'am?' asked Barker.

'Lining up the shot,' said Servalen. 'The scorch mark on the floor from the plasma beam was under the woman's right shoulder and is – now that I can see it more clearly – oblong.'

Confident that she had the angle right, Servalen turned one hundred and eighty degrees and looked up at an angle consistent with the shape of the scorch mark. There, high above them in the ceiling of the sanctuary, was the intake for the smokestack.

'Throne!' said Servalen. She strode over to the hole in the wall, where she found KB-88, who had returned. Perhaps the mastiff had known all along what Servalen was now realising. The scrutinator scratched the metal dog between its ears, which rotated on servos, as she studied the scorch marks on the floor of the cavern outside the hole. The angle of these marks also lined up with the hole in the ceiling.

As she stood there, Servalen heard more of the scrabbling rats she had heard earlier. The sound was fainter, more distant now than it had been before. And yet, KB-88's ears turned immediately at the sound. It cocked its head, looked straight at the hole in the ceiling, and growled.

'Damnit to the sump,' murmured Servalen, causing KB-88 to slink back a step. She stormed over to stand beneath the hole, the cyber-mastiff trotting behind her at a safe distance. It was far too dark to see very far, but the hole was definitely the bottom of some sort of vertical shaft.

'Enforcer,' she called.

'Yes, ma'am,' replied the enforcer, who had gone back to stitching up Barker's arm.

'Get on the vox and recall Nox and the rest of the squad,' she said. 'D'onne never went through that hole.'

'Where did she go?' asked Barker.

'Up.'

Kordon Brann stepped out of the Black Tar, the roughest drinking and gambling den in Sludge Town, and leaned against the metal chute that once poured the thick sludge from the top of the ancient machine-turned-tavern down into a pipe that ran straight through to the pits.

He didn't care that his best suit now had a long smudge down the back. It made a nice counterpoint to the blood and vomit stains down the front. He'd have to burn it. Yet another cost added to the bottom line of this awful day.

At least he'd been able to lowball several down-on-their-luck workers inside whom he had hired to remove all the gore from his offices and from the top of the ramp to the pits. They had jumped at the chance to earn some extra creds on the side after losing their wages in the gambling den. But Kordon was certain the burly workers would come to regret taking the job when they saw the grisly scenes left behind by D'onne.

Their tough luck, thought Brann. Still, it wouldn't be hard work. Load a skiff and dump the bodies in a dried-out vat well away from active refining efforts, he'd told them. The rats and bugs would take care of it from there. Cleaning the blood from his office would be tougher, and nastier. He'd have to cough up more creds, or find someone desperate enough to take care of that chore.

Then he needed to hire more venators. Once word got out that Mad Donna had taken out his protection, every gang this side of the White Wastes would descend on Sludge Town. Even his position as a guilder wouldn't keep all of them away. Brann would be dead – or worse.

He could always cut and run, he supposed. But this operation was supposed to be his big shot at advancing in the guild. And it had been working – albeit slower than he'd promised – before Donna showed up. If he left now, Kordon would have nothing, and someone else would swoop in and take over his operation. His town! He'd made all this happen, and he would be damned if he let some other Pyrocaen lord steal his credit.

So, Kordon sat there outside the Black Tar, mentally adding up all the extra expenses from this debacle, and trying to figure out ways to hide the losses in the books. He was broken from his reverie by the clanking of metal boots down the street. The enforcers, led by that horrible, gaunt woman and her vicious-looking cyber-mastiff, streamed out of the destroyed entrance to the Cawdor sanctuary.

They marched straight down the street towards him. Brann considered slipping back into the Black Tar before they reached him, but it was too late. The woman, Scrutinator Servalen, was already pointing at him. Kordon didn't like being the object of the severe woman's attention, even at this distance.

He decided to make the best of it. He stood up straight and tried to dust the smudge from his jacket, which left his palms black and sticky. 'Damnit,' muttered Brann, reminding himself not to run his fingers through his hair until he bathed.

'Mr Brann,' said the stern woman, as she approached.

'Ma'am,' replied Brann. He thought about extending his blackened hand in greeting, but the fire in the eyes of the mastiff made him think better of it.

'We are leaving,' said Servalen. 'If you come across anything that might be pertinent to my investigation, do yourself a favour and report it immediately.'

'Um, sure,' replied Brann, unsure why there was an official investigation. Brutal gang battles were a daily occurrence in the underhive.

The scrutinator turned to leave, but hesitated. She looked back at Brann with what he swore was a smirk on her face. 'You might send someone in to clean up the Cawdor shrine. It looks a bit like your office.'

And with that, she wheeled around and strode out of town towards the transport lift, which Brann suddenly realised he should probably check on as well. As for the shrine, he would let the Cawdor clean up their own mess. No reason that cost should come back on him.

'I need new clothes,' said Kordon to no one. No way was he going back to his office, and he hated to let the workers see him looking like sludge trash. But as he walked down the street, something about that last conversation with the scrutinator kept nagging at him.

What kind of evidence are they looking for? he wondered. *What was going on with Donna that warranted a full squad and a scrutinator?*

Brann found himself standing in front of the Cawdor shrine, looking at the doors torn off their hinges and lying on the floor. Maybe he'd have a peek inside, and see what the Cawdor had been hoarding while they thought he wasn't looking. It couldn't be worse than the scene in his office.

Brann picked his way past the broken doors and moved inside. Hundreds of bullet holes pierced the pews, walls and windows. A pile of dismembered bodies littered the dais at the far end of the shrine, mirrored by a small mound of dead rats in the middle of the room.

How odd, thought Kordon. He'd seen rats in the shrine during services, and the Cawdor were known to utilise them. But this many, dead like they were? He made to move closer, when the giant hole in the side wall caught his attention. It was an odder sight, and one less likely to twist his already turned stomach.

Of course, as Brann got close to the hole, he saw the gory bits on the floor beside it. One Cawdor had been cut in two, his torso dangling off the edge of the pew and his legs lying in a pool of blood below. Another dead Cawdor, his head split open, lay draped across the top of two pews. On the floor nearby was the body of a third Cawdor with no feet and a hole through her chest.

Kordon dropped to his knees and vomited again. He'd been wrong to believe this scene couldn't be worse than his office. Then, as Brann wiped his mouth on the cleanest section of his suit sleeve that he could find, he noticed something flickering underneath a pair of bloody severed legs.

He crawled beneath the pews into the pool of blood, not caring any more about the state of his suit, and reached underneath the viscera. Beneath he found a glowing data-slate, drenched in blood.

Now that looks like a piece of evidence, thought Brann. *I wonder how much it might be worth – and who will pay the highest price?*

CHAPTER 7

THE LONG CLIMB

D'onne was pleased that the plasma-gun stunt had worked, but she had no idea how much time it would buy, so she started climbing as soon as the enforcers cleared the sanctuary below. The first part was easy. She climbed up Dog's body. Between the ogryn's bulging muscles and armour plating, she found plenty of hand- and foot-holds.

Dog's grunts and groans when her boots ground into the square of his back were icing on the cake. Once on top of Dog's head, D'onne glared into the gloom above her. The shaft rose into blackness, but she knew it reached into the dome above. Even if there wasn't an exit up there, she'd happily cut her way out.

The bad news was that Dog was beginning to slide. Their combined weight was too much for the ogryn, whose fingers and feet were digging into the soot-covered plasteel sheeting in a vain attempt not to slip past the bottom of the shaft and down to the sanctuary floor below.

'Sump me!' muttered D'onne. She pressed her own hands against the shaft, raised her feet off Dog's head, and set them against the walls to brace herself. 'Looks like we shimmy, Dog,' she said, hoping the ogryn's grunt was an affirmative response.

With their backs pressed against the shaft, D'onne and Dog pushed themselves up the sooty smokestack one agonising inch at a time. About halfway to their goal, as D'onne's arms and legs were going numb, she heard what sounded like an echo of their movement reverberating above them. She stopped moving, but the scratching and scraping echoes continued.

'What now?' muttered D'onne. She craned her neck to peer up the shaft. At first all she saw was a writhing mass of shadows descending the shaft. It looked like twilight had come alive and was crawling towards them on a thousand tiny legs.

'Rats!' gasped D'onne as the roiling shadows resolved into a horde of mangy, disease-ridden rodents scrambling down towards her and Dog. The rats poured over the top edge of the shaft above them, making it look like the smokestack was being devoured by a writhing shadow.

They had no way to get out of the path of the rodent swarm. Their only exit was ten metres above, past a mass of filthy fur, wicked claws and sharp teeth. And they had no way to fight. Both Pig and Countless were too unwieldy in this confined space and more likely to destroy the shaft and send them falling to their deaths than to kill more than a dozen of the hundreds of rats.

The time for 'what-ifs' was over, though. D'onne could see the beady, blood-red eyes of the closest rats. But she saw something else as well: fear. Their eyes were wide and wild and their legs were moving so fast they kept tangling together with the rats around them as they climbed over one another to get to the front of the pack – to flee something behind them.

They didn't need to kill the rodents, D'onne realised. They just needed to not die from a thousand frightened tooth-and-claw attacks as the horde ran past and over them.

'Dog!' she called to her loyal companion, 'Hold perfectly still.' D'onne stepped on Dog's head and threw her body against the opposite side of the shaft. Before Dog slid too far from the extra weight, D'onne pushed backwards against the shaft wall and slid down facing Dog, wedging herself in place without having to use her hands.

Then the rats were on them. The first wave climbed onto D'onne's head and scrambled down her face, digging their claws into her forehead, ears, cheeks and jaw. She closed her eyes and reached overhead to flail her arm at the little monsters. She dislodged those on her face, which fell and landed on her corset, where they dug their claws in again.

But the movement of her arms stopped the horde from climbing over her face again. She opened her eyes and glanced up. As the next wave of rats closed on her, she swatted at any approaching her powdered wig, and slapped away any that landed on her shoulders.

The rat horde instinctively understood there was a blockage in its path and started to part above D'onne's head like a wave breaking on a ship's prow. D'onne took a moment to check on Dog, who had taken a different, much more Dog-like tactic to deal with the rats.

She watched with disgust as Dog grabbed rat after rat in either hand and squeezed until their heads and rumps exploded from the pressure. He then dropped the bloody bits of fur and mashed entrails down the shaft and grabbed another pair.

After several agonising minutes, the swarm had passed them. D'onne peered down the shaft to see the writhing mass of bodies disappear into some crack or crevice near the bottom of the shaft, past the waste disposal room.

Perhaps it was some sort of migration, thought D'onne. She decided she would not think about what they could have been running from.

D'onne looked at Dog. The ogryn was covered in bloody rat fur and rodent droppings. The smell was worse than usual.

'I'm going first,' said D'onne as she began inching her way up the wall again. This time, she had no intention of climbing up Dog to save time.

It was slow going. When D'onne's hands reached the top of the shaft, she barely had enough strength left to pull herself over the edge and collapse on the floor of the cavern. Dog crawled out moments behind her.

D'onne felt a surge of adrenaline as the ogryn's enormous, rat-gore-covered bulk came towards her. She rolled out of the way as Dog fell to the cavern floor, spraying bits of bloody fur as he hit the rockcrete.

Scrutinator Servalen strode out ahead of the enforcer squad as they marched back towards the lift that would take them to the top of the cliff overlooking the White Wastes. The rusting hulks of ancient machines dotted the cavern around her.

Dim lights from those that had been converted into dwellings pierced the oppressive darkness through crudely cut windows in their sides. Others were rusted hulks that had succumbed to the ages, listing to the side or falling in on themselves.

KB-88 padded next to its master in silence as Servalen mulled over everything that happened since they had descended into Sludge Town, and worked at cataloguing all the various pieces of information within her well-ordered mind. The mastiff knew not to interrupt. It seemed content to keep pace and be near its master.

Sadly, Nox did not understand the scrutinator's process as well as her mechanical dog did. The sergeant strode up beside Servalen, his metal-clad feet clanking against the rockcrete and matched his superior's pace for several long seconds as Servalen tried to maintain her concentration.

'With all due respect, ma'am–' began Nox after a minute.

Servalen shot her hand out to the side, palm facing the sergeant, to cut him off. She then raised her index finger to indicate he should wait one damn minute as she entered the tunnel that would take them to the lift. The two walked in silence, with the scrutinator's hand extended for several more minutes before Servalen spoke.

'You want to know why we are leaving Sludge Town, correct?' she asked, dropping her hand back to her side, but not bothering to look at or acknowledge the sergeant.

'Yes, ma'am,' replied Nox. 'I do.'

His words were a bit clipped and curt, it seemed to Servalen. *Good*, she thought. *He needs reminding about who is in charge of this mission.*

'We know where D'onne is headed,' she said out loud. 'It is my intention to get there first.'

'We had her back there,' protested Nox. 'We could have trapped her in that shaft.'

She stopped, exhaled slowly and, finally, turned to regard the sergeant for the first time since he had interrupted her thoughts.

'So, you wanted to follow the deadliest woman in the underhive up a narrow shaft, sergeant?' asked Servalen. She began ticking off points that Nox had apparently not considered on her fingers. 'She had higher ground, a plasma pistol that would burn through your armour as easily as it would a slab of corpse-starch, and an ogryn behemoth she would happily drop on anyone who tried to follow her.'

Servalen glanced back at the squad, who to their credit, had come to a quick halt and were busily securing the area, without acknowledging their arguing superiors.

'Is that the type of battle advantage you would have pressed, sergeant?' asked Servalen, drilling her point home. 'Would that have been your tactical advice in the Cawdor sanctuary?'

The sergeant lowered his eyes towards his boots and shook his head. 'No, ma'am,' he said.

'I didn't hear you, sergeant,' stated Servalen sternly, her words more clipped than Nox's had been earlier.

'No, ma'am!' stated Nox immediately, his palanite drill instincts apparently taking over.

'Excellent,' said Servalen. A smile curled across her face that she was certain looked in no way reassuring. 'Now, we must beat D'onne to Dust Falls. She will show up there, I assure you. So, double-time.'

'Yes, ma'am!' said Nox before turning to the squad and taking his frustration out on them. 'Get a move on, you lay-abouts!' he yelled. 'Who ordered you to halt?'

Servalen allowed the squad to pass by before moving forward again. She scratched her metal canine's head between its mechanical ears. It looked up at its master with glowing red eyes.

Servalen pressed a finger to her lips. 'Don't you worry, Eighty-Eight,' she said in a low voice. 'I'm fine.'

Servalen paused, then collected herself, and considered what they knew. D'onne had attacked a seemingly insignificant guilder's assets to get at a Cawdor gang. She'd ignored targets of more value, and stayed in one place longer than she usually did to interrogate a survivor – which she usually didn't leave – about a boy. The boy had been in the sanctuary. The Cawdor said that D'onne had missed him. That fight in the shrine was a diversion, Servalen realised. The low-level Cawdors gave their lives so the elders could spirit the boy away before D'onne got hold of him.

It all made sense now. The Cawdor elders must have left with the boy around the time Servalen was interrogating that idiot guilder, because if they'd left any later Mad D'onne would've run straight into them. What were they trying to keep from her? What could have got the zealots so riled up that they'd risk going against her to protect some random kid? Was the boy a psyker? She'd felt an effect on her mind half a kilometre out. That would take a lot of power!

Wait a minute! Servalen remembered a report coming across her desk. It had been some vague directive to report the discovery of any previously unknown psykers directly to the lord provost marshal. Servalen had thought nothing of it at the time. She always reported intelligence of unregistered psykers up the chain of command. In light of today's events, though, that report indicated the Spire probably already knew about this new psyker.

A psyker of that power level could be of enormous use to the enforcers, thought Servalen. Or to her. She had to find it first. The boy was a prize that everyone who craved power in the hive would kill to possess, which meant everyone in the hive would soon be after him.

Luckily, the scrutinator knew a bit about the ways of Cawdor and how they tended to deal with psykers. She had taken down some Cawdor of a recidivist bent in the past. There were only a few places they would take such a prize, and only one near Sludge Town: the Deep Pyre.

As Servalen followed the enforcer squad out of the enlarged utility tunnel and onto the lift platform, she knew she had to get to Dust Falls quickly, not to beat D'onne there but to have any chance of catching up to the Cawdor elders and the psyker before they placed him on the Pyre.

CHAPTER 8

OUT OF THE RAT PAN

After the long climb and the rat stampede, D'onne wanted to lie on the floor of this new chamber forever, or at least until she could feel her arms and legs again, but something up here had driven the rats down the shaft, so there was no time to rest. She struggled to a crouch to see where they had ended up.

The dim light they could see while climbing came from bioluminescent lichen growing in patches on the ceiling and other surfaces, giving everything a sickly yellow glow. The stench and grime of the smokestack permeated every surface, as whatever outlet had spirited it away in the past had clearly been blocked for decades.

She scanned the cavern. It was no more than three metres high from floor to ceiling and filled with pipes and ducts running in every direction, turning the low cavern into a maze of metal tubes.

It was a utility level, one of those spaces in between domes. They crisscrossed the hive, creating random patterns as they filled in the gaps between habitable regions. Gangs used them to move unseen from base to battleground. Bugs, rats and worse things found their way into them and built enormous colony nests. What a wonderful place to travel through. Nothing dangerous here.

A few metres to one side, D'onne saw a cylinder opening. The large plasteel tube ran off into the distance along the ground. It was the continuation of the smokestack they had climbed. The rest of the utility tubes and ducts were too small for her and Dog to use and none seemed to go anywhere particular for long. They twisted at odd angles around each other as they carried energy, waste, air or whatever else throughout this section of the hive.

D'onne continued scanning for whatever had driven the rats down the shaft. 'Nothing,' she said at last. 'In any direction.'

Of course, she knew this meant that if something had driven the rats down the shaft, whoever – or whatever – they were, they were either still here somewhere, or had given up on the rats and left. D'onne had no illusions they were gone. The trick would be getting out of this cavern with Dog in tow without being spotted by them.

The best option was the horizontal smokestack. D'onne stood and investigated the cylinder. She could feel air moving through it, which meant it connected to some exit – possibly at the cliffs over the White Wastes.

'Interesting,' muttered D'onne. This would hide them from any local residents and should be a short trip. Unfortunately, going this way meant a treacherous climb up the cliffs where they would be totally exposed. Plus, they'd be trapped inside the shaft with no room to fight – again – if and when they were attacked. Fresh air almost assuredly meant someone living near it.

D'onne reassessed. They needed information about the Deep Pyre, and then they'd need to get to it. Quickly. That meant finding more Cawdor, and to be in an accessible enough spot to find their way to the Deep Pyre without added difficulty. There was only one place nearby that fitted that bill. They needed to go up.

'Come on, Dog,' D'onne said, prodding the giant ogryn with her boot. He still lay on the rockcrete ground next to the open smokestack, covered in rat gore on top of Cawdor gore on top of venator gore. He moaned and rolled over. When he got to his hands and knees, he shook himself like a wet animal, spraying blood, fur and guts in every direction.

'Ugh,' sighed D'onne, her boots and leggings drenched in a fresh layer of rat guts. Every day in the underhive was much like any other. Rip your enemies in half and then rinse their blood out of your clothes.

Now, thought D'onne, *assuming the smokestack goes where I think it does…* She oriented on the large pipe and then turned 90 degrees from that line and strode with fresh purpose. *We need to go this way.*

D'onne was happy to see the path forward remarkably clear, giving her confidence in her decision. She and Dog plodded along, picking their way around any pipes and ducts that periodically intruded or crossed their path. The going was slow due to bundles of cables that also crisscrossed the cavern floor.

After a while, D'onne noticed the stench increasing in potency, which didn't surprise her. She'd noticed some gnawed bones on the ground and the odd tattered piece of fabric caught on pipe hooks here and there as they walked. The one downside to her plan was that it would likely require them to fight their way to the exit. But D'onne figured that if she knew it was coming, she could pick her battleground and turn the advantage.

To that end, she kept her cybernetic eye locked onto infrared. The plan would have worked, too, if not for the greenish-yellow light from the lichen and the unexpected intelligence of her foes.

They had walked for nearly an hour when D'onne saw what she'd been looking for: a lift. The shaft housing it was surrounded by a staircase, and the entire thing was enclosed inside a cage. It was an access point into the utility tunnel. It was also the most obvious place for an ambush. D'onne had fought around such structures many times during her gang days.

D'onne drew Countless from its scabbard and nudged Dog, who looked at her dully before slowly grabbing his club and shield. Dog looked wrong somehow, dumber. Perhaps the lichen was having a soporific effect on his tiny brain. Whatever it was, the problem would have to wait, because the unmistakable sound of claws scrabbling against rockcrete erupted all around them, grabbing D'onne's attention.

She scanned the lift shaft and saw nothing there, though. 'Run for it,' D'onne yelled to Dog as she took off at a sprint towards the stairs.

The inward-swinging gate to the stairwell gaped open at the bottom. *What great luck*, thought D'onne as she hurried towards it. As she neared the cage, though, the entire tableau screamed trap. The cramped space in the caged stairwell would hinder the range of Countless and Dog's club, and the stench that permeated this cavern now seemed to be wafting down from above.

D'onne switched off the infrared filter on her cybernetic eye and peered up into the stairwell. Sure enough, up near the illuminated lichen she caught movement. 'Guard my back, Dog!' she yelled as she stepped onto the stairs and swung the gate shut.

It didn't latch. 'Of course,' D'onne spat, as she slammed the gate two more times and watched it bounce back open. From above, she heard guttural war cries. A small army of muties swarmed down, their yellow skin toxic and sickly in the greenish lichen light, brandishing impromptu swords and spears made from broken slivers of metal wrapped in mouldy cloth or tied to the ends of metal rods with what looked like sinew.

At the same time, the claw-scraping sounds from behind them became punctuated by the chittering of teeth. D'onne peered back the way they had come and saw a pack of mutated rats as big as mastiffs loping towards them.

'Sometimes I hate being right,' muttered D'onne. She thought for a moment and devised a quick plan. She went back through the gate and pushed Dog towards it. 'Inside, you mangy cur,' she demanded. 'Guard that gate!'

The ogryn shambled into the cage, and D'onne pulled the gate closed behind him. Dog backed up to hold the gate closed and placed his giant shield in front of his torso.

'Now,' said D'onne turning towards the mutie rats and triggering the chain on Countless. 'Time to deal with you.' About a dozen filthy, scabby rats that had been scrambling straight at her all slowed at once as the screeching whine of the chainsword erupted through the cavern.

As the rats encircled D'onne, she got a good look at them. They were huge in comparison to the rats in the stack, but emaciated from lack of food. However, the fire in their eyes told her they were far enough from their last meal to be ravenous, but not too weakened. 'Come on, you bastards,' she said, but none of them wanted to test the bite of her chain.

Behind D'onne, amidst the clanging of makeshift weapons against Dog's shield and armoured legs – and the guttural whoops, grunts and yelps of the muties trying to get past her bodyguard – a double-whistle pierced the rising rabble. 'That can't be good,' muttered D'onne.

She was right. At the whistle, the rat pack rushed forward. D'onne swung Countless in a wide arcing swath around her, cutting through the twitching nose and ears of the first mutie rat to reach her, down through the front legs of the one beside it, and then back up and through the chest and shoulder of a third in line.

D'onne didn't stop there, though. She allowed the momentum of the swing to twist her body around and leapt into the air. Releasing her hold on the chainsword with one hand, she grabbed the cage with that free hand and pulled her legs up to her butt.

The rest of the pack crashed into the cage below her. D'onne immediately swung her legs to the side and, still hanging from one hand, swung the chainsword down through the scab-covered heads of three more.

The rest backed off out of range, covered in the blood and brains of their nest mates. Another double whistle from inside the cage elicited a chorus of chitters and squeaks from the remaining five rats. Their bared buckteeth were dark in the yellow light and a frothy drool bubbled from their narrow snouts.

Two of the rats ran forward again, their disease-ridden teeth gnashing in anticipation. At the last moment, D'onne released her grip on the cage and dropped to the ground before they reached her. She thrust Countless through one rat's distended stomach, impaling its spine. Before the other rat could react, D'onne slammed its mate into its body with all the force she could muster. The second rat's neck snapped as Countless cut its way out of the impaled creature.

D'onne turned and raised Countless above her head and roared at the last three, who turned and fled. She waited for a moment to make sure they wouldn't return, but after two more double whistles didn't bring them back, D'onne felt safe.

She turned to survey the situation inside the cage, which would have been comical if not for the disgusting and pathetic nature of the muties. Dog was pressed against the gate, practically cowering behind his giant shield.

Surrounding the ogryn were more than a dozen rag-covered, deformed humans beating on Dog's shield with their make-shift weapons. Behind that group another twenty or so tried to push their way down the stairs to get into the action.

It was amazing to D'onne that these poor, wretched excuses for human beings had this much stamina and drive. Most muties were little more than skin and bones. Their paper-thin, yellowing skin hung from their limbs, and most were wasting away if not malformed from their toxic environment.

Had D'onne told Dog to kill them all, they would probably be dead already. But then she noticed one at the back on the stairs that looked stronger, carried decent weapons, and had an idol of bone and scraps of cloth perched on her head. Their leader, surrounded by the strongest of the rest, all of whom had real weapons, no doubt looted from whatever gangers had been unlucky enough to try to sneak through here before D'onne.

They needed to take out the leader and her bodyguards to get out of here alive. 'Dog!' yelled D'onne. 'Charge!'

The ogryn braced one foot against the cage and shoved his shield and upper body forward into the crowd. The effect was like a wave as the muties on the floor all fell backwards at once, knocking those behind them down into the next row.

Dog continued pushing forward, trampling several muties under his enormous feet, while many of those who didn't fall beneath his boot got smashed by their fellow muties as those behind them pushed back to avoid getting crushed themselves.

As soon as the gate was clear, D'onne shoved it open, grabbed Dog by his belt and pulled him back out. She hauled him to one side before leaping across to the other. She brought Countless back to life as the ogryn dropped his shield and grabbed his giant club in both hands.

With the way clear, the muties rushed out of the cage, happy to be free of the trap they'd caught themselves in. Any that came towards D'onne she cut down. Any that ran off, she allowed to escape. She hoped Dog would do the same, but from the blur of his club, she felt he didn't miss many enemies who strayed too close. Once all the cannon fodder had cleared, D'onne pointed for Dog to take up position blocking the gate.

D'onne peered through the cage at the remaining muties. While they all had that sickly yellow pallor, made all the worse by the lichen illumination, and many showed obvious cancerous sores on their faces and limbs, this group was better fed and clothed as well as having decent weapons. D'onne saw a couple of fighting knives as well as a flail and a two-handed axe. The leader wore a battle glove covered with metal plates to use as a shield and fitted with long spikes that impaled enemies with every punch.

'You've seen what we can do,' called D'onne into the cage. 'We don't want to hurt you. Any of you can leave.' D'onne paused, then pointed at the leader behind the rest. 'Except her. So, who wants to be the new leader?'

The leader's guards all glanced at one another, unsure

what to do. D'onne thumped Dog and motioned for him to move to the side again. Once he cleared the opening, five of the six guards ran down the stairs, holding their weapons in upraised hands as they passed, warily, through the gate. D'onne smiled at them as they ran off into the cavern, once again whooping and hollering.

The final guard, who'd stood still as if paralysed, made up his mind. He turned on his leader and swung with his fighting knife, leaving himself wide open to counter-attack. The leader shoved the spikes on her battle glove through the guard's chest, into his heart, and out the back of his emaciated chest, spraying arterial blood and bits of rib and spine across the cage and stairs. After a second, the knife dropped to the floor with a pathetic clatter.

When the mutie leader pulled her weapon free and realised she was all alone, she turned and dropped to her knees.

'Forgive, please,' she said. 'We are hungry. We try to survive.'

D'onne considered what to do. While the mutie leader looked hale and hearty in comparison to the rest of her clan, she was still emaciated and cancer-ridden. The hive was a hard enough place for gangers and so-called normals. She couldn't fathom life as one of these poor wretches.

D'onne thought about it. That glove gave this wretched, mutated woman too much power, though. She had organised a fairly large contingent of muties into a reasonably strong raiding party. The underhive had far too many dangers already to add organised muties to the list.

'Drop the glove and walk away,' she said, coming to a decision.

'No,' said the leader, her already slumping body sagging even further. 'Without this, I am nothing. I am dead.'

'Your choice,' said D'onne. 'Either I kill you and take the glove or you leave it here and take your chances.'

The leader realised it was no choice. She dropped the glove on the steps and shuffled down the stairs and out of the cage. D'onne ran inside and grabbed the fighting knife and returned to the gate. 'Hey,' she yelled. 'Take this and rebuild.' She tossed the knife outside the cage before closing the gate behind her and Dog.

'Dog,' commanded D'onne. 'Secure that gate.' She handed him one of the strips of metal the muties had used as weapons, which he bent around the gate posts.

'Now,' she said. 'Let's get out of this hole.' She grabbed the battle glove and strode up the stairs, confident the worst was behind them.

Several flights up, D'onne glanced back to see Dog lagging behind. She was halfway up from the landing he'd just reached. 'What the sump is wrong with you?' she asked.

As if in answer, Dog slumped face-first onto the metal-grate floor of the landing.

Kordon Brann walked through the first floor of his Promethium Guild offices, barely noticing that the bloody mess hadn't been cleaned up. He made a mental note to check on the workers he'd hired to remove the bodies but knew in his heart that none of that mattered now.

He had bigger rats to roast. His time inside the Cawdor offices above the sanctuary had been unusually enlightening. There was much to accomplish and not a lot of time to do it if he was to get ahead of all interested powers.

Kordon hurried upstairs to his office and sat at his desk. He needed new resources but wasn't sure of the best way to go about finding them. He could venture into the field, but that wasn't his style or forte and, truth be told, he didn't have time. Instead, Brann pulled the large bottom drawer completely out from his desk and turned it over, dumping the contents on the floor. He then reached inside the empty drawer and felt around for the secret latch.

'There you are,' he said. The mechanism was tricky, and he hadn't needed to unlatch it in years, so it took several fumbling attempts to get the compartment open. Inside were a paper ledger, several cones of incense and a small metal box with wires protruding from each end.

Kordon set the ledger aside. He would need the account numbers inside once he located the resources he needed to hire. First, though, he needed the box, which he laid between his terminal and keyboard. It took him a few minutes to light the incense, recall and recite the correct chants, and connect all the wires. Once done, though, he could make contact with some special associates without the enforcers or, more importantly, his rivals, ever finding out what he was doing.

It was said Lord Helmawr had eyes and ears everywhere, and that might well be true, but as far as Kordon was concerned, the lord of Hive Primus was the least of his worries. Brann doubted the old man cared one whit about his minor legal indiscretions in the pursuit of profit. That was what the hive was all about after all. But if his fellow Pyrocaen lords caught wind of Brann's next few moves, he fully expected to find himself being given an up-close and personal experience with the Eternal Flame.

CHAPTER 9

DUST FALLS

Scrutinator Servalen strode towards the enforcer precinct at the entrance to Dust Falls like she owned the place, which she was about to prove true to Precinct Proctor Clause Bauhein and the council there.

A dust haze that had choked the narrow streets earlier had mostly dissipated, but the stench it left behind coated every surface. The scrap-metal shanties that dotted the seedier sections of the Haggle Market needed to be replaced constantly because of the corrosion caused by the dust rain.

Every year, the expanse of nothingness – the vast Dust Desert – surrounding Dust Falls grew a little larger as locals ripped apart the remains of habs built ages past and hauled sections back to town to replace the walls and roofs that had been swallowed.

Depending on the day and the fickle whims of the air circulators, dust either swept out over the walls and across the Dust Desert towards the White Wastes or gathered in swirls at the edge of the Abyss in the centre of town. There it joined the dried-up effluvial waste that flowed from Hive City above, past Dust Falls, and down through the kilometres-deep hole towards Hive Bottom and the great Sump Lake.

The underhive circle of death, mused Servalen as she surveyed the loathsome city that was a constant thorn in her side. On any given day, gangs from every house travelled to or gathered in Dust Falls to spend the creds they'd earned on expeditions into the Abyss, while others with worse luck tried to steal or cheat them. That many gangs in close proximity was a powder keg ready to explode at the smallest spark. One wrong word, or the wrong person fleeced, combined with too many drinks, and Dust Falls would erupt into violence. Servalen had seen it happen too often.

In fact, the scrutinator found herself in this accursed place so often she wondered if it wouldn't be better to wipe it from existence. It wouldn't be easy. Thousands of people thronged the Haggle every day and the guilders stored many times that number of slaves in their pens. It would be a bloodbath, and the Council of Dust would scream their protests all the way up to Helmawr.

But it would be satisfying. All she had to do was give the word. Her superiors might raise their eyebrows, but she could rationalise the decision to them, and then make a scapegoat of whatever house was most hated at the time to deflect their wrath.

But what would be the point? thought Servalen. Dust Falls existed because the underhive needed it to. Gangs and bounty hunters were drawn to the Abyss because of the promised treasures trapped inside the centuries' worth of compressed domes that dotted the kilometres-deep hole. Anyone brave enough – or desperate enough – to go over the edge in search

of riches would come to this spot no matter what Servalen did. Destroy Dust Falls and another settlement would
be built in its place within a month, most likely run by the
very people running it now.

The scrutinator patted her cyber companion on the head
and shook off the reverie. She turned to address Sergeant
Nox and the squad. The sergeant came to attention immediately. Within seconds his squad had formed two perfect
lines in front of Precinct 1313.

Servalen smiled inwardly at the respect she had garnered
from the squad, but kept her eyes and mouth stern, knowing full well that showing a moment's weakness would risk
all the work she'd put into them so far.

'Sergeant,' she said.

'Yes, ma'am?' responded Nox.

'You and the squad are to take direct control of this city,'
Servalen commanded.

'Ma'am?' One of Nox's eyebrows lifted ever so slightly as
he said the single word. Servalen noticed, but let it pass –
for now.

'I am declaring Palanite Law over Dust Falls,' she continued, stating it as a matter of fact and not as a plan that would
require sign-off by the local enforcer precinct proctor or the
Council of Dust.

'Yes, ma'am.'

'While I go and speak with Proctor Bauhein, I want you
to begin coordinating with the Dust Falls enforcers to close
every road into the settlement and shut down all the gates
into the Abyss,' she said. 'No one enters or leaves Dust Falls
without my permission.'

'Are you certain the proctor and the Council will go along
with this?'

Servalen understood his hesitation. She was asking a lot. 'I will make them understand my authority in this matter,' she said. 'By the time I return, you will have the authority to command the entire settlement's contingent of enforcers.'

'Yes, ma'am,' Sergeant Nox said after an audible gulp.

Servalen began ticking off orders. 'Assign two-man patrols to walk the main streets. Concentrate on the areas around the Six Clans drinking hole, the Haggle and the gates. I want to enforce a strict curfew.'

This brought murmurs from several members of the squad, but Nox snapped his hand into the air and silenced any dissent. 'I will take care of it, ma'am,' he stated with a quick salute, which Servalen returned in kind. 'Anything else?'

'Once you have control of the settlement, return here to Precinct 1313,' she said pointing at the imposing multi-storey building looming over the outer wall of Dust Falls at the end of the street. 'I will coordinate the lockdown efforts from there while I try to determine where Mad D'onne is headed next.'

'We're not going to try to take D'onne here in the settlement?' asked Nox. 'You said she would come here next.'

'Yes, she has to come through here,' replied Servalen. 'But, no, we won't try to capture her here.'

'Wasn't that the entire reason for returning here so quickly?' blurted Nox, his face going red as soon as the words left his mouth.

Servalen allowed herself a small smile before answering. 'Have you ever been caught in the middle of an all-out gang war, sergeant?'

Nox nodded. 'Many times,' he said. 'In the pursuit of the Pax Helmawr.'

Servalen cocked her head and raised her hands and eyebrows

as she might when driving a point home to a child. 'Now, imagine that in the middle of Dust Falls,' she said. 'Mad D'onne is a walking, sometimes talking, flamethrower. She'd have every gang in there brawling before you could draw your gun.'

Seeing the light finally igniting behind the sergeant's eyes, Servalen continued. 'Our best bet is to keep Mad D'onne from entering Dust Falls. Barring that, we will allow her to leave as quickly and quietly as possible, hopefully already knowing where she is going so we can intercept her outside these volatile walls. Is that clear, sergeant?'

'Crystal clear, ma'am,' replied the sergeant, failing to keep the sarcasm he'd previously been reprimanded for out of his voice.

'Excellent,' she said. 'You have your orders.' With that Servalen turned on her heels and strode towards the grey plasteel precinct house. KB-88 followed closely, turning to growl at shadows that grew out of nearby doorways.

When one shadow didn't disappear quickly enough into its hovel, the cyber-mastiff left Servalen's side and bolted through the door. Several short, sharp barks, one long growl, the snapping of metal teeth and a scream of pain quickly followed as Servalen waited outside.

A moment later, KB-88 padded back to the scrutinator, a bit of bloody cloth hanging from its metal jaw. Servalen pulled the tattered sleeve free and continued towards Precinct 1313, confident in the ability of her pet to handle any situation she might encounter.

D'onne stomped back down the stairs towards her unconscious bodyguard. Conflicting emotions played through her head. She was alternately angry at Dog for slowing them down and concerned he might be dead – which would rob her of the chance to punish him for whatever he'd done to cause this problem in the first place.

When D'onne reached the supine ogryn, she nudged him with her boot to see if he was alive. When she got no response, she whipped her leg forward and 'nudged' him harder – with a swift kick to the ribs. That produced an audible grunt, which at least answered one question.

'Get up,' D'onne yelled, kicking him again. She was now officially angry. 'What the sump is wrong with you?'

Dog didn't respond. In fact, it was becoming clear to D'onne he was not faking. Her first clue was that he hadn't moved since he fell face-first onto the metal grating. If he'd fallen on solid rockcrete, he would be suffocating right now. The open grating of the step had probably saved his life. Her second clue was the colour of the ogryn's skin. His neck, shoulder and cheek had all turned a sickly greyish-green colour, which looked worse in the lichen light.

'Let's turn you over and see what happened,' said D'onne with a sigh. She got down onto the grating beside Dog and began pushing on his body. It wouldn't budge. His bulk was too much for her to move alone.

'Just great,' she said, and punched him in the kidney for being such a pain in her ass. D'onne sat beside the ogryn and thought. After a minute, she turned his head to the side to allow him to breathe more easily because the sound of his lips vibrating against the grating was driving her crazy.

'I've got to make your bulk work for me and not against me,' she said finally. D'onne got up, grabbed one of Dog's feet and pulled that leg up and over his other leg. Then, using the bodyguard's club as a wedge under his hip, she levered him up until gravity took over and dropped him onto his back.

'There,' said D'onne. 'Now, let's see what's going on here.'

Dog's chest, neck and face were still covered in rat blood, so it was impossible to see anything clearly unless she washed it all off. She had no water, but she did have a bottle of what had looked like primo hooch, which she'd stolen from the Cawdor while searching for Dog. She pulled it out, took a long pull so it didn't all go to waste, and then, reluctantly, began pouring it over Dog's body.

The ogryn screamed and woke up, his eyes flashing wide as he sat up and almost knocked the bottle from D'onne's hands. As she fumbled to keep the bottle from dropping and wasting any more of the sweet, stinging liquid inside, Dog fell back over with an enormous bang onto the grating.

D'onne capped the bottle and then wiped away as much blood and liquor as she could without getting her clothes any bloodier. Then, on the ogryn's neck, she saw it: two sets of long scratches in the soft flesh on either side of his jugular. They weren't deep. He wasn't going to bleed to death. But it wasn't the scratches that worried D'onne.

In addition to the sickly colour of the surrounding tissue, his veins and arteries had engorged beneath the skin, covering the area with a spiderweb of purple lines of infection that was visibly spreading down his arm and up towards his face. One large line was heading straight towards his heart.

Scrutinator Servalen tried to push her way past the seated assistant outside the proctor's office with a wave of her hand. The young enforcer stood and moved to place herself between the scrutinator and her boss' door, but a short bark followed by a long growl from KB-88 stopped her in her tracks at the corner of her desk.

Servalen scowled at the young woman. It was the same

assistant Servalen had shown the lord's personal seal to the last time a lead had forced her to visit Dust Falls on official business. If the woman couldn't remember an official representative of the palanite enforcers, she should be replaced.

'I am Scrutinator Primus Servalen of the palanite enforcers,' she said to the assistant, producing Lord Helmawr's seal by rote. 'I have urgent business with Proctor Bauhein. We are not to be disturbed. Do you understand?'

'I take my orders from the proctor,' the assistant replied, dully.

Servalen sighed. 'And I take my orders from the Lord Provost Marshal,' she told the assistant as she turned towards the grey plasteel door.

'My metal friend here will guard the door. I would avoid eye contact, if I were you.' With that, Servalen turned, opened the door, and marched into the proctor's office.

'You have a problem, Clause,' stated Servalen as she slammed the door closed behind her.

'You're trying to take control of my town,' replied the proctor without looking up from the paperwork littering his desk, 'and close the gates to the Abyss! This is unprecedented. Mistress of Coin Minerva and Narco Lord Van Zep will not stand idly by and let this happen without responding.'

'Okay,' said Servalen. 'You have several problems. I can help you with the big one. If you help me, all the other problems will go away.'

'Besides an assistant who can't keep an overly zealous scrutinator out of my office, what is my big problem?' asked Proctor Bauhein. The large, imposing enforcer looked up from the reports on his desk and locked eyes with Servalen.

To his credit, Clause Bauhein held Servalen's gaze for several seconds before dropping his eyes back to the desk. The proctor shuffled through a few reports to make it look deliberate, but Servalen saw the bead of sweat at his temple and knew she had him right where she wanted him.

'Your big problem is Mad D'onne,' replied Servalen, twisting the stress screw a little tighter into the proctor's nervous mind. 'She is coming to Dust Falls. You think the great zombie plague was a threat to the settlement? Remember what happened the last time D'onne strode into town.'

Proctor Bauhein mustered the will to stand and look, if not directly at Servalen's face, somewhere next to her head. 'Fine,' he said, his voice showing his resignation. 'Close the settlement. I will deal with the Council of Dust. Is that all?'

Servalen shook her head, causing Bauhein to slump back into his chair.

'Look, you don't want me here and I don't want to be here,' said Servalen, trying to take a lighter tone and marginally succeeding. At the same time, she closed the distance between the door and the proctor's desk to loom over the seated man.

The combination of Servalen's more conciliatory tone and intimidating stance had an effect on the proctor. When Bauhein glanced back up, a myriad emotions played across his face: anger, mostly, but also fear and a tinge of hope.

'What do you want?' he said, his voice low and resigned. 'You already have my city. What more can I give you?'

'Information,' replied Servalen. She took a step back from the desk and sat down to look at the proctor on a more even level. 'Mad D'onne is on her way here, but this isn't her destination. She's passing through.'

Bauhein sighed. 'You could have told me that from the beginning,' he said. 'Why all the mind games?'

Servalen smiled. 'Maybe I enjoy them,' she said. 'Maybe I hate this town so much it brings out the worst in me. Or maybe you needed to know who was truly in charge here today.'

'Fine. You win. What information do you need?'

Servalen smiled inwardly this time. 'The Cawdor have something D'onne wants,' she said. 'I need to find it first or at least stop that lunatic from getting her hands on it.'

'Oh, really?' said Bauhein, his eyebrow raised. He began rifling through the reports on his desk again, but this time in earnest. 'Do you know what she's looking for?'

'A powerful psyker. Just a boy, really.'

Bauhein pulled a report from the file and glanced at it. His demeanour was seemingly calm to an average observer, but Servalen noticed the man was practically quivering with restrained excitement.

Servalen stood, leaned forward and put her hands on the desk to loom over the large man. 'What is that report?' she asked. 'Hand it over.'

Servalen snatched the paper from the proctor and skimmed its contents. The report stated that a group of Cawdor had entered Dust Falls earlier this very day with an unsanctioned slave in tow – a young boy in grubby clothes – and had joined up with a larger gang.

The scrutinator sat down and leaned back in the chair to give the proctor a bit more space. 'Impressive,' she said, and mostly meant it. 'You know everything that happens in your jurisdiction. So, tell me, where are the Cawdor keeping the boy?'

From the pained look on his face, Proctor Bauhein was having an argument with himself.

She'd seen this response in numerous interrogations. The man had information Servalen needed – and would pay dearly for – but withholding it in hopes of getting a sweeter deal could simply bring more pain. As always, the fear of spending more time with the scrutinator overrode the subject's hopes for a bigger payday.

'They left through the gates an hour ago,' replied Bauhein without looking up to meet Servalen's gaze. 'They are already on their way down into the Abyss. All of them, the full Cawdor gang and the boy.'

'Thank you,' said Servalen. 'I will take my squad and leave the settlement. You may reopen the roads and the gates.'

She stood to leave, but then turned back one last time. 'If Mad D'onne enters Dust Falls,' she said, locking eyes with Bauhein and willing the man to hold her gaze, 'your enforcers will not engage her, will not deter her in any way, and will allow her to leave the settlement unharmed. Do we understand one another?'

Proctor Bauhein weathered the storm admirably, then broke. 'Yes, ma'am,' he said, his voice barely louder than a whisper.

CHAPTER 10

CLIFFS AND WALLS

D'onne slid the lift gate open and peered into an abandoned room that hadn't seen a human being in at least ten years. A thick film of dust covered the floor and the empty shelves lining the side and back walls. A single door set in the middle of the far wall sat between tall cabinets that had once been locked, but long ago had been jimmied open. Whatever had been inside was long gone.

'Seems as good a place as any to store you, Dog,' she said as she stepped out from the lift cage, which dominated the middle of the room. 'Picked clean and forgotten. Pretty much describes the best places I've ever hidden.'

She looked at the unconscious ogryn inside the lift. It had taken D'onne a long time to lever his enormous bulk into the cage. They were lucky the ancient lift still functioned. From the state of this engineer's shed, it hadn't been serviced in more than a decade, perhaps longer. She hoped it didn't become his coffin. She would miss using Dog as a bullet shield.

D'onne strode across the room, kicking up a cloud of dust that nearly obscured the cage. 'I'll be back with a doc or meds,' she said over her shoulder as she opened the door, taking a step over the threshold onto the tiled floor beyond.

The ground split into a shadowy nothingness and D'onne plummeted feet first into the darkness. Her hand ripped free from the door handle before she knew what had happened. She tried to grab the door jamb with the same hand, but only succeeded in dislocating a few knuckles and slicing a gash across her palm.

She and Dog must have walked far enough through the utility tunnel to get close to the edge of the Abyss. It made sense for the muties to live near that kilometres-deep hole. It was like an all-access pass to the treasures of a hundred levels, not to mention easy pickings of those dumb enough to descend the Abyss without proper protection.

Contrary to popular belief, the Abyss wasn't a vertical drop. Like any hole created by erosion, it sloped from the top down, and twisted to follow the path of least resistance. There was nearly half a kilometre of sloping terrain at the top of the Abyss before it became a sheer drop. This was both good news and bad for D'onne, who slammed into a rockcrete abutment – the edge of some ancient retaining wall sticking out into the Abyss twenty metres below the storage room.

The wall hit D'onne in the chest as she fell past it, driving the wind from her lungs, cracking a rib, and dislodging the spiked glove she had stuck in her waistband. She threw her arms forward to grab the top of the wall but misjudged the distance and slammed her elbows into the rockcrete instead as the mutie leader's treasured weapon tumbled away.

'Damnit,' moaned D'onne, as much from the loss of the

weapon as from her precarious predicament. 'That was going to pay for recharging Pig.'

Pain from the cracked rib and bruised joints shot through D'onne's body, but the impact had slowed her fall. As her forearms scraped down the rockcrete abutment, she scrambled to grab hold with her fingers and slammed her knees and toes into the side of the wall. A combination of friction, strength and sheer determination brought D'onne's slide to a halt.

For a moment, she hung there as she tried to refill her lungs. Every breath was a new adventure in pain, but D'onne knew her arms and legs would soon tire, so she inhaled deeply, tensed her muscles against the strain and began climbing the wall, inch by inch, a foot-hold at a time. Soon, she lay atop the wall, gasping for breath that barely came, her numb legs throbbing from the adrenaline-fuelled blood pulsing through them.

She lay on her back for a time taking stock of all her aches and pains. Her hands and forearms were scraped and bloody. Her elbows were on fire, but a few experimental flexes of the joints showed no permanent damage. A rib was cracked, but her breathing had eased. It seemed her corset had taken the brunt of the impact, and the tightness of the garment was better than any bandage wrap.

All told, it wasn't the worst fall into the Abyss she'd ever suffered. At least she was still conscious. Now for the bad news: the top of the Abyss was at least a two hundred metre climb. And then she'd have to find her way back to Dog, hopefully with meds or a doc. A vet, she thought wryly, and laughed, which hurt like hell but was worth it.

An hour later, D'onne reached the top of the Abyss. The last part of the climb had been the hardest. Long ago, the effluent had eroded away the rockcrete substrata beneath the habs at the edge of the kilometre-deep hole, causing the ground and the buildings at the edge to tip over at ridiculous angles. Most had fallen into the Abyss, but some remained connected to the ground, hanging over the edge at thirty-to forty-five-degree angles.

It was like walking up the surface of a whirlpool towards calm seas, with boats looming all about. The buildings tantalised with their promised safety, but you knew full well that nothing around you was secure, least of all the ground you walked on.

Just before reaching this section, as D'onne made her way through an open expanse devoid of buildings or any debris that could provide cover, she spotted the enforcer squad piling into one of the Dust Falls gate lifts atop the Abyss. If they looked her way they would certainly spot her. She hung there like a black leather-clad spider.

As the lift approached her level, D'onne slid down the Abyss twenty metres towards a section of tangled and twisted plasteel rebar poles that jutted out from the wall like a mangled cage. She grabbed a curved metal bar in one hand and gritted against the pain as she swung her legs through a gap in the snarl of metal. Once inside the makeshift cage, D'onne watched as the lift descended past.

A tall, gaunt woman stood in front of the armour-clad enforcers. She wore a long leather cloak, belted at the waist, that flowed past the tops of her boots. Atop the cloak, she wore an armoured chest plate, but to D'onne's trained eyes, the severe-looking woman was no fighter.

The woman turned, and D'onne swore she stared straight at her hiding place. The hunter pressed her body against the wall, pushing into the tangle of rebar as far as she could.

After a long, tense moment, the woman turned to speak to one of the enforcers and then the lift was past.

Afterward, D'onne extracted herself from the cage and began the long ascent towards the top. By the time she reached it, her body needed a few minutes to recuperate and her mind needed time to decompress from the stress of the climb.

She sat in a heap and took a moment to breathe, get her bearings and burn this spot into her memory so she could find it again later. She was off to one side of the busiest Abyss gates. Behind her she could see the rising silos of the warehouse district and over to the side she could hear and smell the guilder slave pens.

A nearby silo stood open and dark inside. D'onne decided to chance that it was currently abandoned. After dusting herself off from the climb, she headed for the open door, smiling politely at a few burly Goliaths hauling goods on carts from the warehouses towards the Haggle off in the distance.

D'onne was a bit surprised that no one recognised her before she reached the empty silo. She supposed it was possible that random labourers had never heard of her, but before she reached the open silo door, she spotted a couple of local enforcers patrolling between the silos. She was certain they had seen her, but instead of raising an alarm, they turned about face and headed down between two other silos.

This seemed odd to D'onne. Dust Falls security relied on two factors to keep its citizens safe: the wall surrounding the entire city and the local enforcer presence. The wall protected the settlement from external attacks, most notably muties, but occasionally other horrors that crawled out of their holes to search for fresh hunting grounds.

Inside the walls, the local precinct enforcers kept the peace between the gangs so that the guilders and traders (and the

Council of Dust) could continue to profit from the gangs who ventured into the Abyss to bring back its treasures. They were a diligent force, who would no doubt know of D'onne. Because of the enforcers, the streets of Dust Falls were, oddly, among the safest in the underhive, which, admittedly, wasn't that safe.

Over the years Dust Falls had certainly seen its fair share of attacks. It was once nearly overrun by plague zombies, and several times noble houses had made concerted efforts to gain control of the town and so also the Abyss. But, other than one freak riot that D'onne *definitely* had not started (and no one living could prove otherwise), no attacking force had ever taken Dust Falls.

In fact, a gigantic spider mare had once crawled out from the Sump Lake and rampaged through the settlement before being herded to the town's wall. It took the entire precinct's contingent of enforcers and members of five separate gangs to bring down the mare before it escaped Dust Falls.

The black and green-streaked stain of its bloated body could still be seen on the inner wall where the massive creature had died after killing and eating two enforcers, a handful of juves, and one very unlucky guilder. A night of raucous partying inside the Six Clans drinking hole had been held in honour of the brave enforcers and juves. No one had mourned the loss of the guilder.

So, when D'onne found herself inside the walls of Dust Falls, she figured all she needed to do was stay away from the local enforcers – and avoid starting another gang war – and she'd be where she needed to be in no time.

She shrugged at her luck in avoiding the enforcers and slipped inside the open silo, quickly scanning it for other squatters. A few regular-sized rats scurried about, but the rest of the silo was empty. She decided to lie low for a while and watch the patrol patterns of the guards near the Abyss gates before venturing out to find a doc.

Her luck held, because no more than fifteen minutes later, D'onne noticed someone who held the answers to all her current problems: a certain one-armed enforcer who had quite graciously, if unwillingly, aided her previous escape from the Cawdor sanctuary.

For reasons D'onne cared nothing about, this young, formerly fully functional enforcer had not joined the rest of the squad on their descent into the Abyss. Instead, he patrolled the warehouse district, perhaps looking for her. D'onne decided to give him what he wanted.

She crept out of the silo and followed her mark down a narrow alley between it and the outer wall of the settlement. He came to a set of stairs running up the side of the wall and began to climb.

D'onne slunk along the wall beneath the enforcer as he patrolled on top, watching for a secluded spot to launch her ambush. Behind another silo that blocked the view of the wall from the rest of the settlement, D'onne began scrambling up the side, using helpful handholds installed to allow guards to rally on the wall quickly. Once she neared the top, D'onne reached up with one hand and grabbed the enforcer by the ankle. She yanked hard, pulling the man off balance.

He yelped in surprise at his sudden loss of footing, but the sound was muted by his helmet. D'onne swung her arm out wide, still holding the enforcer's ankle, and kicked off the wall, dragging his leg behind her.

They both fell, but D'onne had both feet under her and was prepared for the landing, while the enforcer had no control of his body, one leg grappled and only one arm to cushion his impact. It did not end well for him. His armoured body lay in a crumpled mass on the ground next to D'onne, with one leg bent forward at the knee.

'You may lose that leg, friend,' said D'onne, getting up. 'You have a bad habit of being in my right place at your wrong time.'

The enforcer didn't answer, and D'onne noticed a long crack in his helmet that ran from one ear to the other around the back of his head.

'Now I have to drag your ass back to my silo,' D'onne said with a sigh. 'Thanks for nothing!' She reached down and grabbed the man by his armoured collar and pulled him back to the narrow alley that led to the abandoned silo she had claimed, being careful to stay close to the wall and avoid making a noise when other patrols walked nearby.

Once she got his dead weight inside the empty silo, D'onne returned to the wall to scuff out all evidence of the dragged body. There was no blood, which was good news for the enforcer, but better news for D'onne.

Back in the silo, D'onne got to work. First she removed the enforcer's weapons – a couple of frag grenades and a stub gun – plus his gear belt and pack. Next she set about removing the man's armour, which was a slow process. D'onne periodically kicked him in the head to make sure he remained unconscious.

Inside his belt pack, she found a set of magnacles. Not that useful on a one-armed man, so D'onne improvised. She cuffed the man's remaining wrist to a chain hanging down the wall of the silo used to haul goods up to the second level. She then found the winch and hauled the chain up so he hung from it while standing on his one good leg. The enforcer wasn't going anywhere anytime soon.

A torn strip of the enforcer's undershirt stuffed into his mouth completed the job. Now she could take a good look at the prizes she'd earned for all her hard work. D'onne dumped the contents of his belt pouches and pack on the floor of the silo and began sorting. She felt her smile stretch from ear to ear as she looked at them all.

After applying some of the medic's salves and dressings to her wounds, D'onne began wracking her brain for a trader in Dust Falls whose silence she could buy. Contraband this good could easily buy her a full recharge for Pig.

CHAPTER 11

DOWN TOWN

Strewn across Lord Helmawr's immense oak desk, which was larger than some of the hovels his less affluent subjects called home, lay every report and piece of intelligence his people had ever procured on House Ulanti. The thickest folders were devoted to Sylvanus, the family patriarch, and his youngest living daughter, D'onne.

It disturbed him how much information he had needed to collect on these two nobles over the years, but it probably upset him less than it would Sylvanus and Mad D'onne. While the noble houses on Necromunda wheeled in the dark to find a way to jam a knife in his back, Lord Helmawr made it his business to gather every dirty little secret he could. What did he care why they stood in line, as long as they did?

Yet, with all his intel on House Ulanti, Lord Helmawr knew they were doing the same. Spies who had professed loyalty to Sylvanus had been captured. And executed, of course, but there was always the chance that they had found something unsavoury and spirited it back to Sylvanus before they were discovered.

Helmawr had devoted considerable resources looking for some piece of blackmail that could be used to keep Sylvanus quiet in the event of a disagreement, but had thus far come up empty. Mad D'onne, however, fitted that bill. In custody, she would be his ultimate bargaining chip when dealing with House Ulanti.

As Helmawr mulled over how best he could use D'onne's madness against her father, his lord chamberlain entered the office.

'I have news about Mad D'onne, my lord,' he stated after his customary hair-flipping bow.

'Has she been caught already?' asked Helmawr, a smile creasing his face for the first time in a week. 'Wonderful work, chamberlain.'

The man's crestfallen face, the fleeting look of fear, and the extended pause sent the smile sloughing from Helmawr's face.

'Spit it out, man,' he said, glowering.

'A report from the enforcer precinct at Dust Falls has confirmed there is a purpose behind the Ulanti woman's killing spree, my lord,' he said.

'Cut the preamble, man,' sighed Helmawr. 'What is going on down there?'

The chamberlain gulped and adjusted the tight, ruffled collar around his neck.

'It seems D'onne is searching for a psyker that recently appeared in the underhive.'

'Why would D'onne... What psychic discipline does this new psyker exhibit?' he asked slowly and deliberately.

'Divination, my lord,' replied the chamberlain. 'Our sources say the young psyker can find any lost object. Quite a gift. Remarkable, really, when you think about–'

Helmawr slammed his fists down onto his desk, scattering the contents of the two large files on Sylvanus and Mad D'onne Ulanti.

The chamberlain stared, terrified, as Helmawr gawped at him, wide-eyed. 'Are you feeling well, my lord?' he asked.

'Not at all, chamberlain,' Helmawr replied. Sweat had beaded up on his prodigious forehead, and soaked through his silk shirt under his arms and across his stomach. 'Not at all.'

'Shall I fetch the royal doctors?'

Helmawr shook his head, hardly taking notice of the chamberlain. The wheels had begun turning in his mind. He needed to prepare for the worst because it seemed likely that the worst was racing towards him at interstellar speed.

'Bring the Master of the Psykanarium to me quickly but discreetly,' commanded Helmawr. 'I have important matters of state to discuss with him.'

It seemed to Servalen that she'd spent her entire day on the lift. After the trip down and back from Sludge Town, and her subsequent fact-finding mission at Precinct 1313, she had gathered up Nox's squad and headed towards the Abyss gates to get a lift into Down Town.

'What was the point of having me chase my tail back there?' asked Nox as they descended into the shaft. 'You had no intention of maintaining that lockdown, did you?'

Servalen turned towards Nox and smiled. 'You're learning, sergeant,' she said. 'You tell me. Why would I make you go to all that trouble?'

The sergeant thought for a moment. 'It was a show of force.'

Servalen nodded. 'I needed Proctor Bauhein to know I could take over his command anytime I wanted. It made him much more pliable.'

'You could have let me in on the plan,' Sergeant Nox replied.

'Think of how convincing your performance was when you believed me and were afraid of what I would do to you if you failed.'

That brought the conversation to an end. The scrutinator enjoyed a silent ride the rest of the way to Down Town, through the eight lift changes it took to reach the bottom.

Servalen was more than ready to get off the lift when Down Town came into sight and put some rockcrete beneath her feet again. It wasn't that she was afraid of heights. Servalen wasn't afraid of anything. In fact, she had no fear or any strong emotions at all. She actually felt nothing most of the time.

KB-88 was literally the only being in her life that didn't cringe every time she stood near it. It was her only friend. The cyber-mastiff was her constant companion not just because she sometimes needed a little muscle in her line of work.

As the port city of Down Town stretched out around the lift, Servalen began to realise that, once again, her thoughts had turned inward – and become a bit maudlin. The same thing had happened as they neared Sludge Town.

'He's here!' she said as the lift docked at the platform. 'The boy is somewhere inside the town.'

Nox, who had been supervising the docking process, wheeled round. 'Here? Now?' he said. 'How do you know?'

Servalen hesitated for a second. She couldn't explain it to the sergeant. She could barely explain it to herself. She had a feeling. She couldn't sense the psyker, but her instincts screamed that the boy was close.

She stared at a fixed point in the distance, and concentrated. A large skiff drifted across the sump lake, while others loaded or unloaded cargo onto frantic piers. She worked through what she knew, point by point, and exhaled. 'My source in Dust Falls confirmed the Cawdor escorted the boy into the Abyss to Down Town,' she said. 'They will be looking for transport to the Deep Pyre. They weren't so far ahead of us as to have already negotiated passage, unless they have some other way there.'

It was a reasonable assumption, she thought, *based on all available evidence.*

'Take the squad to the docks, sergeant,' she ordered, 'and search for the boy and his captors there. Interrogate the locals to see if they have already boarded a skiff.'

'Yes, scrutinator!' said Nox, adding a salute. 'Will you be joining the search?'

Servalen shook her head. 'No. I have suspicions the Cawdor have a secret way to reach the Deep Pyre,' she said. 'While you check the docks, I will check out that possibility. If you don't hear from me, I will meet you at the docks. If you don't find the boy, procure us a skiff.'

Nox saluted again and turned to lead the squad towards town. As he walked away, he began tapping on the portable terminal on his arm, most likely to bring up a map of Down Town to coordinate the squad's search. It would be wrong, out of date, but it would be something.

'Come on, KB,' she said, scratching the cyber-mastiff's metal head. 'We know where the Cawdor are taking the boy. We need to find their trail and follow it. Without the squad slowing us down, hopefully we can get there first – maybe even before D'onne descends from Dust Falls.'

The cyber-mastiff cocked its head at Servalen, as if asking if she was sure she knew what she was doing.

'The day I need a squad of enforcers to handle a few Cawdor elders is the day I throw my badge in the sump,' she said. 'If they did contract a local gang up in Dust Falls, we'll call in the sergeant and let his squad take the brunt of the final confrontation.'

Servalen strode off towards the far rear edge of the grubby little town, keeping the sump-slick habs, docks and warehouses on her right as she hugged the cliff walls of the looming Abyss above her. The Pyre lay some way down the Sump Lake past the cliff walls. If there were a secret tunnel leading to it, it must lie between the lift and the edge of the sump. Servalen picked up her pace, the fatigue of the long day evaporating as the challenge of the chase reinvigorated her mind and body.

'I don't understand the issue,' said Kordon Brann through the vox interface on his terminal. The screen showed the gaunt, scarred face of Wicker Crag, the leader of a gang of hive scum that Kordon had hired after returning from the sanctuary.

The image was green monochrome with interference lines running through it, but even so, Kordon could tell Wicker's face was flush with anger, his eyes practically popping out of his nearly skeletal face.

'*Issue?*' yelled Wicker. Spittle flew from his thin lips as he screamed. '*Like there's only one? This whole job smells worse than the sump.*'

'I thought your gang was supposed to be tough,' said Kordon. He pressed on before Wicker could respond. 'Didn't your group take down a spider mare on your first trip to the sump?'

Some of the bluster left Wicker's face. *'Yeah,'* he said. *'We got a bit of a rep after that. We done some things since then, too.'*

'That's what I'm saying,' said Kordon with a smile on his face, although inwardly he was beginning to doubt whether he'd made the right choice with this gang of scum, who imaginatively had named themselves the Circle-Skulls. Still, they were the best he could afford, and they did have a rep. Plus, they were in the right place at the right time. He needed them. 'The Circle-Skulls can do this. It's just a kidnap job. I have faith in you.'

That was the wrong thing to say.

'That's just it, Mr Brann,' spat Wicker, the spittle flying again. *'We ain't talking about a Cawdor gang here. I hear an enforcer squad and Mad Donna are after this boy as well. That's not crazy. That's suicide!'*

Damnit, thought Kordon. *They found out about that*. He'd hoped to keep that little gem of information to himself during negotiations. 'Look. I paid good credits to hire you for this job,' he said, pushing to keep the original deal in place. 'If you can't do it, I'll find people that can!'

'All I'm saying is we're gonna need some extra muscle for this job,' said Wicker. He raised his hand into view and rubbed his thumb against his middle and forefinger. *'Who's paying for that?'*

Kordon turned his head to mask his raised eyebrow and smirk. *So, all of this was a shakedown*, he thought. *This Wicker was a man after his own heart*. The scum leader did have a point about the extra muscle, though. After what Donna had done to Brann's previous gang, he couldn't argue with that. And if the word was out about Donna and the enforcers, he would have trouble finding anyone else to take the job.

'Okay,' said Kordon. 'I will transfer another five hundred

creds to you. Hire some more guns, and spread the rest around to your gangers to ease their concerns about attacking the Pyre.'

Brann keyed off the transmission and sat back in his chair. This business was risky, he realised. But if it should blow up, there was little to point back to him. All his communications had been through guilder channels, and the credits would be virtually untraceable if anyone was inclined to look. Still, he had a lot invested in this venture. He would need someone in Down Town to keep tabs on the situation. Time to make another call.

D'onne hung by her fingertips from the wall of the Abyss, her lower body swaying in the space made by the open doorway to the supply room. She swung back and forth a few times and then let go. Her feet landed inside the room, but the ground shifted, knocking her balance back towards the chasm.

She swung her arms out to catch the inner walls and stop herself from falling to her death, forgetting about the cabinets to either side. Her fingertips scraped along their plasteel surface and her feet started sliding out from under her on the dusty rockcrete floor. Her fingernails caught on the door jamb and a moment later she found herself on her hands and knees inhaling a cloud of Abyss dust.

D'onne stood and coughed for a full minute before she could breathe normally again. A pain in her left hand called attention to the torn fingernail she'd suffered. 'You see what I go through for you, Dog? That's twice I've nearly died!' she called into the cloud of dust. 'I don't know why. You hardly deserve it!'

No response came from the lift cage that dominated the

centre of the room – not even a grunt or the ogryn's horrible snoring, which D'onne swore was louder than Countless running at full speed.

'Dog?' called D'onne. 'Dog?'

She rushed to the cage, shoved open the gate and dropped to the metal-grate floor beside her bodyguard. She fumbled to find his neck and checked for a pulse. It was weak and slow, barely discernible through the ogryn's thick skin. D'onne lowered her ear to his face and listened. His breathing was shallow and she heard a raspy wheeze with every exhale.

Without waiting for the dust to settle, D'onne grabbed a stimm from Barker's pack and jammed it into Dog's inner arm between the bodyguard's plasteel armour plating. She checked the pulse and breathing again after a minute and both seemed improved, but not much.

When D'onne could finally see, she realised why Dog's health had fallen so fast. The infection from the wounds on his neck had spread across his face and all the way down both arms. Worse, the engorged purple spiderweb of blood vessels had almost completely encircled his heart, turning his chest into a sickly maze of infection. His entire body was now a wan yellow colour.

D'onne searched through the first-aid pack she'd stolen and found what she needed. Enforcers had to enter a multitude of toxic environments and face all sorts of contagions in their work. They always had the best antivirals. Not knowing what rat-borne infection worked this fast, D'onne grabbed a strong, broad-spectrum serum.

Given Dog's bulk and the speed of the infection, D'onne figured more would be better. After jamming the antiviral into an applicator, she plunged the needle into Dog's chest and emptied the whole course into the ogryn's heart.

There was no immediate change in his condition, not that D'onne expected to see anything right away. Dog lay there, motionless, showing no physical reaction to the long, quivering needle piercing his heart.

Well, it will either kill him or save him, D'onne thought as she sat back and watched her bodyguard. Either way, she couldn't wait. From the reports she'd heard over the enforcer's vox, she needed to reach the Sump Lake as fast as possible. *Time to see how deep this lift shaft goes.*

CHAPTER 12

A BOY NAMED JEREN

Jeren Jerenson had never been anything special. He was slightly built and slightly short, with arms like twigs and legs no bigger around than skiff oars. On his eighteenth birthday, he still weighed no more than fifty kilos sopping wet. His mother, on her more charitable days, said he would disappear if he turned sideways. On her less charitable days, she wished he would do just that.

He couldn't blame her, though. It wasn't her fault, really. Jeren's mother had wanted a strong son, someone who could join a gang or toil in the corpse-starch factories to ease her burdens – which were considerable, to hear her talk.

Jeren, though, couldn't pull his own weight – literally. He was too soft in both mind and body to handle heavy machinery, too weak to hold a lasgun, let alone raise it and fire it, and lacked any skill one could charitably call useful.

He was a drain on the family, according to his mother, and the cause of his father leaving (also according to his mother).

So, on the day of his sixteenth birthday, she had told Jeren she had no choice in the matter – no choice at all – but to sell him into servitude to the Promethium Guild.

Life didn't change much for Jeren. Instead of his mother haranguing him for everything he didn't or couldn't do, it was now his overseer. He couldn't push a cart, not even down a ramp. He couldn't haul or connect hoses because they were too heavy for him to lift.

In the end, the only job the various foremen he'd been shunted between could find that Jeren could complete reliably was scrubbing sludge vats. Every empty vat had to be brushed clean to ensure every drop of sludge made it to the refineries. This meant working on hands and knees with a rubber-edged tool to squeeze every last drop off the bottom of the vat into the collection pipe.

It was hot, filthy, horrible work. The sludge fumes, which were moderated above the vats by large fans that moved the air in the vat room, concentrated to near toxic levels down on the floor of the vat, making Jeren's stomach convulse and his temples throb throughout his twelve-hour shifts.

At night, he tried to clean his clothes and body to remove the tar stains, but there was only so much his allotted one bar of soap per month (and the toxic liquid that passed for water) could do. Most nights Jeren fell into a fitful sleep to the staccato drum-beat of his blood pounding in his head.

And yet, Jeren Jerenson was thankful. He had finally found something he was good at; a job he could do better than anyone else (even if that was only because no one else wanted to do it). And he was thankful his mother had been repaid for raising him despite all his shortcomings as a son.

So, every night for two years, Jeren Jerenson went to bed content with his lot in life, welcoming the dreams that always followed the cessation of the drums beating in his head.

Everything changed for Jeren one evening when, on a whim, he decided to treat himself to a meal somewhere outside his plasteel-sheet hovel. It was his birthday after all, he had thought.

Jeren sat alone in a Sludge Town slop shack, which was little more than a drinking hole with a hot plate behind the bar. Other workers came and went, some drinking and bois-terous, others quietly seeking companionship for the night. No one paid attention to Jeren. No one ever did. He had the soft, round facial features and thin, scraggly hair that epitomised nondescript. The thick layer of dried-on sludge didn't help either.

He recognised one loud group of male workers. They were on the same crew as Jeren. They used to play cruel tricks on Jeren, but recently had found someone else to torment. Jeren overheard them talking at their table.

'I can't believe you lost it, Morn,' said Drey, the talkative one of the group. 'The overseer is gonna kick your ass!'

'You'll be docked a month's pay at least,' said Keld, a new member of their crew.

Jeren glanced at the group. Morn was holding his head in both hands and moaning. 'I had it at the beginning of the shift,' he said. 'I looked everywhere.'

Without thinking, Jeren pushed his chair back and stood up. He stepped across the sticky floor to their table and, before they noticed his intrusion, said: 'Your respirator is lying beneath a pile of hoses on cart D-1619.'

Everyone at the table stopped talking and looked at Jeren, a mixture of expressions ranging from confusion to anger crossing their faces.

'I hope the foreman doesn't kick your ass,' added Jeren, and he turned to go back to his seat.

'What the–' began Drey. 'Did Jerken just talk to us?'

'How the hell does he know where your respirator is?' Keld asked. 'I bet the little stick took it.'

Morn, the biggest of the group and the chief tormentor of fresh meat on the sludge-pit floor, sat there dumbfounded. 'I remember now,' he said finally. 'I laid it down on a cart when it got hot. Another crew must have dumped hoses on top of it.'

Morn shoved his chair back and stormed over to Jeren. 'We weren't even working on the same floor today,' he said. 'How did you know?'

Jeren shook his head. 'I don't know, really,' he said. 'I think I saw it in my dream last night.'

As the Cawdor led Jeren, surrounded by the burly reinforcements they had picked up in Dust Falls, through a series of tunnels away from Down Town, he thought back to his eighteenth birthday and wondered, again, if he should have kept his mouth shut – and not because of the beating he had received at the hands of Morn and his pals.

Of course, Morn found the respirator right where Jeren had said it was. Jeren had no doubt it was there. He'd seen it clearly in his head. That didn't change anything for Jeren; not at first. If anything, his shift mates avoided him more – to the point of crossing the street as he walked towards them. During shift changes, Jeren walked in a bubble of space that no one dared enter – much as he walked now, shackled to and encircled by Cawdors.

But then Jeren found lost items for other people as well. They didn't ask him to locate them, not at first. He would see the objects in his dreams at night or during the day when he fell into strange trance-like states, caused by the heady sludge fumes. He knew who the items belonged to and where they had lost them. Didn't he have to tell the owners? Didn't they want to know?

Some were grateful. Others lashed out. Mostly, people became increasingly afraid of Jeren. They walked away when he approached. They averted their eyes when they saw him. Jeren feared someone would tell the foreman and he would lose his job.

Instead, the faithful had gathered outside his shack one night. He knew they were coming. He'd seen an object one of the Cawdor had lost several times before they came for him. It was a skull – the skull cap, really, down to the rounded top edges of the eye sockets in the front and just past where the ears would go on the sides.

As they dragged Jeren from his hovel, he tried to tell the Cawdor where they could find their lost skull, but they seemed uninterested. As they dragged Jeren along, he saw Keld standing in the shadows off to the side. Jeren smiled at Keld, remembering the night that Morn and Keld and the rest of that crew beat him outside the restaurant.

After Morn's cronies had left Jeren curled up in the sludge dust on the street, Keld had stopped and looked back at Jeren. His beady little eyes had squinted in the darkness of the street, as if he was trying to pierce the vat scrubber's skull and get a peek inside his brain. At that moment, alone in the street, bleeding from his mouth and nose, his ribs aching from being kicked, Jeren's pounding headache had stopped, just for a moment, while he and Keld locked eyes on one another.

How differently would his life have gone, Jeren wondered

as the Cawdor hustled him through dank and musty tunnels, walls slick from sump condensation, if Keld had not been such a devout Cawdor? Would Jeren be here today, shackled by plasteel chain leads and surrounded by gangers? Most likely not. But Jeren knew in his heart – and in his pounding head – that he was right where he needed to be.

Servalen's search of the cliff walls surrounding Down Town brought her to the edge of the Sump Lake. The Deep Pyre was an abandoned amphitheatre half submerged in the lake. It lay roughly two kilometres down the ragged coastline from where she stood. Between here and there, crumbling rockcrete walls rose out of the deep, toxic lake, cutting off access to anyone who couldn't climb walls or procure a skiff.

And yet, Servalen had often wondered if there might be another way to reach the Pyre. The Cawdor weren't the type to waste creds on a skiff, even if their rituals required a secluded and sacred space.

This far down near the utter bottom of the hive, levels and domes had been compressed to a near solid mass by aeons of pressure. There were no tunnels down here. No access points to hidden domes. No pockets of space at all. Just the sump and the Abyss rising above it. If you wanted to go deeper, you dug or you dredged. At least that was the common wisdom.

And yet, the Deep Pyre had survived. Its arched ceiling rose above the sump back into the compression zone. The wide stage of the amphitheatre arced above the deep toxic liquid, overlooking an audience of spider mares and the odd boat as the sump lapped at the edge of the orchestra pit.

Was it so far-fetched that tunnels might still exist down

here that led to the ancient amphitheatre? And if so, who would know about them but the Cawdor, who claimed the place as their own sacred refuge?

Servalen moved along the wall, scanning for any irregularities that might indicate an opening. The cliff walls of the Abyss rising above her gave no clue, though. The entrance to the tunnel, if it existed, was well hidden. She had an ace up her sleeve, though.

'KB-88,' she commanded as she pointed at the cliff face. 'Find the Cawdor!'

The cyber-mastiff's ears began rotating as it pressed its metal snout to the ground. Analysers inside the plasteel canine's housing tested the air for the rare oils and essential essences used by Cawdor, while its ears emitted active sonar waves to search the rockcrete face for hidden pockets.

It didn't take long for KB-88 to find the trail. The mastiff loped off back the way they had come a short distance and began scrambling up a pile of rubble that had long ago tumbled down from some decaying building above. At the top of the rubble pile, which was deceptively easy to climb, 88 found a hidden gap behind a house-sized chunk of rockcrete that hid the entrance to a service tunnel.

Servalen came up behind the metal dog and surveyed the area. Sure enough, just inside the tunnel someone had etched the symbol of House Cawdor's Cult of the Redemption.

'Good dog,' she said. She patted the cyber-mastiff on the head before reaching for her vox to inform Nox of what she had found. After giving the sergeant directions to the tunnel, the scrutinator headed inside. There was no time to lose waiting for the rest of the squad. KB-88 padded ahead of its master to take the lead in the dark tunnel.

* * *

D'onne rode the lift down through the bowels of the under-hive in almost complete darkness. Beside her, Dog's breathing had improved; his wheeze had turned into a snore loud enough to wake the dead – or, more likely, plague zombies or muties on the lookout for descending food.

Periodically, the lift cage passed through areas illuminated by lichen or the odd functioning service light. When these bright areas loomed, D'onne stood, readied her weapons, and kicked Dog to shut him up. Light usually meant life in the underhive, and life in the underhive's dark places wanted to kill you and then eat you.

The bright areas this deep were mostly compressed utility tunnels with room for nothing but rats. As the lift went ever deeper, she saw fewer of these narrow areas. In fact, it had been a quarter of an hour since D'onne had seen any lights.

Eventually, she saw a faint, yellow, bioluminescent glow below her. She stood and prepared to give Dog a really strong kick but noticed something strange about the light. It filled the entire empty space they were approaching, as if the lichen light was reflecting off a large, mirrored surface.

D'onne's eyes opened wide in horror when a ripple moved across that surface. She lunged for the lift controls, but tripped over the immense, sleeping Dog and fell flat on her face. With her cheek pressed against the plasteel cage floor, D'onne had a great view of the Sump Lake rising towards their descending cage.

Scrambling to her feet again, D'onne slammed her palm into the emergency stop button on the control box. An ancient bell rang for a second and then trailed off like a dying rat as the gears above the cage ground against the cables. The cage lurched and fell three more metres before coming to a stop amidst an odour of burning metal mixed with the foul stench of the sump.

The cage swayed as D'onne stared at the surface of the lake, barely two metres below her feet. Above her, the cage hung free about ten metres below the domed roof above the Sump Lake. Plasteel girders – the jagged remains of the lift's structure – ended below the shaft hole, torn off by hive quakes or scavenged over the centuries.

A corroded plasteel service walkway snaked away from the broken girders surrounding the shaft opening. D'onne had no idea how secure the catwalk might be, but it was their only chance. She punched the 'Up' button on the control box and hoped the gears hadn't completely burned out.

The shrieking of metal grinding against metal echoed across the lake and the lift lurched again. D'onne nearly tumbled to her knees as the cage dropped another metre and began swaying back and forth over the foul, murky liquid bubbling and rippling below her.

Just as she thought the gears might saw their way through the cables and drop her and Dog into the sump, the lift cage began to rise. A long section of frayed cable cleared the gears and the screeching faded, but their emergency stop had stripped away at least half the width of the cable. As the frayed area pulled away from the cage, plasteel wires around the worn spot strained and snapped.

D'onne kicked Dog hard and began yelling at him. 'Dog!' she screamed. 'Wake up, you lousy, good-for-nothing cur!'

Painfully slowly, the cage rose towards the catwalk as D'onne heard the twang, twang, twang of wires snapping. She kicked and yelled at Dog as she watched the catwalk creep ever closer. Finally, about two metres shy of the metal walkway, the ogryn's snores turned to moans and cries of pain.

D'onne saw her bodyguard's eyes open for the first time in hours. 'Get up, you lazy, mangy dog!' she yelled as she stabbed the stop button. Not waiting for the ogryn to move out of her way, D'onne vaulted over him to grab the cage door and slam it open.

The edge of the catwalk was more than a metre away, so D'onne had to leap across the gap. As she did, her momentum pushed the lift away from her. She stumbled on her landing but kept her footing – at least until the lift came rocking back.

The cage hit the walkway with a metallic clang, knocking D'onne to her knees and dislodging a corroded section of the walkway flooring. She tipped forward as the grating fell away beneath her hands and nearly fell through the hole. At the last moment, D'onne lunged forward, pushing off with her feet and knees to clear the hole.

As D'onne scrambled back to her feet, the lift crashed back into the walkway. Inside, Dog was standing, but looked unsteady and still a bit green around the neck and shoulders. He swayed when the cage hit the walkway again but steadied himself and prepared to jump across to the catwalk.

The opportunity was gone, though. The cage hit at an angle and started spinning around the side of the catwalk. D'onne ran down the walkway as the cage spun and rolled along behind her, crumpling the plasteel catwalk in its path. Above, more wires snapped as the strain on the cable increased.

'Jump!' she yelled as she backed away from the spinning cage, which had rotated away. There was precious little walkway left. Dog retreated to the back corner of the cage and raced towards the open gate, jumping at an angle towards the edge of the catwalk.

At that moment, a deafening crack like the sound of thunder clapped the air above them as the cable snapped. The cage fell as Dog jumped. He soared towards the catwalk and it looked like his enormous hands might catch the edge, but his feet hadn't cleared the gate, and it slammed into his ankles as it fell.

D'onne watched in silent horror as the cage and the ogryn dropped away from her towards the Sump Lake. A moment later, a large splash erupted from the lake surface, sending a gout of foul, toxic liquid high into the air. D'onne ran down the catwalk away from the impact site before the geyser peaked and splashed across the catwalk behind her.

As soon as it was safe, D'onne returned to the crumpled edge of the catwalk and peered down at the sump. She saw no evidence of the lift cage or her ogryn bodyguard, though, just the receding ripples of the surface. Soon, the sump bubbled and settled as if nothing had happened.

'Stupid mutt. That kid's psychic abilities damned well better be worth it,' she growled as she made her way around the top of the cavern on the metal walkway.

CHAPTER 13

DEEP PYRE

Servalen hustled down the dark tunnel behind KB-88, keeping the light attached to her autopistol hooded with her free hand to avoid giving their position away. The mastiff's enhanced optics and tracking subroutines kept them on the right path and helped avoid obstacles and dead ends.

With all her preparation Servalen still stumbled several times in the dark, which slowed down their progress enough that they didn't catch up to the group holding the boy until after they reached the Deep Pyre.

Servalen slowed down as she saw yellowish light seeping into the black tunnel ahead of them. She switched off the light on her weapon and crept forward to the end of the tunnel beside KB-88. The floor of the Deep Pyre sloped from the back wall where she stood down to the edge of the Sump Lake, making footing tricky, especially down where the toxic liquid lapped at the edge.

This had been the stage of the amphitheatre before the

dome had partially sunk under the lake. The stage ended beyond the edge of the sump, dropping at least another five metres. A vaulted ceiling rose above it all to meet ornate rockcrete arches that crossed in the middle, dividing the ceiling like a giant pie cut for six people. Chunks of the rockcrete had fallen from it over the years. Most had bounced down into the sump, but several large hunks of debris still littered the stage.

The light came from luminescent lichen that covered most surfaces around the sump. Oddly, there was no lichen within the stage area, which created long, strange shadows on the floor and walls as the Cawdor elders moved towards the altar, still circled around the chained psyker.

A Cawdor gang fanned out around the stage to protect the elders during the coming ritual. Half took up position between the altar and the sump, their eyes scanning the lake for intruders. The other half surrounded the altar at a respectful distance as the elders moved into position.

The Pyre altar was a scrap-built monstrosity of bent and warped plasteel plates cobbled together with wire around a chunk of fallen ceiling arch. Atop it all was what looked like a slab of obsidian. How the Cawdor had afforded such an extravagance or hauled it to the Deep Pyre was a mystery, but it completed the creepy tableau of the ritual space perfectly.

Half of the obsidian shone on the shadowy stage, reflecting the yellow lichen light, while the other half drank in the darkness, like a rectangular black portal from which nothing, not even light, could escape.

The elders surrounded the altar, pulling their chained prisoner against its side. They motioned for two of the gang members to lift the boy onto the slab. The chains rattled as they forced him up. The two gang members then retreated towards the back of the stage as the elders moved forward in unison. They looped the chains through rings welded roughly to the plasteel sides of the altar and locked them in place with large iron locks.

Why is he so passive? Servalen wondered, watching the young prisoner. He didn't seem like much, to be honest. His clothes looked like they were draped on hangers because his slight frame barely filled them out. He seemed strangely resigned to his fate.

Had it not been for the gang, Servalen could have moved in while the Cawdor fumbled with the locks. She and KB-88 could have easily subdued six unarmed recidivists, especially while they were distracted. But the presence of the strong-arms changed everything. She needed to hold position until the squad arrived to back her up.

As Servalen was about to retreat down the tunnel to wait for reinforcements, though, the young prisoner turned his head and looked straight at her. At that moment, the scrutinator realised that the mental strangeness she had felt before had disappeared. He was inside her null zone. If the Cawdors noticed, they didn't show it.

Servalen decided to stay put. The boy's powers, whatever they might be, wouldn't work with her in close proximity, so whatever the Cawdor elders wanted from the boy, he wouldn't be able to deliver. This gave her an advantage she might be able to exploit. At the very least, she could see what they were after. She nodded at the boy, who smiled wanly.

Unfortunately, the elder closest to the boy's face saw the smile as he fumbled with his lock. 'What are you smiling about, you heretical monstrosity?' he bellowed, spraying spittle all over the young man's head.

The psyker's eyes flashed for a moment towards her position

in the tunnel. Involuntary reaction, but it doomed her plan. She slunk back further into the shadows, but it was too late.

'Who's there?' demanded the elder, straightening up and moving round the altar towards the tunnel. 'Guards! Flush out the intruder!'

The two Cawdor gangers who had placed the boy on the altar turned and began advancing on Servalen's position, guns ready. She plastered herself against the wall as their opening shots rang out and bounced off the wall opposite her.

With limited options, Servalen decided to be bold. 'Eighty-eight,' she hissed. 'Attack!' Her cyber-mastiff immediately bolted out of the tunnel towards the two Cawdor gangers, who yelled in surprise and stopped firing into the tunnel to focus on the charging metal monster instead.

Servalen stepped out of the shadows, her autopistol raised, and shot the elder who had spotted her square in the chest. To her left, KB-88 was now standing on the chest of one ganger, who looked unconscious, and chomping down on the arm of the other.

The ganger, probably a juve, judging by his undisciplined reaction, screamed in pain and dropped his autogun, which clattered on the floor. KB-88 slapped its front legs into the juve's chest to push him to the ground. It then grabbed the young ganger by the neck with its powerful jaws.

'Hold, KB-88!' Servalen demanded. The mastiff kept its jaws locked around the ganger's neck and growled. The entire skirmish had taken no more than a few seconds and the rest of the Cawdor elders and Cawdor gangers were still too stunned to react. *Time to press my advantage*, thought Servalen.

'I am Scrutinator Primus Servalen of the palanite enforcers,' she said as she waved her autopistol around at the Cawdor. 'Which one of you Emperor-fearing clowns is in charge here?'

The remaining elders glanced at one another uncertainly. Fear and ambition warred in equal measure.

Damnit, I killed the leader, thought Servalen, *and left a power vacuum. This might still work, though. I have to act fast before they sort themselves out.*

'Here's what will happen next,' said Servalen as she strode towards the altar. 'I will take this... man... off your hands and you all will go home, quietly and peacefully, and pray I don't send an enforcer squad to mop up this little mess.'

To punctuate her authority, Servalen raised her free hand and clenched her fingers together to form a fist. At that command, KB-88 clamped down on the ganger's neck. The ganger screamed, but his cries quickly turned into gurgles as gouts of blood sprayed into the air.

The Cawdor and a few of the gangers looked queasy afterwards. Servalen's show of force had the added benefit of freeing up the mastiff. The scrutinator pointed a finger into the air and twirled it about, indicating she wanted KB-88 to patrol. Her metal companion prowled around the altar, watching for any of the gangers to make an offensive move.

'Now drop your locks and leave,' Servalen said, aiming her autopistol at the closest Cawdor. 'The rest of you, drop your weapons or my mastiff will rip out your throats.'

As a bluff, it was a strong one. She and KB-88 had already killed three people and hadn't broken a sweat. Several cult elders did drop their weapons and about half of the gangers lowered theirs while waiting to see what the elders did. But Servalen knew it only took one foolhardy soul – an overly devout Cawdor or a trigger-happy ganger – to break this uneasy truce, and they had the numbers on their side.

'You have no authority here, you soulless witch,' said an elder standing behind the altar. He may have been the next in line after she killed their leader, or maybe he wanted to stake a claim on the position. The man waved his lock at her for emphasis, but Servalen could see sweat beading on his brow and little twitches on his lips as he made his defiant statement.

'I have authority over anything I say I have authority over,' stated Servalen firmly. To emphasise her point, the scrutinator swivelled her aim and fired, intending to hit the new cult leader between the eyes.

Sadly, she missed – badly – which only served to embolden the man who had dropped behind the altar for protection. 'Cawdor!' he screamed from the refuge of his hiding place. 'Attack the heretic!'

Servalen turned and bolted around the back of the altar, firing at, and dropping, the next Cawdor in line.

She ducked behind the altar as the firing began. She crouched next to one of the elders who had also sought the safety of the ramshackle altar. The two of them stared at each other for a long moment as bullets streaked by overhead. The man, perhaps hoping to be the hero of the day, pulled a ritual knife from beneath his robes and raised it to strike. Servalen shot him between the eyes.

Four down, thought, Servalen. Then, in the distance, she heard KB-88 growl and snap, followed by a scream that was cut short. *Five*. But the scrutinator knew her position was untenable. Soon, the gangers would stream around both sides of the altar and there would be nowhere to run.

Her only hope was to use their desire to harness the psyker's ability against them. She grabbed the chain next to her and yanked on it, pulling the boy laid out on the altar towards her. If she could pull him free from the altar, perhaps she could use him as a human shield and retreat to the tunnel.

Unfortunately, the first elder she shot had locked his chain in place on the other side of the altar, which stopped the boy from tumbling down on her side. Okay, she thought. Plan B. Grab the new cult leader and threaten his life to make him halt the attack.

Servalen began crawling round the altar towards the new leader but came face to barrel with a sawn-off shotgun held by a grizzled Cawdor ganger. Servalen looked straight up into the ganger's eyes, trying to bring the full weight of her null abilities to bear on the man.

He hesitated a moment, but then pressed the barrel of his shotgun firmly into Servalen's temple, forcing her to fall backwards, completely helpless. He pressed his finger against the trigger. 'I hereby revoke your authority, palanite scum,' he said with a snarl.

Before the ganger could finish pulling the trigger, however, his head exploded, spraying Servalen's face with grey and red gobs of gore. Behind her, Servalen heard the welcome voice of Sergeant Nox scream, 'Attack!'

As the enforcer squad streamed out of the tunnel and entered the battle, Servalen grabbed the robes of the dead Cawdor next to her and wiped the mess off her face and out of her eyes. Once she could see properly again, the scrutinator peered over the altar to take stock of the situation.

The Cawdor gangers were hard-pressed by the firepower of the entire squad as well as KB-88, who had chased one to the edge of the sump, where he threw up his hands in surrender only to have a long-las round punch through his neck.

To Servalen's left, the new cult leader rose from his hiding place and climbed atop the altar. He fumbled in his robes before producing his own ritual knife and raising it over his head in both hands.

'Your power belongs to the Cult of the Redemption. The Master of Mankind so decreed!' he roared as he loomed above the chained psyker. 'We cannot allow that power to fall into the hands of infidels. I condemn you to the eternal darkness between the stars.'

Servalen shot the man in the chest and then fired several more times to be certain she finished the job. The elder fell off the altar and crashed to the floor dead, a look of surprise frozen on his face forever.

The battle raged around Servalen. Most of the Cawdor lay dead or dying in pools of blood, but a few fought on. Several enforcers had also fallen under fire and were being pulled to the safety of the tunnel by other members of the squad while the rest mopped up the gangers.

Servalen cared little about any of that. Her sole interest in this matter was the young psyker that so many were willing to kill or die over. She moved around to the other side of the altar, staying low to keep out of sight as much as possible.

As Servalen moved around to the sump side of the altar, the last few gangers made a break for it as KB-88 gave chase. Servalen realised her presence in the field of fire had probably given them the opening.

She dived to the floor, but it was too late. The escaping gangers grabbed the last couple of elders, gunned down an enforcer, and sprinted for the tunnel with the cyber-mastiff right on their heels.

Servalen might have felt remorse about the death of the enforcer, but the squad's safety was Nox's purview, not hers. She had one job here, and that was to secure the rogue psyker.

As the battle continued at the tunnel entrance, Servalen examined the lock the cult leader had clamped onto the chain. Quickly calculating the safest angle, she raised her autopistol and fired, shattering its iron circlet. She pulled the remains of the lock free from the chain holding the boy and flung it towards the sump.

She stood and looked at the young man, who had been lying atop the black stone all this time. He was unscathed – not a single drop of blood had landed on him from all the surrounding death and carnage – but seemed to have fallen into some sort of trance. His pupils had rolled up past his eyelids, giving him a white-eyed stare, and he muttered nonsense syllables under his breath, which came in fits and gasps.

'I'm taking you with me,' she said, unsure if the boy could hear her. She reached out to grab him by the shoulders.

'I have a different plan,' said a gravelly voice from behind Servalen. 'We kill all of ya and then take that damned psyker for ourselves.'

Servalen turned to find two skiffs carrying more than a dozen hive scum had come around the edge of the amphitheatre wall and landed on the stage. They were all clad in flak armour and armed to the teeth. Their leader, a tall, gangly man wearing a respirator over a gaunt, almost skeletal face, jumped out of the lead skiff. He had a scar that ran from one ear down under his respirator and a tattoo of a skull inside a circle etched on his neck.

He levelled a compact heavy stubber in both hands at his hip and began firing.

CHAPTER 14

CONFRONTATION

Servalen dropped to the ground and crawled around the side of the altar as quickly as she could. As she moved, she could hear the screams of the enforcers, who had all been firing at the escaping Cawdor, so were facing the tunnel when the new group arrived.

Once safely round the side of the altar, Servalen turned and took a shot at the leader, hoping to stop the relentless barrage from his heavy stubber. Her shot went wide, though, and hit a scabby young woman who had been climbing out of the bobbing skiff.

The female screamed as the autopistol shot tore through her flesh. She spun about on the bow of the skiff, lost her footing and fell in the sump. The lake surface hissed and sprayed several other members of the gang of hive scum, who winced and screamed as the toxic liquid burned their flesh. As the scabby female sank beneath the waves, her screams turned to gurgles.

The leader glanced at the ripples and flexed his neck muscles, which made his skull tattoo undulate inside the circle. 'I guess you die first,' he said, staring at Servalen. He fired his stubber and advanced on her as she scrambled back behind the altar.

Large-calibre rounds sprayed the stage, hitting the floor, the sides of the altar and the wall behind Servalen, sending huge chunks of rockcrete flying into the air. The last two Cawdor, who hadn't kept up with the more veteran gangers, fell in the barrage, dropping beside Servalen with blood spilling from their chests and arms.

Servalen's errant shot had at least focused the scum leader's attention on her, allowing the squad members remaining after his first barrage to rally. Nox and two enforcers had crawled along the back wall behind the altar and then scuttled forward to take position around the scrutinator. The other two enforcers had retreated into the tunnel. Servalen could see the barrels of their weapons – one high and one low – at the edge of the tunnel wall.

KB-88 had disappeared, though, and Servalen felt a thrum of panic pass through her.

'Where's my mastiff?' she hissed at Nox as he crouched beside her. She could hear the edge of urgency in her voice, betraying the loss of composure she felt over her missing companion.

'It chased the retreating Cawdor down the tunnel,' he reported, somehow completely calm amidst all the chaos. 'That is where you should be, ma'am. We need to get you to safety. Now!'

'Not without the psyker,' she replied, working to regain her stoicism. 'That's the mission. Nothing else matters!'

Nox nodded and then signalled the enforcers to prepare

for attack. 'We'll lay down covering fire, ma'am,' he said. 'You grab the kid and make for the tunnel.'

Servalen gave Nox the thumbs-up. The sergeant raised three fingers for the remaining enforcers to see, and then dropped one and another. On three, all five remaining enforcers stood as one unit and began firing.

Servalen poked her head above the ramshackle altar and pulled the semi-conscious psyker towards her.

'It's not time yet,' he said, rousing from his trance and turning his head to face her. His face was a mixture of despair and resignation. It seemed to be his natural state. 'It's too soon – I can't stop it.'

Servalen felt her eyes go wide at his sudden desperation, and swung to look for the cause. The entire gang of hive scum, a dozen of them bolstered by reinforcements from another skiff, had fanned out along the edge of the sump and begun firing as soon as Nox and his enforcers stood.

Servalen dropped back behind the altar as bullets and las-rounds streamed back and forth across the stage, filling the air with lead, laser blasts, and a cacophony of shrieking ammunition and screaming wounded.

One by one, the few remaining enforcers dropped to the ground around Servalen. The first to go down were the enforcers on either side of Nox, their armour riddled with bullet holes. Blood streamed from a dozen wounds, covering their armour in a bright sheen of glistening blood.

Next, Servalen saw the two enforcers in the tunnel entrance crumple to the floor, their weapons clattering from their lifeless hands as their bodies piled atop one another.

Finally, Sergeant Nox slumped to the floor next to Servalen.

Servalen turned the sergeant to place his back against the altar. His armour was dented all over, but only a few rounds had penetrated. Blood seeped from the wounds, but none were located in critical areas.

'You'll be okay, sergeant,' she reassured him.

A grimace passed across Nox's ashen face. 'You are a terrible liar, ma'am,' he said.

Servalen looked closer and saw a single bullet had passed straight through the sergeant's neck. Blood flowed freely from the wound, pooling up and seeping into the collar of his armour. He was done for.

'I'm so sorry,' said Servalen. 'This is all my fault.'

'Not true,' Nox replied, shaking his head slightly before it lolled off to one side. 'Keep Helmawr's peace.'

'I will. I promise,' Servalen said, but Nox was gone, his eyes glassed over and his chin resting in the blood pooled on his collarbone. How she was supposed to keep that promise, though, was currently beyond her reckoning. She needed a miracle. She needed KB-88.

As if on cue, she heard the cyber-mastiff's metal paws padding down the tunnel. At the same time, though, the hive scum had apparently regrouped and reloaded after their last onslaught.

'Grin, Tank, grab the kid!' the hive scum leader bellowed behind her. 'Rest of you scum shoot anything still moving!'

Servalen peeked out from behind the altar to see two large and well-armed hive scum moving towards the Pyre altar. The shorter of the two carried a rifle with an extra barrel and a hose that wound around to his back. One side of his neck was blackened and blistered. The other, taller and bald with a wicked scar that started between his eyes and ran over the top of his head, wielded a chain glaive. These were some serious scum, perhaps venators that had gone rogue and banded together at Hive Bottom.

'Eighty-eight!' called Servalen, seeing her dog's red eyes piercing the darkness of the tunnel entrance. 'Protect the target!'

The mastiff charged out of the tunnel, grabbing the attention of the hive scum, who began firing again. Servalen, taking advantage of the distraction, moved to the other side of the altar and took a shot at the tall, bald scummer with the glaive, hoping to wing him and make it tough to hold the polearm, but her shot hit his armoured chest, doing little damage.

The shorter scummer advanced, grinning with evil intent as he raised his rifle. A jet of fire gushed forth, engulfing two of the downed Cawdor in flames. The tall one, Tank, apparently, thrust the spinning chain glaive on the end of his polearm into the chest of one of the Cawdor gangers who had been crawling towards the back wall, impaling the ganger and ripping out bones and organs from his chest in a gout of blood.

At the same time, autogun bullets sprayed through the entire amphitheatre again as the rest of the hive scum tried in vain to hit the darting mastiff. The firing tapered off as KB-88 charged Tank and leapt on the tall man's back, bearing him to the ground. The chain glaive bounced on the rockcrete floor and spun away towards the far wall, grinding everything in its path, including one of the other hive scum.

During the confusion, Servalen reached up onto the altar and pulled the young psyker over the edge. This time he didn't resist and slipped easily off the obsidian slab, dragging his chains out of their brass rings and down on top of him. Servalen peeked over the edge to keep an eye on her mastiff.

KB-88, still standing on Tank's back, growled and snapped its head forward, its jaws opening extra wide. It chomped down on the ganger's bald head. The man's thick skull offered some resistance, but it was no match for the cyber-mastiff's pneumatic-powered jaws. After an agonising moment of grinding and screaming, Tank's bald head cracked like an egg with a loud bang that echoed across the stage.

Grin, the ganger with the autogun-flamer rifle, turned and aimed his weapon at the cyber-mastiff. Before the ganger could pull the trigger though, Servalen shot at the canister on Grin's back. This time, her aim was true. The autopistol shot punctured the canister, which exploded in flames. The fire quickly swept down the tubing towards the weapon, engulfing the ganger's torso and arms in red-hot fire.

In a fit of panic, Grin ran towards the lake's edge and dived into the liquid, which made the fire spread and burn faster. Flames leapt ten metres into the air as the ever-present gases above the sump ignited. Soon, there was nothing left of Grin but a burning stain and an acrid layer of smoke that floated slowly down the lake.

'Damnit!' yelled the leader. He pointed at Servalen. 'Kill her! She needs to die. Right now!'

Servalen dived back out of sight as every autogun began firing at her. She heard KB-88 growl and its metal paws scrabble against the rockcrete ground, followed by heavy stubber fire ricocheting off hardened metal.

'Hark!' yelled the leader, a definite note of terror entering his voice. 'Take care of that metal mongrel.'

A lull in the shooting caused by most of the scummers reloading after their third barrage allowed Servalen to peek around the edge of the altar again in time to see a huge mountain of a man wearing spiked, full-body armour and a metal mask with barred eye-slits, step in front of the gang leader and aim his massive stub cannon at the charging KB-88.

Servalen knew the man by reputation only. Krotos Hark was a gun for hire. How these hive scum could afford to pay his fee was a matter for another time. The massive body underneath all that armour was almost assuredly Goliath, but he never worked for the family of giants, preferring to work against them more often than not. He was known to be a ferocious, brawling fighter.

He fired the massive stub cannon, the boom of the large-calibre shot reverberating across the stage like its namesake and shaking dust and small rocks loose from the arches above the Pyre altar. Masonry mixed with rebar sprayed into the air as the slug hit the rockcrete stage floor, showering the surrounding gangers with shrapnel that sliced flesh and dug into armour.

The impact left a metre-wide crater in the floor but missed KB-88. The mastiff had leapt before the shot rang out, flying towards the gigantic bounty hunter and evading the massive slug. Its jaws closed around the gloved hand holding the oversized pistol and clamped down hard, metal teeth tearing into the one piece of the hunter's flesh not encased in metal.

Hark grunted in pain and shook his arm to try to dislodge the beast, but all he managed to do was fling his stub cannon towards the far wall. The massive pistol slid across the stage, dangerously close to the sump.

The bounty hunter had no time to worry about his gun, though. The weight and momentum of the mastiff had twisted him around and pulled him towards the lake's edge as well.

Servalen didn't see what happened next, because the other gangers had finished reloading and shrugging off the effects of the shrapnel explosion. They began firing and advancing on her, forcing the scrutinator back behind the altar.

'Kill that bitch!' yelled the scummer leader. 'And get the kid so we can scram.'

Servalen edged towards the side of the altar closest to the tunnel, looking for an opening she and the young psyker could use to escape. She picked off the first scummer she saw, a fresh recruit from the shabbiness of the weapons, and decided it was now or never.

'Follow me!' she hissed at the boy as she bolted from cover. Too late, Servalen realised the boy couldn't move – quickly or otherwise – while burdened by all those chains. But she was committed now. Firing and sprinting across the gap at the back of the stage, Servalen dived over the bodies of the two enforcers crumpled at the tunnel entrance and slid into the other bodies stacked up behind them.

After extracting herself from the tangle of corpses, Servalen crawled back to the entrance. The scummers had reached the boy and were busy pulling him back towards the sump, but it was the battle between Hark and KB-88 that stole her attention. Her mastiff was their only chance now to salvage the mission.

The giant bounty hunter had freed himself from KB-88's jaws and the two circled around one another near the beached skiffs. Hark kept low, the muscles on his arms tensed and ready to react as he whipped a fighting knife around in front of him to keep the mastiff at bay. KB-88 charged and leapt again, apparently unafraid of the blade, but the Goliath dropped the large knife and clamped his huge hands around the mastiff's neck.

'Got you, you metal monster!' growled Hark. As the mastiff's jaws snapped at his thick forearms, the Goliath whipped his body and arms around one full revolution and then flung KB-88 ten metres out into the sump, where it sunk out of sight, leaving barely a trace of its passing.

Servalen, outwardly as calm as Nox had been at the end, stood and strode out of cover, inner rage swinging her arm from one ganger to the next, emptying her clip into the hive scum standing between her and Hark.

The scum began retreating towards the skiff. The leader raged at them to fight as he desperately tried to jam a fresh ammo drum into place.

'Funny woman,' said Hark with a grunting laugh. 'Where's my cannon?'

'You mean this old thing?' asked a new voice. Everyone turned.

There was Mad D'onne, who had appeared at the far edge of the stage next to the sump. She held Hark's stub cannon in both hands. As the armoured hunter turned towards her, she fired.

The recoil slammed D'onne's back and arms into the wall behind her and sent the weapon bouncing across the floor. The slug slammed into Hark's helmeted head, though, right between his barred eye-slits, sending the hunter flying back onto the edge of the second skiff. He hit hard and tumbled inside, his legs splayed over the bow, twitching.

At that moment, the gang leader finished reloading and opened fire, spraying slugs around the amphitheatre. Servalen dived to the ground and crawled back towards the altar for protection.

'Get the boy on the skiff!' yelled the gang leader as he emptied his second drum of ammo. The shots centred on Servalen and the Pyre altar.

As Servalen crawled behind the safety of the altar amidst the hail of bullets, she heard the crackle and smell of burning ozone from a plasma blast tearing across the stage near the edge of the sump. Instantly, the staccato beat of the heavy stubber stuttered to a halt.

Servalen peered over the top of the altar to see that half of the hive scum leader's compact heavy stubber, along with one of his hands, was gone, replaced with a liquidising mass of metal and flesh. He screamed and dropped the other half of the weapon, which smouldered and dripped plasteel on the stage floor.

'New plan,' he grunted as he grabbed his stump with his remaining hand and fell back onto the bow of the skiff in between Hark's twitching legs. 'Get us out of here!'

CHAPTER 15

COOPERATION

D'onne dived for cover behind a hunk of rubble under the hail of bullets as the scummers made a fighting retreat towards the skiffs. From her hiding place, she saw one burly man with twin scars and mangled ears carry the boy away from her, the kid's chains clanging on the ground behind them like the train of a metal gown.

Another hive scum, just a scabby kid not much bigger than the chain-wrapped psyker, had the presence of mind to pick up Hark's stub cannon. Unfortunately, the inept scummer didn't have the intelligence or the strength to handle such a huge weapon.

As the scummer scrambled aboard the skiff, the cannon fired, sending an explosive shell towards the back corner of the stage where it exploded, bringing several tonnes of rubble crashing down to bury the tunnel entrance. The kickback sent the scum flying back into the sump, while the cannon clattered down into the skiff.

Hoping to take advantage of the moment of chaos, D'onne drew Pig and peeked out from cover as the skiffs scraped free of the stage, but a short female hive scum with a long, grey-streaked mohawk and a longer black rifle knelt near the front edge of a skiff, her weapon propped on the bow and pointing right at D'onne's head.

D'onne dropped back behind cover as the sniper's shot put a neat hole through the rockcrete rubble where her eye had been. She heard two more shots – one that ricocheted behind her hunk of rubble and nearly took off one of her toes, and another that hit somewhere else on the stage, causing the enforcer woman to grunt and scramble for cover, judging by the sound of boots scraping against rockcrete.

After a few moments of silence, D'onne peeked again, but from the other side of the rubble – just in case. The stern of the rear skiff was disappearing around the corner, taking with it the surviving gangers and the prize she sought. She was too late.

D'onne stood and surveyed the carnage. Cawdor gangers and hive scum lay dead or dying in pools of blood scattered from the lake edge up to the Pyre altar along with more than a few enforcers. Another set of bodies, all dressed in blood-soaked Cawdor robes, were strewn about the altar.

'Hell of a party I almost missed,' said D'onne as she moved through the carnage, kicking bodies to check for life and weapons to scavenge.

As she reached the first ganger, whose head looked like it had been cracked open in a vice, D'onne noticed movement from behind the altar. She ducked down, Pig ready, and waited to see who emerged. It was the tall, gaunt enforcer woman, who crawled towards the sump, seemingly without noticing D'onne.

D'onne tentatively lowered Pig. She considered blasting her away, but stopped herself. There were dead enforcers here, true, but there could be more en route. More gunshots would give her away. D'onne also felt something else – a strange sense of nothingness – coming from the woman.

D'onne watched the scrutinator reach the edge of the sump and begin scanning the bubbling lake. Holstering Pig, she began to check the bodies of the fallen. If any of them were still alive, they might know where the hive scum were fleeing to with her prize. Even the dead could still be holding secrets.

As Servalen stared at the bubbling sump, looking for any sign of KB-88, the turmoil inside her mind began to subside a bit. She still felt the loss of the mastiff, as well as Nox and the squad, but now she could see their loss as more of a pragmatic issue than an emotional one.

They were gone. Nox was gone. The squad was gone. KB-88 was gone. She was the only one left. She exhaled, turned, and saw D'onne behind the altar, staring down at the bodies of Servalen's dead companions.

Servalen raised her autopistol and fired twice. Both shots impacted the altar, spraying black rock into D'onne's powdered wig.

'What the sump?' D'onne yelled. She crouched behind the altar, out of view. Servalen stopped moving and scanned the top and sides of the altar, waiting for D'onne to reappear.

'Come out, D'onne,' Servalen called to her, her autopistol in hand and pointing at the Pyre altar. 'You're quick, but you've got nowhere to go. Let's talk.'

D'onne chuckled. 'No sign of your little pet out there in the sump, eh?' she called from behind the altar. 'The undertow probably grabbed it. Not much of a paddler, is it?'

The goading wouldn't work. Servalen had lost this battle, but while she had D'onne there was a way to snatch victory from this. She owed Nox and KB-88 that much. But she was stuck here in the Deep Pyre with the maddest woman in the hive, while a group of scummers paddled away with the prize both women wanted.

A kernel of an idea suddenly began forming in the back of Servalen's head. D'onne had a bad habit of escaping from every crazy situation her madness got her into. Servalen had to do whatever she could to get the psyker back and bring D'onne to justice, even if it meant trusting the mad woman – for a time.

'Look,' Servalen said. 'I think we need each other here, for the moment. I will stand down if you do the same. Do you trust me?'

'You can't trust anyone in the underhive, least of all your allies,' said Mad D'onne. But the bounty hunter stood up behind the altar, her plasma pistol drawn but pointing up in the air.

'I guess you would know that better than most,' said Servalen. 'You've turned on every friend you ever had.' The scrutinator couldn't resist the jab. This woman had been a thorn in her side for a month or more. But she also raised her weapon to point the barrel into the air.

The two women faced off. Servalen studied D'onne's face, but it was as inscrutable as ever, especially framed under that ridiculous wig, the powder spattered with dust, dirt, blood, and what looked like rat fur.

D'onne snorted a short, sharp laugh. 'I killed them all,' she said, with a slight smirk, 'because they all turned on me first!' She holstered her weapon and moved around the altar. 'What I'm saying is, don't turn on me.'

For a moment, Servalen considered emptying her autopistol into D'onne's chest, even though the woman had holstered her weapon. The very thought of trusting Mad D'onne was insanity itself. But she had a mission and the mission came first.

The pragmatist inside Servalen won out. She had nothing to lose, for now. It was an alliance of convenience, nothing more. And Servalen would never forget that D'onne was, at her heart, a ruthless killer who did whatever it took to survive.

Servalen nodded and holstered her weapon. 'To be clear,' she said, pointing a finger at D'onne, 'when this is over, you face justice *and* the boy goes with me.'

D'onne shook her head and shoved her own finger into Servalen's face. 'What, so you can lock him in the Psykanarium and throw away the key?'

'I would never...' replied Servalen but faltered before she completed the thought and gave D'onne more information than necessary. Instead, she pointed at the rubble blocking the tunnel.

'It's all moot if we can't get out of here,' she said. 'Can you cut through that rubble with your plasma gun?'

D'onne shook her head. 'Doubt it. Pretty sure I'd consume Pig's entire charge before it burned away all that rockcrete, even assuming the roof didn't cave in as we cut through.'

Servalen nodded. She glanced at the sump. With the skiffs gone, that didn't seem a viable escape route either. As she studied the motion of the lake, a twang of remorse over KB-88 stabbed Servalen in the chest. She shoved it down into the recesses of her darkened soul to focus on immediate problems.

As she stared at the steaming surface of the sump, a thought occurred that probably should have surfaced earlier. 'How did you get here?' she asked, turning back to face D'onne. 'You appeared at the edge of the lake.'

D'onne smiled a wicked smirk and strode off towards the far corner of the stage. When Servalen didn't follow immediately, the hunter turned and crooked a finger.

'This was the fun bit,' D'onne said as she stood, back to the sump, dangerously close to the lake's edge. She pointed up and motioned for Servalen to look.

The scrutinator moved to the edge, but well outside D'onne's reach. She leaned out and looked up at the wall. High above hung a rusted, plasteel catwalk that ended near the edge of the opening to the stage.

'How did you...?' started Servalen, looking at the distance down from the catwalk to the stage. 'You jumped from there?'

D'onne nodded.

'You could've died!'

D'onne nodded again.

Servalen moved down the sump edge to peer at the wall on the Down Town side of the Deep Pyre. Unfortunately, the catwalk didn't continue on that side. As Servalen wracked her brain for some way to scale the slick wall, she heard D'onne rushing up behind her. Servalen twisted around as D'onne bowled into her, wrapping the scrutinator's arms tight to her leather corset in a bear hug, and bearing her to the ground.

When they hit, D'onne rolled away from the sump, taking Servalen with her before releasing her grasp and rolling to a crouch beyond the enforcer.

'What the hell?' roared Servalen. She scrambled to her feet and drew her weapon.

In response, D'onne aimed her plasma gun and fired. The beam crackled through the air past the scrutinator. Behind her, Servalen heard a spine-chilling roar. She turned to see the glistening wet bulk of a spider mare that had climbed onto the stage right where she had been standing.

The beast's bulbous eyes rotated in their sockets above its slavering mandibles, where two-metre-long pincers clacked together excitedly. D'onne's plasma bolt had seared off one of the creature's eight legs, which twitched on the rockcrete floor.

The beast roared again and charged.

With the sump to her right and D'onne on her left, Servalen had little room to manoeuvre. She backpedalled away from the mare, but even on seven legs, the huge spider was fast. She fired wildly towards the creature's head, but her first shot glanced off its carapace. Her second shot burned out one of its eyes, but did little to deter its charge. She was running out of room on the stage and the beast was almost within pincer distance.

With the snapping pincers closing fast, Servalen considered diving beneath the beast, but the mare's massive thorax nearly scraped the rockcrete floor as it ran, giving her no room for error. Then, from the side, a crackling beam of purple plasma streaked past Servalen.

D'onne's weapon claimed another leg, disintegrating one of the mare's bulging knee joints. The loss of a second limb while scuttling at full speed caused the spider to skid towards the sump. As the beast foundered on the edge, Servalen scrambled away and sought safety behind a fallen piece of rubble.

'Keep targeting the legs!' called Servalen. 'I'll do what I can to keep its attention while you ground it.'

The mare roared and pulled itself into the sump as Servalen pressed the trigger on her autopistol. Her shot bounced off its hardened hide again, but the beast seemed to be swimming off. Perhaps the two women had done enough damage that it decided to seek easier feeding grounds.

Servalen moved clear of the rubble and glanced at all the blood and bodies littering the stage. *That was what it was doing*, she thought. *Looking for an easy meal*. With all the fresh meat strewn around the Deep Pyre, she knew it would be back.

Sure enough, a moment later, the mare shot out from beneath the sump, breaching the surface in an arc that would carry it to the back of the stage. D'onne shot at the beast as it flew over their heads, but her plasma bolt missed the flailing legs, tearing a deep gash in its thorax.

Servalen held her shot until the spider extended its legs for the landing and then fired twice quickly in succession. The first shot slammed into a rear leg, right where it met the creature's carapace, but didn't quite sever it. The second shot went right into the joint inside the carapace, finishing the job. Three legs down.

The mare tottered on its remaining five legs as it landed on top of the altar, but somehow it kept its balance. As it twisted around to face the two women, D'onne fired again, removing its other front leg below the carapace.

The beast focused on the wild woman with the large hair and big weapon. Before Servalen or D'onne could fire again, it roared and leapt, pushing off with four legs to fly in a perfect arc towards Mad D'onne.

D'onne fired wildly as she fell backwards. Her shot clipped one of the beast's pincers, turning the pointed front half into a molten stump of cartilage and bone. Servalen shot before it hit D'onne. She hit another leg, but the autopistol was too weak to burn through the mare's thick limbs in a single shot.

Servalen couldn't fire again for fear of hitting D'onne,

who lay prone underneath the behemoth. The beast lowered its head to bring its pincers to bear on D'onne's body. It snapped them together around D'onne's head as she tried to raise her arm to fire at the mare's mandibles.

With half of one pincer gone, though, the spider couldn't decapitate the hunter, try as it might. After several attempts to bite D'onne's head off, it roared, reared its head and drove the remaining pincer straight down.

Servalen fired at the remaining pincer as it hurtled towards D'onne's head. The bullet didn't penetrate the bone, but it chipped off a hunk of cartilaginous exoskeleton. More importantly, the shot drove the pincer to the side, where it slammed into the rockcrete floor next to D'onne, who had squirmed in the other direction.

We can't count on that working again, thought Servalen. She needed to find a way to distract the beast somehow so D'onne could escape and burn through the remaining legs. Servalen recalled that the scummers had some larger weapons. She glanced around to see if anything was near, but all she found was a severed foot.

With a shrug, Servalen grabbed the bloody foot. 'Catch, you disgusting creature,' she screamed as she threw the foot at the spider. The blood-stained boot sailed through the air, spraying blood.

Some of the spray splattered across the spider's face as the boot flew over its head. The mare reared up, pushing its thorax clear of the floor – and D'onne's chest – to catch the meaty morsel, freeing D'onne to roll out from beneath it.

Once clear, but still lying prone on her back, D'onne raised her plasma pistol. Holding onto it with both hands, she fired a steady stream of plasma at the rearing beast. After burning through one leg, which clattered to the floor next to her,

Pig's beam continued across the mare's thorax to another leg, severing it below the shoulder joint.

For her part, Servalen took aim with her autopistol and finished the job she'd begun on the leg she had hit earlier. Reduced to a single leg, the spider toppled over, forcing D'onne to roll and scramble away to avoid getting crushed again.

The beast lay on its back, its last leg and the remains of its pincers waving in the air as brown and yellow ichor oozed from it.

D'onne studied her weapon for a moment. 'Burned through another charge,' she grumbled before holstering the pistol. She drew her chainsword from its scabbard and thumbed it on. 'Guess we have to finish this up close and personal.' She moved towards the mare's still-snapping pincers.

'Why?' asked Servalen, pointing at the spider legs strewn about the stage. 'It's not going anywhere now.'

'And neither are we until we kill this thing,' replied D'onne. 'Now grab that chain glaive over there and start cutting.'

Unsure what D'onne was up to, Servalen didn't move. Did she want to take the mare's eyes? Sure, they were valuable, but she'd heard the process was tricky and took hours.

D'onne sighed and thumbed her blade's grinding chain back off, dropped the tip of the sword to the ground, and leaned on the hilt. 'Look,' she said. 'These things float, okay? That's how mare hunters get them back to Down Town. We can ride the damn thing, using its own legs for oars. Now get that damn chain glaive and help me gut this scavving beast.'

CHAPTER 16

CHAIN OF COMMAND

'You requested my presence, lord?' asked the master of the Psykanarium upon being ushered into Helmawr's office by the lord chamberlain.

The master was a nondescript man despite dark, brooding eyes that seemed to pierce the soul, the long, angular nose that made it seem he was looking down on everyone around him, and the straight, black hair that seemed eternally plastered to his head, as if oil oozed from his scalp. And yet, no one who had ever met the man could describe him in any detail the moment he left their presence. It was as if he had never existed once he exited a room.

Being in the man's presence was a completely different matter, though. If the pariah, Scrutinator Servalen, made Helmawr's stomach quail when she was near, the master of the Psykanarium made him feel as if he'd been laid bare on a slab with his chest cavity open and his entrails trailing onto the floor. Lord Helmawr swallowed to keep his lunch down in his stomach and tried to clear that imagery from his mind.

'I did,' he said, forcing himself to look at the master for a long moment before turning back to the chamberlain. 'Leave us, chamberlain, and secure the office – completely – on your way out.'

After the chamberlain had bolted the office doors and Helmawr could hear the hum of the interference generators running behind the walls, he spoke again.

'We have an issue developing at Hive Bottom that may need the attention of specialists,' Helmawr began.

'Mad D'onne and the young divination psyker?' asked the master.

Helmawr was not surprised that the master of the Psykanarium knew about the presence of a new psyker, especially if recent reports about the boy's power level were accurate, but he steeled his face to remain passive in the face of the master's knowledge. He did not maintain control over Necromunda by giving any adversary an upper hand during negotiations.

'Exactly,' he said. 'The enforcer in charge of the operation has lost control of the situation. Her squad is dead and the psyker has been taken by a group of heavily armed hive scum.'

'I can retrieve the psyker for you, lord,' said the master, an almost ghoulish glint flashing across his eyes. 'But it won't be easy, and it won't be pretty.'

'Do what must be done,' replied Helmawr. 'Unleash the full power of the Psykanarium upon the underhive if you must. But bring me that boy!'

'I swear it will be done,' said the master as he turned to leave.

'One last thing,' called out Helmawr. 'Instruct your psi-hounds to leave no trace of the young psyker behind. Wipe the memory of him clean from the hive.'

'As you wish, lord.'

The office door opened as the master reached it, allowing the man to sweep through unimpeded. The lord chamberlain peeked inside shortly afterwards.

'Do you require anything else, my lord?' he asked.

Helmawr nodded but didn't respond immediately. First, he stood and maneuvered around his desk, before heading towards a hidden door in the side wall. He turned to face the lord chamberlain before pressing the button that would open the secret door.

'I am retiring to the royal residence,' Lord Helmawr decreed. 'Report to me there every hour, or as news develops about the Mad D'onne situation.'

'Yes, my lord.'

Helmawr opened the secret door and stepped through but turned back to the chamberlain one last time.

'Oh, and chamberlain?' he called back through the door. 'I was never in the office today. I stayed in the residence the entire day. I met with no one and requested no reports. Understood?'

'Understood, my lord.'

Kordon Brann had been brooding in his office, which amounted to working his way through a bottle of spider wine while picking at random things on his desk. Nothing really got accomplished when Kordon was in this mood. Stacks of paperwork got moved around and his desk tidied up a bit as the spider venom in the wine numbed his body.

He knew he should stay sharp and sober, but everything

was in flux and his nerves had got the better of him. He'd lost the venators he'd hired to guard the sludge pits and, instead of using the reserve creds in his guilder account to hire more guards, he'd thrown a thousand credits into the sump on a group of bottom-of-the-pit hive scum on the chance they might be able to beat Mad D'onne, a squad of enforcers and the Cawdor to the prize. What the sump had he been thinking?

Right. What a boon that psyker kid would have been to business, thought Kordon as he took another swig of wine. *Not to mention my future prospects within the Promethium Guild.* He had started his second bottle at this point so it took him three tries to grab the bottle and raise it successfully to his lips.

Kordon had asked around town and people said the kid could find anything you'd lost and even things you didn't know you were missing. Most people had asked for small things: lost shoes, weapons. But what if the kid could take it further and find lost archeotech? Or hidden reserves of promethium? The possibilities for exploiting this psyker's powers were infinite to someone with any business sense.

'What a waste,' Kordon said out loud. If the enforcers got hold of him, Helmawr would turn him over to the Psykanarium. They would warp that beautiful power into something simple and murderous. There was value in that, but they'd have destroyed so much potential.

Kordon had to face it: the psyker was gone, and the money, too. He hadn't heard from Wicker in hours. Kordon *might* be able to hide the thousand-credit loss in the books this month and recoup it from the guild's coffers, but he was already being watched for weakness. It would cost at least as much again to replace the venators Mad Donna had killed, and even trying to do so would risk exposing his position.

If only he'd known about Jerenson's ability earlier, before

it got to the point where everything went off the rails. Things would have gone differently if any of the workers loyal to him had discovered the kid's talent instead of that damned Cawdor zealot, Keld. The Cawdor had infiltrated every corner of the pits. It had become impossible to run his business without them exerting undue influence.

As far as Brann was concerned, Church and business should never mix. It wasn't that he had any particular problem with Redemptionist views or philosophy. It was just that zealots never saw the big picture when it came to business.

Hell, I'd work with muties if they had any need for money.

Kordon's train of thought trailed off. After a few minutes of not moving, his mind returned to the office. Brann blinked twice and tried to focus on the bottle, but it seemed to be oscillating back and forth on his desk like a mirage.

Perhaps I've had enough spider wine. Kordon went to cork the bottle and was pleased it only took him a couple of tries to get it right.

As he debated whether to try to make it across town to his home and bed or to let his head drop onto the desk, Kordon noticed the light blinking and the buzzer sounding on his private vox connection.

'I don't need any more bad news!' he screamed as he pawed at the box until he finally hit the receive button. The screen came to life, showing the distorted face of Wicker Crag. 'Go away! We're closed!' yelled Brann.

'*About scavving time!*' yelled Wicker at the same time. '*I've been calling for five minutes!*'

To Kordon's spider-venom-addled brain, Wicker's Circle-Skull tattoo looked like it was glowing and rotating on his neck. He stared, transfixed by the vision for ten full seconds before fully registering that the ganger had spoken to him.

'Give me… a minute,' Kordon said as he rubbed his eyes and searched his desk for a mug of old coffee or some water to splash on his face – anything to sober up enough to make the tattoo on Wicker's face stop staring at him.

'*We don't have another minute!*' screamed Wicker. '*I've got the psyker kid, but we suffered major losses and Mad D'onne and that nasty scrutinator are not far behind us. If you want the kid, we need to act now!*'

That did the trick. Kordon's business mind wrested control from his brooding, self-pitying mind – at least temporarily, while the adrenaline kept the spider venom at bay. 'What are you saying? What do you need? Just bring the kid to me!'

'*Wrong,*' said Wicker. His face was almost, but not quite, as animated as the skull tattoo. '*We're still here in Down Town. We need reinforcements before we try to ascend the Abyss. The sump only knows how many other gangs are after this kid. Set me up with another thousand creds to restock and recruit and then we'll bring the boy to you.*'

The mention of funds sharpened Brann's brain a bit more. 'A thousand is pretty steep,' he said. 'Why so much?'

'*'Cause this needs to be done quick, man,*' said Wicker. '*I don't got time to haggle, and I need to gather every bounty hunter and hive scum I can afford, plus plenty of weapons – ones that can stop Mad D'onne, which ain't gonna be cheap.*'

What assurances do I have you can deliver? was what Brann should have asked. Perhaps, if his brain hadn't been three-quarters embalmed by spider venom, he might have even said, *why should I throw good money after bad?* or *this will likely ruin me.*

Instead, what Kordon Brann said to Wicker Crag was, 'The funds will be in your account immediately. Get that kid up here. If you meet Mad D'onne, you can keep the bounty on her for your troubles.'

After transferring the funds, Kordon laid his head down on his desk and fell asleep, with his cheek pressed against a stylus and three tacks, which he wouldn't feel until the nerves in his numbed skin began firing again.

Servalen had never seen Down Town from the surface of the sump before. She'd always ridden the lifts from Dust Falls. From above it looked like every other dirty hole in the underhive: haphazard rows of dust-covered hovels surrounding a dirty town square. The only difference between Dust Falls – or Sludge Town – and Down Town was the sump, which from above looked like an oily stain leaking out from the edge of town.

From the surface of that stain, though, Down Town had a kind of a grim beauty. The rundown, ramshackle buildings, moist from sump spray, shone in the lichen light. The skiffs, some lined up neatly at the docks and others dotting the reflective surface of the sump, gave the 'hole at the bottom of the hive' the air of an old-world port. Above it all, the Abyss loomed over the town, looking more like a grand, natural-rock formation stretching into infinity than the compressed accumulation of decaying rockcrete and plasteel domes.

It was at this moment, as Servalen and D'onne rowed the sump spider carcass into sight of Down Town, that the scrutinator realised the psyker and, by extension, the hive scum gang that took him, must be somewhere nearby. The pressure inside Servalen's head had returned, bringing with it the strange, wistful thoughts the kid's presence always seemed to provoke within her null psyche.

The question was, of course, where they would take him next. More to the point, who had hired them? Hive scum didn't do anything unless paid to do it. They definitely would not have taken on a squad of enforcers unless they had good reason to. No. No one was that stupid. Somebody had paid them a lot to kill Sergeant Nox and the squad. Who had that kind of credits to throw around?

The answer was obvious: guilders. And she knew one guilder in particular who was greedy enough – and stupid enough – to think sending a gang of hive scum against Mad D'onne and the enforcers made good business sense.

If that was the man that had hired them, then the gangers would be heading to Sludge Town. The problem was she and D'onne were still in the middle of the sump, rowing a spider mare.

At their present speed, it would take another half an hour to reach the shore. Plenty of time for the hive scum to haul the kid onto the lower lift.

Maybe Servalen could buy her and D'onne some time. She had to hope Proctor Bauhein would answer her on the vox.

Servalen placed her leg-oar on top of the carapace and detached the vox from her belt. She keyed it to broadcast at long range on a frequency reserved for precinct proctors.

'Proctor Bauhein,' she said into her hand vox. 'This is Scrutinator Servalen. Please respond.'

Nothing. D'onne stopped paddling and whipped her head around to stare at Servalen over her shoulder. Several loose strands of her powdered wig slapped the hunter across her cheeks. She blew them out of the way with a puff of air. 'What the hell are you doing?' she hissed.

Servalen held a finger up to her mouth to shush D'onne. After making sure the vox channel was closed, she said. 'The hive scum were hired by the guilder in Sludge Town. Who else could know about this? Who else worked with the

Cawdor? Bauhein can shut down the Abyss gates, and that should buy us time to catch up to them.'

'What do we do then?' asked D'onne. 'That scum and their pet Goliath killed your entire squad!'

'I'm sure you'll think of something,' said Servalen, pointing to the spider mare carcass they were riding. 'You always do.'

'Okay, I might have a plan,' said D'onne smiling. 'But, assuming we can pull this off, what do I get out of this?'

'The chance to screw me over and get away with the psyker,' Servalen replied, matter-of-factly.

D'onne looked taken back by the reply, but Servalen saw the grin pulling at her face. 'Sounds fair,' she said. 'Continue.' D'onne waved at Servalen dismissively with the back of her hand as she turned around to continue rowing.

Servalen keyed the vox transmitter back on and tried again. 'I know you can hear me, Clause,' she said. 'No need to reply. Just listen. A dangerous psyker is headed up the Abyss. You need to close the gates. Believe me, you don't want a psyker of this power inside your walls.'

There was no answer, and Servalen realised she needed to sweeten the deal. 'I know closing the gates costs the council a lot of credits,' she said into the vox. 'Do this for me, and I will give Mad D'onne to you. That should more than compensate everyone.'

D'onne whipped her head around again and scowled at Servalen. The scrutinator held her hand up to silence her objection.

'Think about it, Clause,' she continued into the transmitter. 'If you capture the underhive's most dangerous woman, they'll promote you to proctor majoris. No more dealing with the Council of Dust.'

If there is one truism in any hierarchy, military or otherwise, it's that the best way to manipulate anyone is to dangle a promotion in front of their eyes.

A moment later, the vox's receiver crackled to life. *'Why should I trust you?'*

'Look, all I want is the psyker. He is my mission. D'onne was just an annoyance. I'll be glad to be rid of her.'

'How do I know you even have the mad Ulanti woman?' asked Bauhein. 'How could you defeat her in combat?'

'KB-88 did most of the work,' said Servalen.

That lie stung a bit, but luckily Bauhein snorted and said, 'I bet he did!'

'I'll prove I have her,' said Servalen. She snapped her fingers to get D'onne's attention and then mimed stabbing her, while holding up the vox receiver.

'Ow!' D'onne yelled after a moment. 'Stop that, you soulless, mutie-spawned b–'

Servalen gave D'onne a thumbs-up and waited for Bauhein to respond.

The vox remained silent for several minutes, during which time D'onne was able to paddle the spider mare into a secluded section of beach at the edge of town. Just as Servalen was about to give up on Bauhein, the vox crackled back to life.

'You have a deal,' came the response. Bauhein then laughed a long, hearty laugh. *'You certainly aren't as sharp over the vox as you are in person, though.'*

'What do you mean by that?' asked Servalen, a gnawing pit beginning to form in her stomach.

'The gates have already been closed. The order came from above. Sounds like you're not the only one looking for that psyker.'

The vox connection cut off, leaving Servalen stunned to silence. 'That can't be good,' she said finally. 'Think it's a trap?'

D'onne shrugged her shoulders and climbed off the spider. 'To be honest, I act like every situation in the underhive is a trap. Pick your moment and roll with it, I say.'

It was surprisingly sage and sane advice coming from the mad woman of the underhive. 'So, what do we do now?' Servalen asked as she walked across the spider's back towards the shore.

'What else? We set a trap ourselves!' replied D'onne.

CHAPTER 17

MIND GAMES

D'onne banged open the bowed door to the Bottom of the Barrel, the oldest and most (and least) respectable ganger hole in all of Down Town. The old, iron-strapped door slammed into the rockcrete wall behind it so hard that pieces of rockcrete flew off the wall.

The Bottom of the Barrel was famous for two things, neither of which was the quality of its alcohol. The first was the door, which had been cut from a huge cask of ale found floating in the sump at least a hundred years ago. Legend had it that the original owner, a Goliath named Karg Gangrol, had pulled the three-metre-tall barrel from the sump with his bare hands and served the dark, dank liquid inside to the first patrons, many of whom lived to tell the tale. Common wisdom said that the ale served by Karg's granddaughter, Karga (not a lot of originality in the Gangrol family) was only slightly better-tasting and less toxic than that original brew.

The second thing the Bottom of the Barrel was famous

for was for being neutral ground. Karga maintained a strict 'no gang violence' policy inside the hole. It was open to all houses all the time and anyone caught fighting inside was banned forever, which is to say violators were carried to the sump by one of Karga's brothers and tossed in.

This policy was instituted by the second Karg, called Two by his four brothers, who while not big and strong enough to pull a four-tonne cask out of the sump, made up for it by being the smartest Goliath in ten generations (and the best shot with a las pistol as well).

Two understood there was money to be made by serving every ganger who came looking for fortune in Down Town, not just the Goliaths. Having four huge brothers meant he could outsmart them and force them to do his dirty work.

Karga, who was Two's eldest, and the smartest and best shot amongst her five siblings, had carried on her father's tradition of serving everyone in Down Town and forcing her brothers to do her dirty work.

So when Mad D'onne slammed open the door to the crowded and noisy bar, Karga was not only the first to notice, but she immediately pulled the nearest lasgun out and levelled its long barrel at the chest of the wild woman.

Every last ganger in the hole went dead silent as soon as the crowd heard the whine of the lasgun heating up and saw who it was pointed at.

'Drop your weapons, Donna, or I drop you where you stand,' demanded Karga. 'No one comes in with weapons, especially not you!'

D'onne raised her hands to show she came in peace – at least until the shooting started – and took a step back, just in case. 'Look,' she said. 'I'm not here to start anything. I'm not even inside.'

'Then turn around and leave,' said Karga. 'Boys? Help her out!' She nodded her head towards two of the largest Goliaths D'onne had ever seen, lounging against either end of the bar. As big as they were, each glanced at the other and then at their sister with a wide-eyed, rat-in-the-crosshairs look of terror at the prospect.

'There's no need for that,' D'onne said, and the relief that washed over their faces warmed her heart. She'd remember that in case she ever did need to start something inside the Bottom of the Barrel. 'I don't want any trouble. I have a proposition for you and your patrons – a very profitable proposition. One that takes place completely outside this very stout door.'

'Spit it out then leave,' said Karga, who spat on the floor to emphasise her point. 'Hurry up about it. My trigger finger is getting bored with your presence.'

D'onne, realising she would rather take on all five of Karga's brothers than fight the Goliath woman alone, began her prepared spiel. 'It's an opportunity for you,' she began. 'A spider mare crawled out of the sump and made it to the lift platform.'

That got the attention of everyone in the Barrel. Stools and chairs scraped across the rockcrete floor as entire gangs excitedly scrambled to get to their feet first. D'onne was glad that none of them had their weapons, or they would probably end up killing one another in their rush to be the first through the door.

'Wait!' D'onne yelled, and suddenly her chainsword was in her hand. The Barrel went silent again. She took another step back and held up her hand to silence Karga before continuing. 'There's a hired gang of hive scum at the platform too,' she said. 'Why do you think I came here instead of killing the mare myself?'

'What do you want?' growled Karga. She'd come around the bar and pointed her lasgun at D'onne's head.

'Any gang that helps me rescue the prize from those scavving hive scum – and the fat, rich guilder they work for – will get to share in the spider's very valuable eyes,' D'onne replied. She switched off the chain on Countless and sheathed it. 'All I want is a single eye. The rest you all can divvy up as you see fit.'

With that, D'onne backed out of Karga's line of sight, before turning and running back towards the lift platform. Her only regret was that she wouldn't still be hanging around when these gangs were left 'negotiating' over who got to keep the eyes.

Servalen was getting concerned. D'onne had been gone a long time and there was still no sign of the mob she'd promised. Whatever was happening up-hive could change at any moment and once someone above Bauhein ordered him to open the gates, the lifts would begin running again.

There were too many uncontrolled variables for Servalen's liking. In addition to the chaos that involving gangers would create, and the distinct possibility that a stray shot could kill the psyker they were trying to capture, Servalen had to figure out D'onne's endgame.

The mad woman would definitely try to double-cross her, that much was obvious. But how? The plan was so nebulous that the possibilities were endless. Servalen was used to keeping her work and world tight and orderly. She researched and planned everything ahead of time and made sure she controlled every aspect of any mission she went on.

She never asked a question in an interrogation that she didn't already know – or suspect – the answer to, and she never left any piece of any plan to chance. Not until today, at any rate. This mission had made Servalen fly by the seat of her pants at every turn. She wasn't sure if D'onne or the young psyker were to blame. She suspected mostly the former.

Her only choice at this point was to go along with the plan to a point but keep a constant eye on D'onne, to stay one step ahead for as long as possible. She had one ace in the hole, at least. D'onne did not yet know that the psyker's power exerted some sort of mental pressure on Servalen's mind that allowed her to sense his presence.

From her vantage point at the opening of a tunnel above the lift platform, Servalen could see the hive scum and the boy. He looked none the worse for wear. His shock of dirty brown hair fell about his ears and eyes like wispy strands of wire weed, while his sludge-stained shirt and trousers hung on his thin frame like sackcloth.

He could use a few meals, thought Servalen. At least he was only dragging two of the six chains from the Pyre. The rest had been removed, but the last two connected the psyker to a couple of new, low-level scummers.

The leader had added a few more well-armed scummers to his gang as well since they'd escaped with the boy. The stump of his arm had been bandaged and his weapons replaced. He paced the lift platform like a caged animal, no doubt getting more and more anxious about the lack of movement from the lifts above him.

That nervousness would play into D'onne's plan well, but only if the leader didn't give up on the lifts and go and hole up for a while. *Where was the mob?*

At first, Servalen had been relieved to see the scummer on the platform when she and D'onne had arrived at the tunnel entrance. The trip through the tunnel had been circuitous and seemed to stretch on forever. More than once, Servalen wondered if D'onne was leading her into a trap.

But Servalen had to admit that D'onne's knowledge of hidden routes through the backwaters of the underhive was quite impressive. This spot was perfect for their plan. If Servalen didn't have orders to bring the mad Ulanti noble to justice, D'onne would make a great asset. Perhaps something to consider if she got out of this alive. Not that D'onne would ever agree to work with any official hive authority.

Still, it might be worth considering...

'Damnit,' muttered Servalen, becoming painfully aware, again, of the psychic pressure inside her brain. 'That damn kid's presence keeps making my mind wander.'

Servalen checked the path leading from the lift platform down to the edge of Down Town for any sign of D'onne's promised mob. She could see the leading edge of a large group of gangers coming into view below the lift level on one of the final switchbacks that wound up the mound of rubble from town to the platform.

The group was huge, though. Much bigger than D'onne promised. The hunter had said it might be twenty or so members of a few different house gangs. The mob Servalen saw spanned an entire switchback and numbered at least sixty gangers from a dozen or more gangs.

Did D'onne know there would be this many? wondered Servalen. *Was that part of her plan to screw me over?* This fight would get out of hand quickly. She needed to alter her part of the plan.

But first, it was time to throw a spider-mare-sized wrench into the hive scummer's day – and do something D'onne-level crazy to try to stay ahead of the mad noble. Before the gangers rounded the last switchback, Servalen retreated from the edge of the tunnel, moving carefully around the hollowed-out husk of the spider mare to avoid the legs, which were wedged into cracks in the carapace to make the spider appear complete.

To Servalen, the spider was obviously a dead husk, but it only needed to fool the scummers and the gangers for a few seconds to spark the initial fireworks. Greed and the natural animus between gangs would take it from there.

Servalen pushed the spider mare carcass slowly across the rockcrete floor of the tunnel towards the opening. When she felt it begin to teeter a bit on the edge, the scrutinator grabbed hold of a loose section of carapace with both hands and shoved with all her might to slide it all the way out of the tunnel.

A moment later, Servalen and the spider carcass were plummeting towards the lift platform below them. As the spider mare landed with a loud thud, Servalen rolled to the ground behind the bulk of the mare.

As Servalen huddled behind the mare, the scummers began shouting and firing their weapons at the carcass.

CHAPTER 18

SNEAK ATTACKS

'How much longer are we going to stand here?' asked Dani, one of a pair of venators Wicker had hired to replace Grin and Tank. The large blonde woman was equipped with a hand-flamer and a two-handed hammer and wore head-to-toe leather armour. A dozen leather straps crisscrossed her armour but seemed to be present to make a statement more than do anything practical. She had no ammo or grenades hanging from any of the belts.

'As long as I say,' replied Wicker. He was getting tired of Dani's constant complaining, but he had to admit that he wasn't happy with the situation. He just didn't have to admit it to a subordinate.

'We can't wait around to be gunned down like a bunch of juves,' chimed in Brak, the other venator. Brak was a big ape of a man with the beard and body hair to match. He carried a blunderbuss casually in one massive hand as he scratched at the unruly mass of hair beneath his chin. While Dani had no grenades, Brak carried at least a dozen and they were all clipped to the tangled hair that covered his torso.

Wicker sighed. The two venators complained like an old married couple. They were definitely veterans and their glory days could well be behind them, but Wicker knew that to live this long in the underhive, the pair was either very good at surviving or very good at killing – probably both. That was exactly what Wicker needed right now, especially since the rest of the new recruits were little more than juves.

Wicker had put two younger recruits on guard duty near the edge of the platform because he wasn't sure they could handle anything else, and the psyker didn't seem much of a flight risk. Wicker wasn't sure the kid could lift his own shirt over his head, he looked so small and weak.

'How much longer?' whined one of the scummer juves guarding the kid. He swayed back and forth, putting his weight on one leg and then the other, over and over.

Watching the kid fidget on guard duty finally made Wicker reach boiling point. 'Everyone shut up and follow orders or Hark here will turn your heads into a fine red mist.'

Hark nodded his helmeted head and placed his hand on the giant stub cannon holstered on his hip.

At that moment, a resounding impact from the platform behind Wicker made him stumble forward a step. All around him, the new recruits began yelling and firing their weapons.

Wicker whirled around, fully expecting to see Mad D'onne and her enormous ogryn bodyguard tearing through his recruits. Instead, a giant spider mare had appeared in the middle of the lift platform. The sight astounded the scummer leader, leaving him speechless and motionless for several long seconds as his mind sorted out the image.

The scum, startled by the sneak attack, had opened fire

without orders. Autopistols, shot guns and autoguns filled the air with a cacophony of ordnance, little of which had any effect on the spider. Most of their shots ricocheted off the thick carapace.

By the time Wicker assessed the scene, even the veterans and Hawk, Wicker's sniper, had opened fire. The mohawked scummer's first shot put a hole clean through the mare's skull, while Brak's blunderbuss removed a large chunk of carapace near the middle legs. Oddly, the creature didn't react at all, not even to those deep wounds.

Amidst all this chaos, the two juves tasked with guarding the young psyker had panicked and pulled the kid by the chains back to the edge of the platform, apparently to get as far away from the nightmare spider as possible.

Within a few moments, though, Wicker realised the spider mare was dead and had been so for quite some time. Its legs were splayed to the side and not supporting its weight. The eyes were dull and glazed. No fluids flowed from the fresh wounds his scummers had inflicted. The beast had already been gutted.

As Wicker was about to call a ceasefire, though, several loud voices began shouting behind him. 'There it is!' yelled one voice, 'Get the eyes!' Another screamed, 'Don't let the guilders steal our spiders!' Several more cried out orders: 'Get 'em!' or 'Attack!' or 'Open fire!'

Wicker spun around to see several score of gangers with weapons brandished and venom in their eyes charging the platform. Every house was represented in a strange, marching mélange of colours that surged and shifted as each gang vied to lead the riot converging on the platform.

'Forget the spider!' Wicker bellowed. 'It's dead! We're being attacked from behind. It's an ambush!'

Wicker dived for cover as the first shots rang out from the charging mob. He crawled towards the spider mare, hoping to use the corpse as a protective wall. As he crept forward, Wicker heard one last cry ring out loud and clear from the exuberant mob: 'Mad Donna was right!'

It made sense. D'onne had riled up the locals and then dropped the mare on their heads to create chaos. Once safely behind the dead spider, Wicker scanned for the psyker prisoner and his two juve guards, figuring that's where D'onne would be, but he couldn't find them through the mass of bodies, bullets and blasts.

The leading edge of the mob reached the platform. Half a dozen large gangers, including several Goliaths and one enhanced abhuman, drew heavy melee weapons and charged into hand-to-hand combat with the front row of his young recruits. Wicker was glad he'd filled the ranks with fodder now.

The rest of the mob surged forward, engulfing the space around the platform. Those at the front tried to scramble up the sides of the platform or stood on their own wounded and dead to climb over the edge and reach their spider prize.

The scummers were badly outnumbered and trapped with their backs against the tallest wall in the known worlds, but for the moment Hark, Hawk, Dani and Brak were keeping most of the gangers at bay.

Dani stood by the head of the spider, spraying fire in a wide arc across the platform to hold back the advancing line while Hark's booming stub cannon blew holes in the surging mob. Every explosion blew body parts and rubble into the air around the platform. Hawk had climbed up onto the mare and found a spot from which she could snipe, concentrating on the biggest targets near the front of the mob. And

Brak ripped grenade after grenade off his chest and flung them into the crowd, spreading gas, smoke and deadly metal fragments through the mob, creating his own bit of chaos.

Still more gangers were streaming towards the platform from the top of the switchbacks. Even his veterans wouldn't be able to hold out long enough. Once their ammo ran out, they were all done for. Wicker needed a way to turn the tide or the psyker wouldn't be the only thing he lost today.

He glanced around, looking for an opening in the enemy lines or a leader to take down that might demoralise the mob, but it was, at its essence, a riot, which wouldn't end until everyone was dead or dead tired from the constant exertion.

Or, he thought, *once the mob got what it wanted*. The beginnings of a plan began to form in Wicker's mind as he edged his way towards the head of the spider mare corpse.

D'onne waited off to the side of the lift platform in the shadow of the kilometres-high encircling wall of the Abyss. After leaving Down Town from a side street, she had climbed the rubble pile to get close enough to the lift platform to strike when the time was right. She now hid behind a room-sized chunk of rockcrete buttress that had once been part of the foundation of some large building.

From the looks of it, the buttress had only recently plummeted to the bottom of the Abyss. For one thing, it wasn't completely coated with the slimy residue of the sump. For another, less than a quarter of the structure had been scavenged for building materials. There was still enough left of this hunk of rockcrete to hide behind and it provided D'onne with a good vantage point.

The hunter had been watching the scummers while waiting

for the gangs she'd enticed with dreams of an easy paycheck mixed with some guilder payback. It was a beautiful plan full of symmetry and chaos.

It wasn't all about death and destruction for D'onne; that's what most people got wrong about her. She wasn't a nightmare or a spectre of death at all. She was an artist, and the underhive was her canvas. She painted it with blood to illuminate the transience of life. She played the roles thrust upon her – mad woman, noble daughter, gang member, bounty hunter – to lay bare dark truths about hive society.

In many ways, D'onne's life had been formed and moulded by the people and relationships in her past. She was the woman she was today because of what men – and some women – had said to her, done to her and made her do, to fit her into the mould they had set. It wasn't until recently she had realised – and more importantly, accepted – the truth that she had long been controlled by her past. No more.

'Where the sump are those gangers?' she wondered out loud. It had been nearly thirty minutes since she had left the drinking hole. She was worried at the time that the mob would beat her to the lift platform, because she had to take a roundabout route. But there was still no sign of anyone from the Bottom of the Barrel.

'How long does it take a score of gangers to gear up?' she asked the buttress, speaking to it not for the first time. At least the wait had given her time to observe the scummers and choose her approach. *Those two guards are fresh meat and standing way too close to the edge of the platform for their own good*, she thought.

Plus, the other new faces in the scummer gang were keeping the leader busy with their constant talking. 'That's why

I don't lead gangs. I'd kill my own gangers every time they annoyed me,' she told the buttress.

'Ooh,' continued D'onne, thumping the buttress with an excited fist bump. 'Here comes my angry mob while the scummer leader is distracted. Perfect timing, don't you think?'

D'onne looked at the rockcrete foundation, half expecting it to at least glint or crumble a bit in response. 'Right. Not Dog.' She sighed and crept from her hiding spot as the spider mare crashed onto the platform.

As all hell broke loose on the platform, D'onne raced across the rubble field, practically skimming the rough edge of the Abyss cliff. She needed to beat the mob to the edge of the raised lift platform without alerting the scummers to her presence.

What D'onne hadn't told Servalen was that the mob's secondary job was to cover her escape, not her approach. If all went to plan, she and the psyker would be long gone before Servalen ever reached the platform. She'd dragged that carcass through a long, circuitous tunnel for a reason. Symmetry amid chaos. It made her smile as she ran.

There, she thought, seeing the psyker being pulled away from the spider mare by his two guards. They each had a chain locked around their wrists to keep him from running, but that wouldn't slow D'onne down any.

D'onne drew Countless from its scabbard as she reached the edge of the platform but didn't activate the chain yet. Instead, she slunk around the platform towards the kid and his guards, who were watching the spider battle intently.

Everyone knew mares could leap great distances, so they were probably soiling themselves worried about being tethered to the kid should that happen. They should have been more worried about what might be behind them.

D'onne reached up with her free hand and grabbed the psyker by the ankle. With one mighty heave, she pulled his foot off the edge of the platform. He flailed his arms to try to maintain his balance, but D'onne kept pulling and there was nothing the kid could do but fall off the edge. D'onne released her hold on his ankle and caught the psyker in a one-armed bear hug around his slim waist.

Before the two distracted guards knew what was happening, the chains attached to their wrists went taut and pulled them off balance as well. With one final heave on the chains, D'onne pulled both young scummers off the platform.

They landed on their backs with twin thumps beside D'onne, slamming their heads hard on the jagged rubble. She released the psyker for the moment, flicked on the thrumming chain that whirred around Countless and raised the chainsword over her head. With two quick strikes, D'onne severed the chains just clear of the guards' wrists.

She raised Countless over the unconscious guards again, but before she could behead them, the psyker spoke.

'Don't!' he pleaded, his voice almost too small and weak to be heard over the commotion raging around them. 'Don't kill them,' he said.

'Look, kid,' said D'onne, 'I don't have time to argue. They need to die, and you need to come with me. Right now.'

The psyker moved between D'onne and the two young scummers. 'If you kill them, I won't come with you,' he said.

'I don't need your permission,' she replied. 'You weigh less than Countless here.' To prove her point, D'onne shoved the kid out of the way with her free hand.

'I won't help you!' he said as D'onne raised her blade again. 'If you kill them, I will never tell you where to find it.'

Now that was a different story and made D'onne hesitate.

After a moment, with the mob rushing towards the platform, D'onne sighed. Shuddering at what she was being forced to do, she slammed her favourite weapon down twice more, but turned it at the last moment each time to hit the young scummers with the flat of the blade. 'Happy?' she asked.

The kid nodded.

Still, 'not killing' didn't exclude delivering a little pain, and D'onne examined her handiwork. Both strikes had indeed been with the flat of the blade, but the leading edge of Countless had taken off an ear apiece. *At least they now had battle scars to prove they were real gangers*, she thought.

Pleased with her work, D'onne grabbed the chains and pulled the psyker along behind her as she ran towards her buttress. Behind her, the mob streamed onto the platform and chaos erupted in her wake, again. *Mission accomplished*, D'onne thought as she ran.

CHAPTER 19

ESCAPE PLANS

Servalen crept along the back edge of the platform behind the spider mare as autogun and shotgun rounds bounced off the outer shell on the other side. She needed to get clear of the carcass before the scummers brought anything heavier to bear.

Sure enough, as she reached the back end of the dead mare, high-calibre rounds began slicing through the head and carapace behind her, embedding and ricocheting off the rockcrete wall of the Abyss. Servalen had no choice but to dash across the open space between the mare's splayed back legs and the side of the platform.

As she did, an explosion rocked the Abyss as one of Hark's shells rocketed through the empty shell and detonated on the Abyss wall, sending shards of rockcrete and bits of metal from embedded rebar spraying across the entire back side of the platform. The shockwave of the explosion sent the scrutinator sprawling forward off the side of the platform.

As she lay on the rocky ground beside the platform, Servalen took quick stock of her wounds. She found nothing broken and no shrapnel gashes. Luckily, her cloak and armour had taken the brunt of the impact. The scrutinator picked herself up and hurried towards the sloping side of the rubble mound while the dust from the blast still covered her escape.

Servalen huffed and coughed as she ran down the side of the rubble mound. Although fit and capable – enforcer training required nothing less than impeccable physical fitness – Servalen wasn't built for this kind of exertion. That was more D'onne's area of expertise. The scrutinator had read reports of the mad hunter dangling from plasteel beams over the Abyss, battling a noble war vet in power armour on the wing of a speeding lighter or, more recently, climbing a smoke stack to evade an enforcer squad.

Servalen's talents lay in breaking people psychologically, not chasing them endlessly through the underhive. However, she had to find D'onne quickly, so this was no time to slow down. As she saw it, she needed to get around the mob to the other side of the platform as quickly as possible.

She had watched for D'onne's return during the build-up to the ambush and hadn't seen her anywhere around the top of the mound. The rubble mound fell away quickly on the side Servalen had crossed, which was part of the reason she had chosen that route, as it covered her escape. But D'onne would have needed to get to the boy quickly during the initial confusion, so would have approached from the other side, which had a flatter field of rubble.

Servalen scrambled around the side of the mound and reached the switchback road that led down towards town and up towards the platform. She ran up the sloping path that had been vacated by rioting gangers.

From the top of that switchback she could see the battle on the platform. The scummers were completely surrounded with their backs pressed against the carcass of the spider mare. Their first-line defence of juves and young hive scum had been reduced in number and pressed back into the veterans with their heavier weapons.

One female scummer tried to force the mob back with bursts of dripping, liquid fire from her flamethrower, but it only provided short reprieves because two enormous Goliaths wearing salvaged plates of plasteel as armour had taken command of the middle of the line on either side of a huge, muscle-bound abhuman monstrosity nearly as big as D'onne's ogryn bodyguard. The Goliaths swung heavy mauls in wide swaths, forcing the scummers – including the one with the flamethrower – to dive out of the way to avoid broken bones.

Anytime Hark or the older veteran with the blunderbuss raised their big guns to try to take down the Goliaths, their weapons got swatted aside by those mauls as well. Meanwhile, the muscle-bound abhuman picked up juves and young scummers by the neck and shook them around before tossing them to the ground. It had been filled full of holes and sliced by a dozen deep cuts, but nothing seemed to slow it down.

The only thing working for the gang of hive scum was their mohawked assassin, who was picking off gangers left and right from her vantage point atop the spider. Sooner or later, though, she and the rest of the scummers would run out of ammo and the mob would converge to rip them apart.

With the attention of all combatants centred on the platform, this was Servalen's best chance to get around to the other side. The final switchback was still half filled with gangers, though, and she knew the sudden appearance of an enforcer into this chaotic battle would ignite the mob like a powder keg. So, Servalen began climbing the mound, doing her best to keep out of sight.

Wicker ducked behind the spider carcass as an ambitious ganger let loose with a barrage of autofire rounds from a heavy stubber. As the scummer leader crouched there, he heard the booming crack of Hawk's long-las rifle above him followed by a dull squelch in the distance and the cessation of the stubber fire.

'Thanks,' Wicker grunted as he stood and once again tried to remove the spider's head from its body. But, with no bladed weapon and one hand, it was impossible. He briefly thought about unleashing a torrent of slugs from his stubber into carapace-covered cartilage, but he was certain he'd die from ricochets before severing the dead beast's neck.

He needed Hark but taking him off the front line would doom them as well. The bounty hunter had switched to his hunting knife, which was as long as one of his legs, and had already cut down one of the two Goliaths terrorising Wicker's young scummers and had begun slicing up the second as Dani kept the abhuman at bay with her fire. That left Brak, who had switched on his chain glaive and was using it to mow down any gangers who got too close to Dani.

As Wicker tried to come up with some way to sever the spider's head so he could use it to distract the mob, he spied a group of gangers climbing onto the platform near the edge of the cliff face and had to deal with the immediate problem. Resting his compact heavy stubber on his bandaged arm, Wicker sprayed slugs into the advancing group of gangers. The heavy ordnance cut skull fragments and brain matter from the first three gangers to splatter into the faces of those following, who dropped out of site.

'I need help!' Wicker called emphatically. 'Hawk! Gangers doing an end-around at your three o'clock.' In response he heard the boom of her rifle and a las-shot streaked above him. The blast went straight through the edge of the platform, and was followed by a grunt and a gout of blood.

'And if anyone knows how to remove a spider mare's head,' he called out, 'tell me now.'

Wicker fired another salvo from his stubber towards the side as more of the mob had reached the Abyss edge of the platform and scaled its side. The heavy weapon bounced all over the place on his bandage, shooting pain from his stump straight up his arm and sending his ammo spraying high and wide. But he'd found if he aimed low and kept firing, he generally hit someone. It really wasn't that different from how he usually fought.

'I have a crazy idea!' yelled Brak.

'Will it get us killed?' Wicker called back.

'Probably not,' replied Brak as he stood up beside Wicker. He had apparently dropped to the ground and crawled under the mare's head to reach his leader's side.

At that moment, Wicker spied a third group of gangers working their way towards the right flank. He ordered Hawk to handle the threat so he could concentrate on getting them all out of this alive.

'So, what's your idea?' Wicker asked. Above him, Hawk's long-las cracked again and again and again. 'All I have is my heavy stubber and my stump. Not ideal cutting tools.'

'A krak grenade should do the trick,' replied Brak.

Wicker snorted derisively. 'And that "probably" won't kill us?' he asked.

'Not the way I plan to use it,' replied Brak.

Above them Hawk stopped firing for a moment. 'Whatever you two are planning, do it quick,' she said. 'I'm almost out of ammo.'

'Okay,' Wicker said. 'Do it.' It was a crazy idea, but it might just be crazy-brilliant. In fact, Wicker thought Brak's idea might solve the other problem of his plan: delivering the head to the crowd. 'Let me get clear first.'

As Wicker slipped around the carcass towards its back legs, he called up to Hawk, the last remaining member of his original gang. 'Hold on tight!' he hissed at her. 'It's about to get bumpy up there.'

Hark and Dani and the few remaining low-level scummers were overwhelmed by the sheer number of gangers pressing forward on the platform, not to mention the behemoth abhuman commanding the centre of the line, but Wicker had no way to get word to them about what was about to happen without alerting the entire mob. If they survived, great. If not, he wouldn't shed a tear. He hardly knew them.

Once in position, well away from the coming explosion, Wicker gave Brak a thumbs-up. The grey-haired veteran scummer yanked the pincers apart, grabbed a krak grenade clipped to his chest, and shoved it as far down the beast's gullet as he could reach.

Brak yanked his arm out quickly, the grenade's pin flying free of his fingers. Wicker could see something was wrong from the look on the scummer's face, though. The mare's mouth had remained open, and Brak's plan called for the force of the explosion to be contained. Thinking fast, Brak grabbed a hunk of rockcrete that had broken off the wall behind him and wedged it into the mare's mouth.

'Fire in the hole!' Brak called as he dived to the ground.

The explosion rocked the carcass, sending it skidding backwards several metres. The legs, which had been wedged into cracks in the carapace, rocketed out the sides. Two legs shattered on the cliff wall to either side of Wicker, making his heart skip a beat.

The battle seemed to freeze as the mob stopped to watch the spider mare's head, with its valuable eyes, soar away from the battle. It cleared the back edge of the mob and kept going until gravity finally brought it down onto the rubble more than five hundred metres to the side of the lift platform.

Wicker stepped out from behind the dead mare and yelled to the crowd. 'There's your prize!' His voice boomed over the stunned and silent mob. 'First gang to reach the head keeps all the eyes!'

Of course, Wicker had no way to enforce that promise, nor did he care. The gangs could (and would) tear each other apart to claim those eyes. *Better them than us*, he thought.

Almost immediately, the mob turned and raced for the edges of the platform, brawling with one another to improve their odds of being first to reach the head. *Time for us to be elsewhere*, thought Wicker. *A bar, maybe. Frag that damned kid. I need a drink and a plan.*

Wicker found Hawk standing next to him and motioned for the sniper to follow him off the side of the platform. Before he turned to leave, the scummer leader saw Dani pull Brak to his feet. He waved at them to follow as well.

Despite their complaints, Wicker needed the elder duo, because the rest of his recruits were dead or gone. Wicker scanned the retreating mob and was unsurprised to see Hark cutting his way towards the mare's head.

'Where to, boss?' Hawk asked as she stowed her long-las in the holster hanging down her back.

'We can't go back to Down Town,' he said. 'Not yet anyway. Not until the survivors forget about us.'

'Dani and I know a spot where we can hide out for a while,' Brak said as he hobbled up to them, supported by Dani. Both were walking wounded, but they looked like they'd keep.

Wicker nodded. The two of them had proved their worth in this battle. As far as he was concerned, they were Circle-Skull now. From behind them, Wicker heard the sounds of the battle starting anew. The negotiations over the eyes had already broken down. The scummer leader shook his head.

Look what greed does to gangers, he thought, *and everyone else consigned to live in this hell-hole at the bottom of the world.* Wicker decided revenge would be a fine replacement for greed – for a time anyway.

CHAPTER 20

TRUDGING TOWARDS INEVITABILITY

'We can't leave them there,' Jeren Jerenson said in the most commanding voice he could muster. Sadly, even he knew it sounded whiny and pleading. He yanked on the chains to stop the female hunter, but all he accomplished was losing his balance. Stopping the tall, muscular woman was like trying to halt a runaway sludge cart.

Jeren fell face-first onto the rough rubble and bounced along behind the woman, who didn't slow down. D'onne – yeah, that was her name. He must have heard the other woman – the one who made him feel like his skin had turned to spiders, but who also made his headache disappear when she got close – say it at the Pyre altar. 'They'll die... if you leave... them there,' he said between bumps.

'Get up!' D'onne growled after dragging Jeren for ten metres. She turned and glared at him, her eyes beautiful even when angry under all that big hair that wasn't her own. She pulled out a large pistol that also didn't belong to her – at least not originally – and pointed it at his head.

'Get up!' she said. 'Or I swear I will blast your head right off your neck!'

Jeren smiled despite the threat. He understood. Mad D'onne wasn't crazy. She wasn't angry either. Well, she was angry most of the time, but she wasn't angry at him right now. In fact, Mad D'onne might be the most contented person alive. She knew her place in the world, her role to play, and she played it with gusto.

'You're not going to kill me,' Jeren said. He ignored the gun in her hand, which wavered slightly as he pulled himself to his feet and dusted off his trousers. A new-found confidence was beginning to grow inside him despite his pounding headache.

'You want to use my power,' he continued, 'and I can't tell you anything if you kill me.'

D'onne moved the barrel of the weapon to aim at Jeren's left hand. 'I might not kill you,' she said, 'but I can hurt you plenty and make you give me what I want.'

'Fair enough,' he replied, 'but I told you I will never give you what you want if those two guards you knocked out die, which they will, in four minutes and forty-seven seconds, if we don't go back.'

'How do you know that?' D'onne asked.

Jeren pointed at his temple and smiled. 'Four minutes, thirty-nine seconds.'

D'onne holstered the weapon and sighed. 'Fine,' she said. 'Just keep up!' She turned and ran back towards the lift platform, pulling Jeren along behind her.

By the time they got back to the platform, the mob had reached the front edge and the battle was raging. They hadn't spread to the sides of the platform yet, but it wouldn't be long before that happened. Jeren could see in his head that many items – weapons, armour and a few limbs – would soon get lost on the spot where they stood.

D'onne grabbed the unconscious guards by their armour and lifted their torsos off the ground. The bounty hunter certainly was strong and luckily his guards had been little older – and bigger – than Jeren. 'How much time?' she asked.

Jeren had lost count. It had taken maybe a minute to get back. 'Um, three minutes and twenty-three seconds,' he replied after a quick calculation and a bit of guessing.

D'onne shot a quick, questioning glance as she began hauling the two guards behind her by their collars. Their legs bounced on the rubble as D'onne dragged them away from the platform.

'How far?' she huffed.

'What?' asked Jeren.

'How far... do I need to drag... these idiots?' she said between heaving breaths. They had reached the edge of the cliff about a kilometre away from the platform. Nothing but rockcrete and plasteel debris lay between them and the mob, but the rolling pitch of the field of rubble had obscured the platform.

'This should be good,' replied Jeren, who only now noticed that D'onne had dropped his chains when she grabbed the guards. He'd been following her on his own volition ever since. *Interesting*, he thought. He hadn't felt this excited and alive his entire life. 'Let me see what I can see!'

D'onne dropped the young scummers and bent over, hands on knees. She breathed heavily while Jeren kneeled between his former guards and laid a hand on each of them. He could feel that they were safe now.

'This will do,' he said. 'Thank you.'

'I didn't do it for you, kid,' replied D'onne. 'I did it for what you can give me.'

'Everything leads us somewhere,' said Jeren. 'All this will mean something in the end. Something important. It must.'

'The universe doesn't have a plan, kid,' D'onne said as she grabbed him by the chains again. 'All you can do is try to survive all the bullshit. You know, like the load you gave me about those two morons dying in five minutes.'

Jeren's cheeks flushed. 'You're right. I generally can't tell when things will be lost. Only that they will be or have been,' he said as D'onne began pulling him along behind her again. 'I didn't lie about their deaths, though. I saw them lose their heads.'

D'onne glanced back at him. He saw genuine concern in her eyes, quickly replaced with something else, something darker. Then, in one swift action, she drew her plasma pistol, aimed it at him, and fired.

Karga, the Goliath bartender, watched the streets of Down Town empty outside the large, banded door to the Bottom of the Barrel as gang after gang rushed off on Mad Donna's fool's errand. Normally, Karga loved a good gang battle. Afterwards, the victors wanted to celebrate and the losers wanted to dull their pain. It was easy money. Of course, only one side or the other would show up at her hole.

A battle like the one about to happen, pitting all the gangs against a bunch of useless hive scum, could well be the best thing that ever happened to the Barrel. Sure, some of her customers would die today, but there was a constant flow of new gangers to Down Town, so they would soon be replaced.

The winners would be flush with creds and plenty eager to spend them.

She figured she could ride this money train for a couple of days, maybe more if the fighting was particularly bloody and everyone ended up with some gangers to mourn. It would only be right that Karga help them spend that newfound wealth, and get them over their various losses.

That was the thought that kept gnawing at Karga as she planned how to spend the creds she hoped to soon be raking in. *When did Mad Donna ever tell the truth?* The answer was obvious once Karga stopped to consider the question: Donna only told the truth when it benefitted her in some way, and even then the crazy hunter only told enough of the truth to get other people into trouble – and help her get out of trouble.

Karga stepped back inside the Bottom of the Barrel and began looking for her brothers and sons. 'Boys!' she called, 'I have a job for you.' As she waited for them to gather, Karga silently thanked her dad, Two, for passing on his smarts to her. If Donna's call for help had been a ruse of some sort, she wouldn't show her face in Down Town again – not for a long while. And if whatever Donna was after was worth more than a spider mare's eyes, Karga wanted a piece of that action.

Luckily, Karga had an idea where Donna might be found after the mob had done her dirty work. While tending bar, Karga listened to every story from every ganger and scummer that set foot inside the Bottom of the Barrel. Sump knows she didn't do it to be friendly. Information was currency in the underhive, and someone was always buying. She remembered one story that at the time was worth nothing, but now might be priceless: a story about a Hive Bottom hidey hole and a Mad Donna sighting.

So, Karga sent her brothers and sons out to cut the mad noble off before she disappeared into that hidey hole. 'Bring her back alive!' she told them a third time. Then, recalling some other information she had recently received from up-hive, Karga added, 'And bring back anyone with her alive as well.'

Karga gave her eldest brother, the smartest of the bunch excluding her, a special gift to help them follow her orders, a strange weapon she had taken in trade a while back, wondering if she would ever have use for it.

After the boys left the bar, Karga had to spend half her time serving drinks. Luckily, with the riot raging up the hill, there were only two groups of gangers in the Bottom of the Barrel. They had both missed the initial call to arms, and each had come to the decision that all the pickings would have been already plucked.

One group had been successful and the other had not, but both had wild tales to tell about their day. Karga treated them the same, as she did with every gang that entered her hole. Just because one group was down on its luck was no reason to show them the door (unless they asked for credit, that is; that offence normally brought swift justice).

The more successful group, a smallish Van Saar gang outfitted in shiny armour and fancy lascarbines, had brought in an intact spider mare without losing a single member of their raiding party. Their boasts were so incredible as to be unbelievable, even with the quality of their weaponry. The leader crowed about landing on the creature's back with his grav-chute and delivering the final blow.

To Karga's experienced eyes, though, they all looked a bit young and green to take down such a large mare without so much as an injury between them. Once she got them drunk enough, though, an even stranger tale emerged, that seemed only slightly more plausible than their boasts.

'It floated down the middle of the sump with a giant standing on its back.'

'He was riding it, Marik, like it was a seahorse or something.'

'Yeah, the giant was riding the mare, like Sanjun said. But it was already dead. He'd killed it!'

'But he had no weapons,' added Sanjun. 'The giant musta killed the thing with his bare hands.'

'Before we got close, the giant jumped off the mare and climbed the wall of the sump,' added Marik, 'right up into some hole overhead.'

'He didn't even have any equipment,' said Sanjun.

'No, he had armour,' said another Van Saar ganger.

'Yeah, but it was bolted on,' replied Sanjun. 'Not like he was wearing it.'

After hearing the story, Karga realised she should work hard to remove all the earnings from these poor Van Saar saps before they went out on another hunt and left the credits to go to waste in some abandoned dome. It was her civic duty.

As strange as that story had been, though, the Delaque gang had a more bizarre one. This group had staggered into the Barrel shortly after the rest of town had emptied out to join the riot at the lift platform. Karga thought about sending them on up to the fight, but they had seen enough battle already.

Their armour was in shreds and there were bandages on all four surviving members of the gang.

'What in the sump happened to you lot?' she asked as she poured them their first round.

'Some sort of ghost creature!' one of them said and then

went silent. He raised a bandaged hand whenever he wanted a refill but never spoke again.

Karga eventually got most of the story out of the others, but it was patchy at best. They were rowing up the sump from a day of boredom and stench when something jumped into the boat. There was some debate on the description of the creature. Whatever it was it moved like lightning and had razor sharp claws and teeth. It glistened and shone in the lichen light and a burning haze enveloped it from head to tail, making it impossible to describe.

The creature sprayed sump water on all of them as it landed in the skiff. Then it tore into them in a feeding frenzy (although Karga noted that none of them seemed to have any visible bite marks).

Two of the crew went overboard before the rest steered the skiff to a landing, thinking they might have a better chance fighting it on solid ground. But as soon as the skiff beached, the ghostly creature leapt onto the shore and loped off into the darkness.

At this point in the story, the gang's cash ran out. Because she had enjoyed their story, though, and because her bouncers were all out, she politely asked them to leave at the end of a lasgun barrel, after forcing them all to remove their gear and leave it on the table. It was obvious they wouldn't last long working the sump, so Karga figured she would do them a favour and send them packing before they suffered a grisly death down there.

While waiting for her brothers – and the survivors of the riot – to return, Karga filed their stories away with the others she had collected recently. Who knew, maybe Nemo was looking for that spider-mare-riding giant or the ghost creature that lives beneath the waves of the sump.

Later, as she was cleaning the bar and checking the charges on all her hidden lasguns, Karga was summoned to the back to answer a vox call from one of her up-hive contacts.

CHAPTER 21

NEGOTIATION

Something had kept Mad D'onne alive all those years. Skill and drive only get a hunter or ganger so far. Eventually a lasgun blast or needler dart catches up with everyone. And if you didn't die in a running battle with a rival house, there were still a lot of other ways to get yourself killed in the underhive.

Tunnels that had been used for years suddenly collapsed, crushing people who were going about their business. Factory accidents destroyed limbs and lives far too often to count. Hivequakes opened holes to long-lost domes, sending anyone standing in the wrong place to an early grave. Rusting steam pipes burst, boiling the skin off hapless passers-by. Everyone ended up under the carving knives of the Corpse Guild eventually.

Lethal accidents happened almost as often in the underhive as gang battles, and people died every day in the most gruesome and bloody ways imaginable. Yet, despite taking crazy chances with her life on a regular basis, Mad D'onne had survived everything the underhive had thrown at her. She had once jumped off the edge of the Abyss to escape death at the hands of an abhuman behemoth, figuring she liked her chances on the way down better than going toe to toe with a foe twice her size.

Some said D'onne had a sixth sense that warned her of danger. A few professed she was just too damned stubborn to let the underhive beat her. Others thought she was the luckiest person alive and that someday her luck would run out. Generally, those were the ones who believed that today would be their day to capture or kill Mad D'onne.

D'onne caught a glimpse of movement at the edge of the curving rubble pile while talking to the psyker kid. Perhaps it was a trick of the light coming off the distant sump or possibly a flare of sump gas in the air around her glinting off the polished barrel of a weapon. Whatever warned her, she saw the ambush coming right before it happened.

She fired Pig. As she did, D'onne realised she probably should have warned the kid. The purple plasma beam streaked past the young psyker's head, sizzling and crackling as it tore apart the oxygen and nitrogen molecules in the air dangerously close to his ear.

Her aim was true, though. The blast from Pig removed the spiked mohawk and more than a few centimetres of skull and soft tissue from the head of a Goliath ganger as he crested a rise in the rubble pile behind them. To the psyker's credit, he stood as still as a rockcrete buttress while the beam burned past him.

'Get behind me,' she yelled. When the kid didn't move fast enough, she grabbed him by the elbow and pulled him back, stepping up as she did to shield him. This was going to get ugly fast, and she wasn't about to lose her prize so soon after winning him. At least that's what she told herself.

Whatever plan this new Goliath gang had for attacking D'onne, her shot disrupted it. About half of them dropped to the ground and began firing, while the other half held their fire and charged, fanning out to cut off her escape.

The curvature of the rubble field made it hard for those lying prone on the slope to get clean shots, so they seemed to be mostly firing blindly. At the same time, the gaps in the line made those charging fan out further, putting them between D'onne and the blind shots of their allies. After two charging Goliaths dropped, screaming and writhing on the rubble, with blood streaming from bullet wounds in their massive calves and thighs, the rest fell back.

A deadly calm took hold of the battlefield as everyone scrambled for defensible positions. How long the respite would last was anybody's guess. D'onne crouched behind the closest piece of sizable rubble and scanned the enemy forces to assess the real threats.

Two large Goliaths wielding two-handed hammers had been the first to retreat. Their combat movements tagged them as veterans of many battles. In fact, D'onne recognised them as two of the bouncers from the Bottom of the Barrel – Karga's younger brothers Korg and Kerg. The rest of the Goliaths must have been more of the family.

If those two were here, then so were Karga's older brothers Karg Three and Kairg. She'd heard stories about those two. They had supposedly killed a spider mare on the docks with their bare hands when they were younger and had defeated a full-strength Escher gang. Surrounded and outnumbered six to one, Three and Kairg had charged the encircling gang and cut them down two at a time until they met at the Escher leader.

'You're surrounded, D'onne,' called Three. 'Drop your weapons. We won't kill you. Move and we start blasting.'

She might have her back literally against the wall, but D'onne had no intention of going peacefully or dying here today. A quick scan located a vulnerability in the gang's line. Kairg and his big brother were crouching to her left. To her right stood Korg and Kerg.

Between the brothers, though, stood only two young Goliaths who wielded stub guns in their trembling hands. They and the two wounded juves lying on the ground must be nephews or sons of the older ones, and none of them looked like they'd seen much combat yet.

'Come on, kid,' D'onne hissed over her shoulder. 'We're making a break for it. Stay close.'

When the psyker didn't answer, D'onne glanced back to find nothing but rubble behind her. The kid had retreated back to where she had dropped the two unconscious scummers, near the foot of the Abyss wall. 'Damnit,' she said. *Was he still trying to save their worthless lives?*

It didn't matter. D'onne's survival instincts screamed at her to move before some twitchy nephew started shooting and everything went to hell. She had one shot to get free of this trap. She had to take it and worry about the kid later.

D'onne raised her hands over her head, indicating a willingness to surrender, while keeping an eye on Three, who had found cover behind a large hunk of rockcrete. The short muzzle of his giant rivet cannon rested in a notch of the rockcrete, aimed right at her. As Three stepped out from behind his cover the heavy barrel dropped out of the notch. At that moment, D'onne sprinted towards the two nephews in the middle of the line.

She slammed her shoulder into one, sending him tumbling

down the rubble slope, and grabbed the other by the wrist, twisting it behind his back as she turned him to face his uncles. In D'onne's deathlike grip, he dropped his weapons. He tried to slam his fists back into D'onne, but an additional, bone-cracking twist of his wrist convinced him to settle down and behave.

'If you all leave now,' D'onne called as she backed down the slope, pulling her meat shield along with her, 'I won't kill your nephew here.'

'You think we care about him?' asked Three. 'His fault if he dies here. Only the strongest Kargs survive!'

With that, the brothers opened fire. Red-hot rivets hit her Goliath shield in the hip and thigh, causing him to fall to one knee. D'onne glanced over at Korg and Kerg, who had dropped their hammers and drawn stub cannons. A stream of rivets from Three's cannon flew over D'onne's exposed head.

D'onne didn't wait around to see who would fire next. She sprayed plasma from Pig towards the elder brothers, burning through Kairg's shoulder as he fired a boltgun. His shot went wide and tore off a chunk of rockcrete next to D'onne.

D'onne turned and sprinted down the slope towards a low wall of rockcrete at the bottom, zigzagging back and forth as bullets and bolts crisscrossed around her. She kept expecting another barrage of rivets to shred her flesh but it never came. When D'onne reached the bottom, she dived over the wall, looking for some easy cover, but found a huge sinkhole instead.

D'onne rotated her body mid-flight and grabbed for the top of the wall to stop herself from tumbling into the gaping hole. Her fingertips caught the edge, wrenching her shoulder as it slowed her descent. Holding on for dear life, D'onne slammed into the far side of the wall. She slid down the surface and landed on a narrow ledge.

She was trapped, but at least she had a defensible position and, thanks to Barker's creds, a full charge for Pig. She was glad she had purchased two. From here, Donna could cut the brothers down easily as they came down the slope. Goliaths were big targets.

She watched for Goliaths, taking pot-shots up the slope, but none seemed keen on running into the line of fire.

'Got you!' said a young, booming Goliath voice.

She turned and found the other nephew coming up beside her. He was smiling and holding some small, shiny weapon in his hand instead of the axe he'd previously held.

'You have that backwards,' replied D'onne. She raised Pig towards the young Goliath's chest.

Before she could burn a hole in the nephew's chest, though, he fired the shiny weapon. A stream of netting pinned D'onne's weapon arm against her chest, and took her to the ground.

That blasted Goliath had a web pistol. The entire set-up had been a trap – probably devised by Karga. D'onne had run headlong into it.

Servalen found D'onne's trail on the far side of the platform.

Once comfortably beyond the mob again, Servalen glanced back to make sure none of the gangers had seen her, but they were all consumed with fighting over the mare's head and its valuable eyes. It looked like the head had rolled down the side of the rubble pile – or been thrown during the chaotic melee – because the battle had shifted almost to the bottom of the mound. Bodies and weapons littered the slope and the mob was half the size it had been at the peak of the riot.

D'onne's trail was odd and far too easy to follow. Every few metres the scrutinator found tiny bits of leather or twine fluttering atop a particularly jagged piece of rockcrete rubble. They were hardly noticeable unless you had a keen eye and were actively looking. They also weren't just random bits of detritus brought down with the Dust Rain, either. They appeared too regularly and maintained a consistent direction away from the platform.

The odd part, though, was that there were two distinct sets of leather scraps with slightly different colours and thicknesses. Plus, the scraps sometimes appeared to the left of the trail and sometimes to the right. It was as if Mad D'onne had been dragging two dead bodies behind her when she left with the psyker, whom Servalen was certain was walking along on his own. She had also noticed plasteel shavings left behind on many rocks from the kid's chains dragging through the rubble.

It was all very strange and Servalen wondered several times if the mad woman had planted the evidence to throw her off the scent. It made more sense than D'onne dragging bodies with her during an escape, and the kid following after her of his own volition. She wished KB-88 were here. She knew she could trust her metal companion to follow the true scent.

The evidence corroborated what Servalen already felt, though. The boy was close. She could feel the pressure in her head and her thoughts had been in turmoil since she had reached the far side of the mob. The sight of KB-88 sinking beneath the surface of the sump plagued her, making the scrutinator wonder if that was why she had so quickly agreed to work with D'onne. Was the mad woman filling a void, a need for companionship that Servalen was now admitting to herself? No. At least not entirely. These thoughts, she knew, were the side effect of the psyker's proximity.

He was close and the trail would lead her to him. She would finish the mission, file a report, obtain a new cyber-mastiff, and return to her orderly, pre-D'onne life. As Servalen trudged on, watching for the next scrap on the trail, she heard weapons fire in the distance ahead of her. The scrutinator hurried forward towards the sound.

'This isn't really Goliath style, Three,' Donna said through gritted teeth, the webbing tight across her face. The eldest brother stared at the hunter through a break in the wall down from where Donna had been webbed. 'I see Karga written all over this plan. What's the matter? She didn't trust that you could actually best me?'

'Don't listen to her, Three,' said another brother from behind the wall. She thought it was Kairg. 'Stick to the plan. You know how Karga gets. Keep your head.'

Donna heard Kairg climbing atop the rockcrete wall but couldn't move her head to see him. Three, however, cracked his neck, his hands twitching for his weapons.

This would be a lot easier if Dog was here, thought D'onne. The hunter would never admit it, but she missed the ogryn. He was a steadfast companion who could take a mountain of abuse on a regular basis and keep coming back for more. That, she realised, had been Dog's best quality. *Just like him to get himself killed when I need him most*, she thought. *Guess I'll have to do this myself.*

'You taking orders from your little brother now, Three?' she asked. 'I guess that's better than being told what to do by your sister. She must've been real worried you'd get your ass handed to you to put him in charge.'

'Go help the others find and web that kid we saw,' Three ordered Kairg. 'The Karg family backs down from no fight. Ever.'

'Maybe I should stay, just in case–' began Kairg.

'Go!' roared Three. 'D'onne is mine and mine alone!' Loose shards of rockcrete slapped against D'onne's webbed body as Three ripped out a hunk of wall and threw it at his brother. He began fumbling around inside his belt pouch for something.

'Do not dissolve those webs, Three!' yelled Kairg. He jumped off the wall and stood over D'onne to block his much bigger brother. 'Karga will have all our–'

'I am the oldest!' yelled Three. 'I have father's name!' He balled his hand into a fist and slammed it into Kairg's face, sending the other Goliath flying out of D'onne's view. She heard him scrabbling to avoid falling into the hole. At the point of contact between Three's fist and Kairg's jaw, a small vial flipped out of the older brother's pouch and dropped onto the webbing covering D'onne's neck.

This had worked better than she'd planned, she realised. Now she needed to find a way to open the vial and dissolve the webs before the two arguing Goliaths realised what had happened. *A diversion would be nice right about now*, she thought.

Once again, the universe decided today was not the day that Mad D'onne's luck would run out. Behind her, up over the hill of rubble, the rest of the Goliath brothers and nephews began yelling and firing their weapons.

Three looked at D'onne and then up the hill. She could hear Kairg scrambling in the rubble to get back to his feet. 'Leave her for now,' he yelled. 'You can have your honour battle later! I promise I won't tell Karga.'

Three drew his rivet cannon and followed his brother up the slope, leaving D'onne webbed on the ground behind them, unattended.

CHAPTER 22

THE BIG SQUEEZE

A stabbing pain lanced through Jeren's skull when D'onne grabbed him by the elbow and pulled him back. It could have been an aftershock from the plasma beam ripping through the air beside his head a moment earlier, but Jeren knew better. He'd felt this pain before.

It never got any easier, but at least he knew it wouldn't get any worse. When the visions came, they brought searing pain with them that made the constant pounding headaches he lived with every day pale in comparison. It felt like white-hot picks plunging into each temple and bursting back out through his eyeballs. The pain radiated through his sinuses down into his teeth and out through his ears.

A cascade of lights exploded behind his eyes, blinding him momentarily to the outside world, but freeing his mind to see beyond present reality and into the endless, spiralling miasma of future possibilities. The battle between D'onne and the Goliaths brewing in front of Jeren dissolved into a gruesome scene filled with severed limbs, torn-open bodies, and bloody entrails laid bare and fought over by rats, which seemed terrible to Jeren's young, inexperienced mind.

Down the rocky slope, past the worst of the carnage in Jeren's vision, the young psyker saw the remains of D'onne's two most prized possessions: Countless, her chainsword, and Pig, her plasma pistol. The sword lay in pieces, as if blasted apart. The chain had flown at least ten metres from the scattered pieces of the hilt and blade.

The plasma pistol seemed mostly intact, although the fat cylinder encircling the length of the barrel had split open at the end as if the weapon's energy had built up and exploded inside the chamber. Between the burst Pig and the broken chainsword lying at the edge of a pool of blood filled with bits of skin and floating pieces of viscera, Jeren could clearly see D'onne's large, powdered wig, streaked by dark red stains.

Then, as quickly as the vision flashed into his brain, it was gone. The piercing migraine that radiated through his head would take longer to recede, Jeren knew from past experiences, but he had no time to worry about that now. The standoff between D'onne and the Goliaths was about to turn hot and if he didn't act fast, his vision would come true.

The old Jeren might have cowered in fear only to later bemoan how his lack of courage caused needless deaths. That regret would have spiralled him down into darker recesses of his mind from which he might never escape.

Today, though, he had stood up for himself to arguably one of the most dangerous people in the underhive. He, Jeren Jerenson, had convinced Mad D'onne Ulanti to do something she didn't want to do. How many people had ever done that?

If it wasn't for me, Jeren told himself, *my two guards would be dead.*

And that was the answer. He saw it in his mind as clearly as a vision, except without the pain and twisting colours flying through his head. While everyone argued about D'onne's surrender – *what were these gangers thinking?* – Jeren skulked off towards the tiny crevice where they'd left his two guards. He had a plan. If it worked, he might be able to save Mad D'onne.

With no one watching her, D'onne tested the webbing to see how much she could move. Her right arm was held tightly against her chest, Pig in her hand aimed into her left armpit. She could move her legs slightly but decided not to flex them yet. As the webbing continued to harden, it would constrict at the slightest movement.

Now the big question: could she move her head? She had a plan, but if she couldn't twist her head to the side, all bets were off. She tried to slide her jaw back and forth to see if the webbing around her face was soft enough to shift. It stretched against her cheek.

Next came the tricky part and then the painful part. The small vial was tucked under her chin, sitting on the webbing stretched across her neck. Moving slowly, she rolled her chin down and to the side, hoping to trap the vial between her chin and collarbone.

Slow, patient movements were not D'onne's forte. Sweat beaded up under her chin, making the entire area slick. Behind her, she could hear the Goliaths shouting and firing along with returning lasgun fire.

Who the sump are the brothers fighting? D'onne wondered. *Not my immediate problem.*

Whoever it was had bought D'onne some time, but she had to move quickly. She felt the vial slipping and starting to roll off her neck. It was now or never. Gritting her teeth for the coming pain, D'onne slammed her chin onto her clavicle.

The webbing around her face and chest constricted and hardened almost instantaneously. She heard a loud pop and swallowed a scream as the webbing wrenched her arm and dislocated her shoulder. She could taste blood from the tight webs cutting into her nose and lips and her temples began to pound as blood forced its way through constricted arteries.

Then she heard a crack and a rush of liquid running down her chest. At first, D'onne feared she'd broken a rib, but a second later a black mist rose around D'onne's face and surrounded her head. Mercifully, the pounding in her head stopped, the blood flowing from her nose and lips lessened, and the pain in her arms and shoulder receded slightly as the pressure lifted.

The solvent inside the now-cracked vial was spreading across and dissolving the webbing. D'onne coughed as it entered her lungs, but her head and chest were free.

D'onne sat up and surveyed her body. She grimaced as the pain from her dislocated shoulder shot into her chest. She also had a cut on her neck from the vial shattering, but it had missed major blood vessels, so she could ignore that for now. She needed to fix her shoulder and get her legs free before Three came back. Half the solvent had spilled on the rubble, so only her torso had been freed. The webbing still held her legs in place.

Gritting her teeth, D'onne reached across her body and grabbed the elbow below her dislocated shoulder. Holding tight, she slammed her body into the ground, yanking the elbow as she hit. A loud pop – and accompanying searing pain – told her the makeshift treatment had worked. D'onne lifted the arm to test it and nodded. The pain had lessened considerably. Enough to handle what needed to be done.

If there was enough slack in the webbing round her legs, she had a chance. Fighting the urge to yank them free, which she knew would end in disaster, D'onne dropped Pig and pushed against the rough rubble with both palms to lift her backside off the ground so she could drag her legs out of the tattered ends of the webbing.

After several long minutes of inching her way out, D'onne's legs were free.

The sounds of the battle over the crest of the hill had abated, which could be good or bad for her and the young psyker. Knowing her luck, D'onne counted on it being bad. She grabbed Pig and scrambled up the hill. As she climbed, she crouched low to avoid being seen. Cutting and running was always an option. She might have a reputation for taking crazy chances, but D'onne was 'mad', not 'crazy'.

When things got really bad, D'onne would sacrifice anyone – no matter how much they meant to her – to save her own skin. It might sound harsh, and D'onne rarely admitted it – even to herself – but her life story certainly had borne out that single truth. It was the reason she worked alone after years of trying to find a place, a family, somewhere.

Everyone who got close to D'onne died, and she bore the guilt for all those deaths. Even Dog, the most loyal companion she'd ever had, was gone, leaving D'onne alone again, which was as it should be. The only reason she was still thinking about Jeren was because she needed him.

Might as well take a look before I write him off, she thought as she neared the top of the rubble mound. She crawled up next to a young Goliath who'd been shot during her escape attempt. *Hope this works out better for me than you,*

225

she thought, looking at the corpse. During one of her darker days, she might have carried on a longer conversation with the dead ganger, but today she had work to do.

From her vantage point at the edge of the battle, D'onne could see the fight had ground to a halt. To her right, the four Goliath brothers had taken cover behind several large chunks of rockcrete. To D'onne's left, crouching behind their own hunks of rubble, was a new squad of enforcers.

'Surrender Jeren Jerenson or die, Goliath scum!' yelled an enforcer sergeant.

'Never!' responded Three. 'Take your bodies back up-hive or we'll send them there ourselves.'

D'onne could see that this impasse could last a while as neither side knew where the kid was, and both wanted him alive. It was obvious that after the initial shock of running into one another, both sides had retreated to assess their options.

In the middle of the rubble field between the opposing groups lay all the younger Goliaths as well as several enforcers, cut to pieces by weapons fire and blades. D'onne could see lasgun burns on the chests and faces of the gangers, while one enforcer lay on the ground with a hammer embedded in his skull and the other two had been gutted, cut down by large, heavy blades. The carnage would have delighted D'onne if she didn't have more pressing concerns.

D'onne didn't see the kid anywhere, which concerned her. But then she saw him waving at her from the recess in the cliff wall where they had dropped the guards. How he knew D'onne was behind the boulder – and looking at him at that moment – she had no idea.

Also, where had the scummer guards gone? Their bodies were no longer where D'onne had dropped them. She scanned the battlefield but saw no sign of them.

Have they wandered off? D'onne wondered. *No. The kid. He set them free.* That's why he had left her at the beginning of the Goliath fight – to save the lives of those two wretched scummers, again.

At least the psyker was safe where he was for now, so she could beat him later on for turning on her after all she had done for him. But the kid had a knack for getting himself into trouble. And sure enough, there trouble was. Skulking behind a piece of rubble near the crevice was that pesky scrutinator that D'onne thought she had ditched back at the platform.

That sure explains a lot, D'onne thought.

D'onne considered dropping the enforcer woman with Pig, but as soon as she fired, she would give away her position. Plus, at this distance, her odds weren't great.

'Screw it,' D'onne muttered. 'Time to do something mad.'

D'onne aimed and fired.

CHAPTER 23

BATTLES LARGE AND SMALL

Servalen drew her autopistol as she hurried towards an uneven mound of rubble ahead of her. She scrambled up the side, following the shouting and weapons firing. One of the voices was definitely D'onne's, but the other voice boomed like only a Goliath's could.

Who in the Spire is that? Servalen wondered. *Some new faction after D'onne and the psyker? Good luck to them.* If the scrutinator had any back-up, she would have been willing to let the battle play out, pick up the pieces afterwards. But it was only her, and she had to ensure the safety of the kid. Perhaps she could turn the confrontation to her advantage, though.

Servalen slowed her pace and picked her way to the top of the rubble field at the edge of the cliff face, seeking a sheltered vantage point where she could observe the battle.

She arrived in time to see D'onne charge two young Goliaths, knocking one down the slope and grabbing the other to use as a shield. The other Goliaths kept firing, though, so D'onne turned and fled down the rocky hill with two larger Goliaths in pursuit.

That left at least four more Goliaths atop the rubble mound – and no sign of the kid. Servalen scanned the mound looking for him. He must be here somewhere. She worried that he might have been hit and was lying dead beneath one of the Goliaths.

But then something strange happened. Two scummers emerged from a crevice in the Abyss wall and ran towards the far edge of the rubble mound. Servalen recognised them as the two guards who had been holding the young psyker at the platform before the riot broke out. The Goliaths immediately began shouting, firing and chasing after the two escapees.

Had D'onne dragged those two scummers all the way here to use as a distraction? Even by her standards, that was absurd. Significant physical effort for no guaranteed gain.

Then Servalen saw the young psyker peering out from the same crevice the scummers had fled. He looked right at her and waved and then beckoned her towards him.

What the sump? Servalen wondered. *He knew I was here. This kid's power is truly impressive.*

While the Goliaths were distracted by the escaping scummers, Servalen moved out of hiding and began picking her way towards the kid. Before she could reach him, though, lasgun blasts echoed from the far side of the mound, followed by several enforcers chasing the Goliaths up it. Servalen ducked behind the nearest hunk of rubble before anyone spotted her and watched for an opening to assist this new group of enforcers.

A short, brutal battle ensued. The lead enforcers cut down the three younger Goliaths quickly with their lasguns, but then fell themselves when two of the larger, older Goliaths closed on them. One raised a two-handed hammer over his head and bashed it into the skull of one enforcer, where it stuck. The other Goliath sliced through a second enforcer with a mighty swing of a huge fighting knife. As Servalen took aim with her autopistol, the third enforcer got too close to both Goliaths, making it impossible for her to get a clean shot off. They grabbed the young enforcer and ripped the woman in half with their bare hands.

Two more Goliaths crested the mound as the second wave of enforcers charged up the slope. Weapons fire erupted as both sides retreated to more defensible positions. The Goliaths scrambled back behind large chunks of rockcrete to Servalen's left as the enforcers spread out and took position on the far side of the mound.

Servalen moved around her own hunk of rubble, resolving to keep from being spotted by either side. The slightest spark would reignite this powder keg, and she didn't want to end up caught in the middle of the chaos.

Apparently, though, D'onne wanted exactly that.

D'onne's plasma beam burned through the top of the chunk of rockcrete that Three was hiding behind, leaving the elder Goliath brother exposed. The enforcers immediately opened fire on the unprotected Goliath. Before D'onne dived to the ground behind her own cover, she saw Three get hit by las blasts several times in the chest and shoulder.

As much as D'onne wanted to watch the brothers get what was coming to them, she also didn't want to get caught by enforcers, so she scrambled back down the rocky slope away from the mayhem she'd ignited.

From the shouts and weapons fire she could hear coming

from the top of the mound, it didn't seem like the fight was going well for the Goliaths. Lasgun and stubber blasts far outnumbered the stub guns and other light ranged weapons the Goliaths had brought to the fight. They had brought hammers to a lasgun battle and had no other option but to run.

D'onne watched as the brothers scrambled down the slope to her right, Kairg holding Three upright as they ran. The enforcer squad followed a few moments later, chasing the brothers across the rocky field of rubble back towards the platform.

If any of Karga's brothers had her intellect, they would have charged the enforcers instead of fleeing, trusting their immense bodies and thick skins to take a few hits so they could close on their enemy. But with Three wounded, they must have panicked.

It had all worked out for her, D'onne thought. *Amazingly well. Almost like she had planned the entire sequence of events.* With the battle running away from her, D'onne was free to go for the kid. Only the scrutinator stood in her way, and D'onne still had one trick up her sleeve – or rather, lying on the ground up the hill.

After the enforcers chased the Goliaths down the slope to her left, Servalen emerged from hiding and began moving towards the psyker again. She had no idea who that enforcer squad was or what their mission might be, but her twin missions were to bring in this unlicensed psyker – Jeren Jerenson – and stop Mad D'onne's rampage through the underhive. The boy was her main priority, and nothing would keep her from him now.

At that moment, a thunderous crack echoed around and above the scrutinator. She looked up at the towering wall of the Abyss and gasped in horror. Some stray heavy stubber fire had cut through a horizontal girder that supported a shelf of compressed rockcrete above the crevice where she'd seen Jeren earlier. Shards of plasteel and rockcrete showered the rubble-strewn ground and the shelf shifted. Servalen could hear plasteel creaking as tonnes of rockcrete pressed down on the compromised girder, twisting and crumpling its metal structure.

Servalen scrambled backwards as the plasteel beam collapsed with a horrible screech. Above her, a ten-by-fifteen metre section of rockcrete sheared off the cliff wall and plummeted to the ground. The concussive force knocked the scrutinator off her feet. She crab-crawled away across the jagged terrain.

After the dust settled and the thundering echoes died away, Servalen stood and picked her way carefully towards the blocked crevice to see if the psyker was still alive. She sighed when she heard a plaintive cry for help emanating from somewhere behind the fallen ledge.

As she picked her way along the cliff face, Servalen kept an eye out for D'onne. She knew the mad noble wasn't as crazy as most people thought. The plasma shot that had reignited the battle between enforcers and Goliaths had been a ploy, she was certain of that.

No. Mad D'onne was still in play, and unaccounted for. Servalen held her autopistol ready as a precaution as she crept back towards the crevice where Jeren was trapped, but the young psyker's cries for help had stopped.

'Damnit,' hissed Servalen under her breath. Had D'onne beaten her to the boy? No, that wasn't possible. She hadn't had enough time to get around the battle. Then, Servalen realised the pressure in her mind, that ever-present reminder of Jeren's proximity, had been silenced. In her panic, the scrutinator ran forward and clawed at the rockcrete, afraid the young psyker had been buried.

'Is that you, scrutinator?' called Jeren from somewhere behind the fallen wall of rockcrete.

'It is,' replied Servalen. She rapped the wall lightly to indicate where she stood.

'I knew it,' he said, the pitch of his young male voice rising almost to a squeal. He rapped on the wall as well and Servalen moved down to stand opposite the knocking. 'My headache was replaced by an uneasy feeling in my guts a moment ago. I knew you were close.'

Servalen nodded. Her presence effectively nullified his psyker abilities and, apparently, the painful side effects of those powers. 'Are you okay?' she asked. 'Can you get out?'

'I'm fine,' he replied, 'but there's no way around and I don't think I can climb out on my own.'

'I'll come help,' Servalen said through the wall. She was no Goliath, but she had enforcer training and, more importantly, a custom-made, folding grappling hook that fitted in her belt pouch along with fifty metres of light, strong plasteel rope.

It didn't take Servalen long to secure the grappling hook and climb to the top of the rockcrete wall. From there, she lowered the rope to help Jeren climb out. The opening between the top of the wall and the crevice was so narrow that the boy, who was little more than skin and bones, still had to squeeze to get past the blockages.

The chains were another problem and Servalen had to reach down past Jeren to grab them and used them to help him climb the last few metres. Finally, he sat on top of the wall next to Servalen, who couldn't quite believe she'd got her hands on him. Now if she could deliver him to the new enforcer squad before D'onne found them, this might all be over.

'Stay right there, scrutinator,' called D'onne from below. 'I'll be reclaiming my prize now.'

CHAPTER 24

LOST AND FOUND

The darkness surrounding Jeren felt strange. The world seemed smaller, like one of his senses had been turned off. He imagined this was how it was for people who lost their sight or hearing. He could imagine the larger world where he was connected to all objects by invisible filaments that spanned both time and space, but that sense was now cut off.

For months, Jeren had been burdened with the knowledge of loss. He could see anything of importance that had gone missing – or would go missing – from anyone around him. The flood of information assailing his mind had turned him into more of a recluse than his childhood filled with disappointment and beatings.

That assault of data also made his temples throb constantly. It was as if jackhammers pounded away at his skull, trying to crack it open and release the daemons his mother had always told him were there. Jeren had tried it all: drugs, alcohol, even concussions – with some help from his co-workers. Nothing had dulled the pain one iota.

Jeren had reached the point where he was certain the only thing that would release him from his personal hell was the cold embrace of death. That was why he hadn't resisted the Cawdor when they came for him. He'd seen the ending; seen himself losing his skin and then his limbs, and finally his organs. The vision always concluded the same way: with Jeren's still-beating heart in the hands of the head Cawdor zealot as it pulsed its slow, final beats.

But then scrutinator Servalen had appeared beside him at the Deep Pyre and everything changed. When the female enforcer came close, it was like someone had flipped a toggle in his brain that turned off his object sense. The larger world that Jeren experienced dissolved away in that moment, leaving him crouching in the dull-grey reality of the underhive. He had marvelled at its beautiful filth and glorious grunge.

The accompanying uneasiness and itchy skin were well worth the respite. For a few minutes, Jeren Jerenson was a normal person again, and not someone burdened with great power; not someone hunted by formidable factions from up and down the hive; not a tool to be used by the rich and greedy before being discarded once they got what they wanted.

So, when Servalen found him in the crevice and he felt the prickly sensation creep across his skin, along with the cool calm of normality inside his mind as the visions and headaches winked out of existence, Jeren had rejoiced, even though her arrival meant he could no longer see the myriad stories of loss playing out around him, and even though he felt the push of what she was, like a punch to the gut.

It wasn't that Jeren could see people's futures, per se.

Occasionally, though, he received vivid images of the last, most personal pieces of themselves that people would ever lose. He particularly hated those visions.

It had been invigorating for Jeren at the Deep Pyre, no longer knowing how the battle would end, because in those moments the future was unfolding and changing. He got to experience the fight like anyone else – terrified for his life and the lives of everyone around him. But he also knew if he'd had his power during the battle at the Deep Pyre, he would have seen Hark flinging Servalen's metal dog into the sump and might have been able to warn her.

Now it had happened again. As Jeren pulled himself to the top of the rockcrete shelf that had nearly entombed him in the crevice, he was as surprised as the scrutinator to see Mad D'onne pointing two pistols at them.

'That's a webber,' Jeren said to no one in particular. 'I knew that young Goliath would lose it and you would pick it up – if I could wake the hive scum guards in time to flee and draw everyone's attention, that is. Otherwise, you would have died when the new enforcers showed up.'

'Sure, kid. Whatever you say,' replied D'onne. 'I had the situation handled.'

'Riveting conversation,' Servalen said. She gave D'onne a withering look that should have had her doing anything to get away, but didn't faze D'onne one bit.

'I don't know what you think your play is here, D'onne,' the scrutinator continued. 'One shout from me and this mound is crawling with enforcers who will drop you where you stand. Surrender now and I guarantee safe passage to a nice dark cell.'

Servalen grabbed the grappling line and prepared to climb down the rockcrete wall.

'Not so fast!' barked D'onne. She shot a patch of webbing at the wall, turning a small section of rockcrete below Servalen's foot into a sticky mess.

'I'm taking the boy and you're staying here,' she continued. 'I'll web you to the wall before you can scream. I bet your enforcer "friends" will get a good laugh out of you hanging there like a spider snack.'

'No, you won't,' Jeren said. 'We all go together or you will never claim your true prize, D'onne.'

D'onne pointed the webber at Jeren and trained her plasma pistol at the scrutinator. 'I don't think you understand who's in charge here, boy!' she growled at him. 'You think this enforcer will protect you? She'll hand you over to Helmawr to gather her few pieces of silver and go on living her own miserable life. I'm your only hope of getting out of this alive.'

'And then what, D'onne?' asked Servalen. 'As soon as you get what you want, you'll abandon him. That's what you do. You don't give a damn about anyone but yourself.'

'That's where you're wrong,' spat D'onne. 'I don't give a damn about myself either.'

'Stop it. Both of you!' cried Jeren, doing his best to quell the terror that erupted in his chest when both of them turned to stare at him.

'I know what you care about, D'onne Astride Ge'Sylvanus of House Ulanti,' he said, only wilting slightly. 'You've been searching a long time. I can help you find it, but only if we all leave here now, together.'

D'onne seemed to consider his offer, which was at least progress. Her weapons wavered a bit, but she didn't lower them. 'Is this like the two scummers?' she asked. 'Have you seen how this all ends?'

Now it was Jeren's turn to waver. D'onne asked a good

question he hadn't anticipated. He assumed that dangling the thing she craved in front of her would be enough. The Mad D'onne he'd heard tales about never considered if an action was safe or not. She acted and then dealt with the consequences.

Jeren wasn't sure whether the truth or a lie would work better so, because he hated the thought of getting caught lying to the most dangerous woman in the underhive, he decided on the truth; just not all of it.

'No. I don't know how it will end,' he said. 'But I know if we don't all leave together, I will never tell you how to find your heart's desire, so lower your weapons and let us climb down. Now!'

Jeren's voice cracked a bit as he pleaded with D'onne, which probably made him look pathetic while he was trying to act strong. Still, his plea must have worked because D'onne holstered her plasma pistol and stashed the webber under her coat.

Jeren sighed, but that was only half the problem. He turned to Servalen. 'After I give D'onne the information she wants,' he said, 'I will come with you. So, no calling for the enforcers and no throwing her into a dark cell after.'

Servalen hesitated a moment and stared at Mad D'onne, the scrutinator's eyes narrowing, which somehow made Jeren feel even more uncomfortable inside his skin. But then she looked at him again and nodded.

'Good,' he said, grabbing the rope from the enforcer. 'Now we need to find somewhere safe to hide before the other enforcers return.'

'I know a place,' said D'onne. 'We'd be there already if you hadn't forced me to save those two idiot scummers.'

'Don't trust her,' whispered Servalen as she helped wind

the rope around Jeren's body so he could rappel down the wall. 'Keep an eye on her at all times.'

'I imagine she will tell me the same about you,' replied Jeren as he began descending the wall. 'It's probably good I'm here to keep you two from killing each other.'

Once the obvious argument over who should lead had been resolved by Jeren pushing both women ahead of him, side by side, so he could make sure neither stabbed the other in the back, the curious trio left the rubble mound and trudged away from the lift platform, hugging the cliff face.

Jeren's plan involved staying alive and close to Servalen for as long as possible. He was certain there were still some kinks that needed ironing out. One of these became clear on their way to D'onne's hidey hole.

'Did you know your superiors were sending reinforcements?' D'onne asked as they picked their way through the ever-present rubble strewn at the base of the Abyss. 'Or did you call for them yourself so you could double-cross me at the platform?'

'I had no idea another squad of enforcers had been dispatched,' replied Servalen. 'And, if you remember, you betrayed me at the platform.'

'You told me I could,' spat D'onne.

Both women trudged in silence for a time before D'onne spoke again.

'I only ask because it would be great to know how many squads were sent to clean up your mess.'

'Oh, they're not sending more enforcers,' Jeren replied. 'A team of psi-hounds was dispatched to hunt for me. The enforcers are here as back-up.'

Both women stopped halfway up another of the endless mounds of rubble they'd traversed today and turned to face

Jeren. 'Psi-hounds?' they both growled at him together. The expressions on their faces told Jeren that this was a much bigger deal than he'd realised.

'Where are they now?' asked D'onne, but Jeren had no way to tell. Next to Servalen, he was blind to the world beyond this one.

'They will kill us both to take you, even if we give ourselves up,' Servalen said. Psi-hounds weren't dispatched into the underhive lightly. They were hideous, misshapen figures with potent psychic abilities that terrorised the general populace when released to do their master's bidding.

Bred in the depths of Helmawr's Psykanarium, they were spliced together from dozens of the most powerful psyker bloodlines. Their powers were then further augmented through the implantation of psychic-enhancing neural-crowns, which, in theory, also kept them docile enough to obey orders. Many dead handlers and even entire towns attested to the truth, though. The programming didn't always hold.

Psi-hounds were built to be weapons of war, and most were shipped off-planet to serve the Imperium. But it was an open secret within the ranks of the enforcers that Lord Helmawr saved the most gifted for his own use. Only Helmawr and a few of his most trusted servants could order their use, which meant that the Lord of Necromunda had given up on Servalen bringing him in. She had been cut loose.

As the reality of that troubling thought sank in, Servalen heard servos firing and plasteel appendages scraping across the rockcrete rubble from over the crest of the mound they were climbing. She grabbed Jeren by the hand and turned to flee. 'Run!' she yelled at D'onne.

'Too late,' D'onne yelled.

Servalen glanced over her shoulder but didn't slow down. At the top of the hill stood a fleshy creature that could only be called humanoid because it had a discernible face atop a massive mound of pink, blubbery flesh. Rolls of fat cascaded down its pear-shaped body. It had no organic limbs, just a huge bulbous torso and head.

The monstrous creature floated through the air via suspensor implants protruding from its bulbous, fleshy body at various points to keep it aloft. Two mechanical appendages hung from its distended stomach, ending in robotic hands. Further implants girded the psi-hound's torso, housing inducer rigs that supported the beast's bodily functions. Without them, its organs would shut down from the severe strain of its grotesque bulk.

Grafted to its head was the spiked neural crown, which might have looked regal if not for the hoses implanted into the creature's temples and cheek and the bulbous rig attached to the back of its head.

'Ortruum 8-8,' muttered Servalen. It was worse than she'd feared. Helmawr must want Jeren badly if he sent his most powerful and dangerous psi-hound to the bottom of the hive to hunt him down.

'There's only one,' cried D'onne. 'How bad can it be?' She drew her plasma pistol and fired at Ortruum 8-8, who had stopped at the crest, hovering there as if assessing the situation. He seemed an easy target.

Servalen knew better. The plasma beam scorched through the air but missed the massive mound of flesh by a full metre. Ortruum's suspensor units fired at the exact moment D'onne pulled the trigger, zipping the psi-hound out of the path.

'He can read your mind, D'onne,' called Servalen. 'You can't hit him.'

'We'll see about that,' she said, holstering her pistol and drawing her chainsword. She charged towards the grotesque blob of Ortruum 8-8.

Servalen wished D'onne luck, but knew it was nearly impossible for a single combatant to defeat a powerful psi-hound with brute force. Still, the mad woman might keep him busy long enough for Servalen and Jeren to get away. As a null, Servalen couldn't be touched by the psi-hound's psychic abilities. It was as if she didn't exist within the warp at all. Thus, Ortruum 8-8 wouldn't be able to track her.

It was also entirely possible the psi-hound couldn't track Jeren when he was with Servalen. When Servalen was near Jeren, her null zone shut down his abilities, which might confuse Ortruum.

That might actually work, Servalen thought as she pulled on Jeren to get him to keep moving. But it also meant this was most likely a trap. Ortruum must have been told they were moving in this direction. Still, running was their best plan, but the boy didn't budge. Was he going to make her go back to save D'onne, as he'd made D'onne bring her along?

That was unacceptable. If they were caught, Jeren would go to the Psykanarium to be dissected and turned into the next Ortruum or worse. She wouldn't wish that on anyone, especially a young kid who so obviously wanted the world to be a better place.

'Come on!' Servalen hissed, yanking on Jeren's hand again. When he still didn't move, Servalen turned and stared into the boy's eyes. They had become glassy and vacant, as if no one was home inside.

'Damnit!' said Servalen. Ortruum must have mind-locked the young psyker. Jeren might have had a chance to fight off the psi-hound's mental attacks if his own powers hadn't been compromised by standing next to her – although without training, it would have been a long shot.

If Servalen had any chance to get herself and the boy out of this situation, she needed to fight beside D'onne, again. She drew her weapon and trudged up the hill, looking for a clear shot past D'onne. Ortruum couldn't read her mind, so he couldn't use prescience to avoid her attacks. She only had the autopistol, but it might be enough to slow him down.

The noble woman was a frenzy of motion between her and Ortruum, though. She weaved and bobbed too fast to get caught by Ortruum's whirring mechanical arms, which flailed ineffectively as D'onne feinted left, ducked right and spun around the psi-hound's enormous girth looking for a way to surprise her opponent and get in a shot he didn't 'see' coming.

But, try as she might, D'onne couldn't land a blow. Her buzzing chainsword was a blur in front of her, whipping around, slicing and thrusting at Ortruum's jiggling flesh again and again, only to find air on every attack.

Unable to find an angle to fire past D'onne, Servalen ran up the hill, hoping to get close enough to shut down the psi-hound's abilities.

As Servalen climbed, D'onne raised both arms over her head, waved her spinning blade Spirewards, and screamed unintelligibly; she was clearly frustrated. Ortruum took that moment to lunge towards the bounty hunter, grasping at her straight, stiff body with both his spindly mechanical arms.

D'onne dropped to the ground and rolled beneath the floating psi-hound. Coming up behind him, she sliced her chain blade in a swift upward arc that cut through Ortruum's main suspensor nozzles, which hung from his back almost like a tail.

Servalen, a bit taken aback by D'onne's bold move – and

her ability to surprise a telepathic opponent – almost missed her chance to shoot at the open target. Recovering quickly, the scrutinator raised her autopistol and fired, aiming for the large nozzle attached to Ortruum's cheek.

Her aim was off and the shot tore through the psi-hound's teeth, stunning him for the moment. He fell to the ground, and rolled onto his side, facing away from D'onne.

'Take his head off!' yelled Servalen. D'onne swung her blade again, but it hit and bit into Ortruum's neural crown and lodged there. With a massive yank, D'onne pulled her chainsword free and rushed around to the front of the monstrous creature.

D'onne hauled her blade back in both hands, grimacing and grunting in pain as she prepared to thrust. Before she could plunge the spinning blade through Ortruum's face, though, his eyes fluttered open.

An instant later, D'onne and Servalen were flying through the air. They hit the rockcrete rubble hard and tumbled down the rocky slope into Jeren. Servalen came to a stop on her stomach. Pain shot through her arms and legs from multiple bruises and cuts, but at least nothing was broken.

D'onne moaned next to her. 'What the sump was that?' she asked. 'And why didn't he lead with it?'

'That was a force blast,' replied a voice from behind them.

Servalen opened her eyes to see a sergeant standing over them surrounded by her squad of enforcers. 'His job was to keep you here long enough that we could do this.'

The sergeant snapped her fingers and two enforcers stepped forward and slapped force cuffs on D'onne, who, Servalen noticed, had stopped moving and had the same glassy-eyed expression Jeren had a few minutes earlier. The young psyker was already wearing force cuffs.

'Thank you for the assist, sergeant,' Servalen said as she rolled over onto her hands and knees. The two enforcers who had force-cuffed D'onne had name badges stating they were Mauch and Geoffers. They stepped over to the scrutinator and grabbed her arms as she worked to stand up.

As Servalen was about to thank the enforcers again, they twisted her hands behind her back and clapped force cuffs on her as well.

CHAPTER 25

PRISONER DILEMMAS

'I demand to know the meaning of this,' growled Servalen as Mauch and Geoffers hauled the scrutinator to her feet. 'I bear the seal of Helmawr himself. No one can detain me. Not even a palanite enforcer.'

Sergeant Vessa stepped in front of the shackled scrutinator and waved off her two grunts. Mauch and Geoffers saluted and retreated immediately. She wanted to keep them fresh and alert and knew they would not be able to withstand the effect of the null for long. The uneasiness was already rising inside her own head, making her skin crawl and her brain itch. But she was made of sterner stuff than the average enforcer.

'It's funny you mention Lord Helmawr,' Vessa said, emphasising the 'lord' that was missing from Servalen's statement. 'Considering we're arresting you on his orders. If you have any questions, you can take it up with him.'

Vessa grabbed Servalen by the cuffs and dragged her, lurching and stumbling, over to the Abyss wall where the other two prisoners had been tossed. There, she loomed over the three prizes – D'onne, the hive's most wanted criminal, Jeren Jerenson, the strongest psyker to appear in the underhive in a generation, and Servalen – the pariah wunderkind that every aspiring enforcer hated. The sergeant had no idea how Servalen had got on the wrong side of old Helmawr, but she was happy to be the one to take the scrutinator down a few pegs.

Around the sergeant, the squad secured the area while her medic and engineer tended to Ortruum 8-8. She did not envy them that task. The further she could keep away from the monstrous psi-hound, the better. It was bad enough she had to remain this close to the pariah and the psyker.

Sure, these abhuman monsters had their uses, but what they did – what they were – just wasn't natural. Breathing the same air as Servalen for more than a minute made her skin crawl. It was exhausting. Servalen walked and talked like a normal person, mostly, but she was an empty shell. There was nothing inside. No soul. That was creepy as hell. She might as well be a servitor; albeit a servitor who thought she was smarter than everyone else.

Vessa had the upper hand now, though. She'd outsmarted the vaunted Servalen in this little game of cat-and-rat. The sergeant kicked the scrutinator in the side to get her attention.

'I knew you'd be skulking around behind that creepy psyker,' she said, 'but I never thought I would see the day that a palanite scrutinator would team up with Mad D'onne. You should be ashamed of yourself. Can you feel shame? Probably not. That's a human emotion and you're not human, are you?'

Servalen glared up at her from the ground. The sergeant had force-cuffed the scrutinator's ankles together as well and she looked ridiculous crumpled against the wall, but the force of the pariah's gaze still made Vessa shudder.

'My mission was to end D'onne's rampage, which started with the appearance of this psyker,' Servalen said. 'Of course you found me with them.' The scrutinator's aggravating monotone made Vessa angrier. She couldn't have the pleasure of getting a rise out of her. 'Or does the truth not matter to you?'

'I don't need to be bothered by truth,' replied the sergeant, rage overwhelming her distaste of Servalen. 'Truth be damned. Delivering the three of you to the Spire is a career day for me.'

'The end of your career, you mean,' said Servalen. 'I know who you are. I've read reports. You may be ruthless and heartless, but you're not stupid.'

D'onne snorted beside Servalen. She too was bound hand and foot, but the defiant fire in her eyes still burned hot. 'Don't engage with her,' she said, turning to the scrutinator. 'It's a waste of time and breath. She'll be dead soon enough.'

Now it was Vessa's turn to laugh. 'I'd heard you liked to boast, D'onne Ulanti,' she snorted, 'but that is ridiculous overconfidence. You're bound. You're surrounded. And you have no weapons!'

'When have I ever needed weapons?' she asked, baring her teeth.

'You sure as hell won't try anything with broken wrists and ankles,' replied Vessa. She kicked D'onne under her ribs to prove she couldn't protect herself.

'You do that,' said D'onne with a grimace. 'Go right ahead and try.'

'You'd like that, wouldn't you?' asked Vessa. 'I get too close and you pull some crazy stunt that gets everyone but you killed? I'm not as dumb as you think I am.'

'I think you are exactly that dumb,' said D'onne. 'Doesn't matter. Bound or not, I will ruin your *career* day by ripping your fool head off and drinking a toast from your skull!' She spat a gob of bloody spittle on Vessa's boots.

The sergeant faltered for a response. Luckily, before the pause between D'onne's taunt and her response dragged on any longer, Vessa was saved by the arrival of Jankins, an engineer.

'Vaundon has healed the psi-hound's wounds,' reported Jankins. 'I should be able to get its repulsor jets working again by scavenging a few of the squad's weapons and using some wound foam to patch it back together.'

'Do it,' replied Vessa. The sooner they got that monstrosity up and running again, the better. A couple of weapons would be a fair trade for not having to haul that thing back to the lift platform where its underlings waited for it.

The engineer saluted before hustling off. Vessa turned and pretended to take an interest in the work being done up the hill to avoid getting dragged back into conversation with her prisoners. *Just a little longer*, she thought. *Up the lifts to Dust Falls, toss their sorry butts in the transport waiting there, and then back to base to celebrate.*

Vessa was certain to get a promotion out of this mission, which would take her one step closer to captain and her own command. Then she could dictate who she worked with. One thing was certain: she would never again be forced to work with abhuman scum.

As she daydreamed about having an office and sergeants to boss around, she stepped away from the prisoners in an attempt to clear her head of the needles caused by proximity to the pariah.

'I thought you said *not* to engage with her,' Servalen said when the sergeant stepped away. She had to admit she enjoyed watching D'onne goad the woman. She was a pig who epitomised all the worst traits of enforcers.

'I meant *you* shouldn't engage,' replied D'onne. 'Besides, I wasn't engaging. I was pushing buttons. In my experience, doing something is better than doing nothing.'

'Well, this looks pretty hopeless,' said Servalen. After D'onne had embarrassed Vessa, the sergeant had sent her two grunts to slap more force-cuffs on the women. Servalen had never seen anyone bound so tightly. Both women were restrained by four pairs each: one on their wrists, one on their ankles and two more connecting arms to legs to truss them up in permanent foetal positions.

'I don't see any way out of this mess,' added the scrutinator, eliciting a heavy sigh from Jeren. Servalen turned her head to look at the boy, who had put himself into a foetal position without the extra restraints. It looked like the fire he had shown earlier when bossing her and D'onne around was all spent.

'Don't worry, Jeren,' she said, trying to nudge him with her feet, but failing. 'We'll figure something out. We need a plan. Luckily, planning is my strong suit.'

'Planning gets you into trouble,' said D'onne, 'I don't plan. I act.' A hard edge tinged her voice as she continued. 'And if we don't act soon, I'll be handed over to my father to be a spectacle in a public demonstration of his power. You'll be tossed in a cell and forgotten – at best – and the kid will be sent to the Psykanarium to be dissected – or worse.'

At that, Jeren began to whimper softly to himself. Servalen felt sorry for him. He had such a talent. It would be a shame to mutate him into another Ortruum. He could be so much more, if only she could save him from that fate. But she wasn't sure she could even save herself from her own fate.

'So, how do we act when we're bound hands to feet?' she asked, trying to find something to spark her mind back out of the stupor caused by her unexpected incarceration, and realising D'onne was the only game in town. 'It's up to us. No one is coming to help. My mastiff is dead, and your bodyguard is... where exactly?'

'My dog is at the bottom of the sump, same as yours.'

Jeren whimpered beside them, making Servalen wonder if the young psyker was responding to D'onne's and her loss, but it seemed the boy had fallen unconscious again and was whimpering in his sleep.

Servalen felt that pang, though. A faithful companion was something to be treasured, she now realised. 'Sorry,' she said.

D'onne shook her head. 'Nothing to be sorry about. He was useful. Now he's not. Life goes on.'

'That was your point before,' said Servalen. 'It might not. Not unless we save ourselves. I might be able to convince some less gung-ho members of the squad that my arrest is irregular at best, but they're more scared of Ortruum than me, which puts me in unfamiliar territory.'

'That's where I live,' replied D'onne. 'Don't overthink it. Watch for your chance to act and when it comes take it. It's that simple.'

'Is it really?' replied Servalen, who knew that D'onne's crazy, carefree attitude towards life always came at a cost, usually to others. 'You think you can do whatever you want, whenever you want and get away with it, don't you?'

D'onne shook her head. 'Not at all,' she started. 'I do whatever I want whenever I want because I accept the possibility of any and all consequences my actions might bring. People might die? Fine. I might die? So what?'

Servalen was taken aback, but what did she expect from a mad woman? She was about to put an end to the conversation, but D'onne continued.

'Look, you have to come to terms with the reality that to get out of this alive, you may have to turn on your precious enforcers. Believe me, I won't be squeamish about killing them and they won't think twice before killing us when our push comes to their shove. The only thing that matters in life is to make a stand for what you believe in, no matter the consequences – to anyone.'

'And what do you believe in, Mad D'onne?' asked Servalen.

'Myself.'

Servalen sighed. Although they had worked together, and the psyker seemed to believe in D'onne, the mad noblewoman had not changed one bit.

'You may be right,' replied Servalen. 'Some enforcers may have to die, but not at my hands. I still believe in the palanite system of order. Without it, the hive would fall into chaos. We protect the people, both good and corrupt, from disorder. Your wanton destruction harms everyone, not just the corrupt.'

'What do you know?' spat D'onne. 'You're part of the corruption.'

'I am an agent of justice,' replied Servalen, 'or was. I fear to see a future where enforcers like Vessa are in charge. I tried to punish the corrupt – I've torn down entire cults.'

'Only because you were told to,' said D'onne. 'Only because they were a threat to the power of the Spire dwellers. Your justice did little more than help a corrupt oligarchy maintain its stranglehold over an entire world.'

Servalen had no answer to that and felt no compunction to talk to D'onne again. This entire situation was her fault. Servalen's life was working just fine until Mad D'onne decided she needed to kidnap a young psyker.

One thing was certain. Whatever D'onne wanted Jeren to find for her couldn't be good. It would mean death and pain, without doubt. Perhaps it would be better for everyone if the boy went to the Psykanarium, even if that meant Helmawr made Servalen disappear or tossed her onto a Black Ship while D'onne was served up as a sacrifice to the noble houses.

Corrupt or not, the system kept Hive Primus running. The total anarchy Mad D'onne would unleash could kill tens of millions, or more, before any sort of order was restored. Servalen didn't think she could live with herself if that came to pass. No matter what, she needed to keep Jeren away from the mad noblewoman or die trying. Today, that was what she believed in.

Jeren didn't remember much about his dad. His 'old man' was gone well before most of Jeren's earliest memories had formed. It had been him and his mother for as long as he could remember. But one memory had lodged deep inside his brain beneath the years of being browbeaten for being such a huge disappointment.

It was the memory of the day his father left. Something D'onne said during her argument with Servalen brought that memory rushing to the front of his mind as he lay whimpering beside the two women.

Mother and father were arguing, and it felt like the argument had been going on for hours, and for years before that. The angry words tossed back and forth were lost to the cobwebs of the forgotten corners of his brain, but he could see them clearly, faced off across the plasteel kitchen table. Their faces were flushed red and their hair flailed about wildly.

Fingers were pointed and voices were raised to the point that neighbours above, below and beside all banged on the walls.

And there was little Jeren, stuck in a crib in the corner of the only other room in their Hive City hovel. It was living room, bedroom and nursery all rolled into one. As he watched them fighting, a feeling of complete helplessness had washed over him, accentuated in his dream by the prison cell bars of his bed.

After the argument, Jeren's mother stormed out the door and his father came to him. Jeren must have been crying, although he couldn't remember if he was or not. He must have cried, but in his memory, he had remained silent, much as he would for the remainder of his youth.

Jeren's father picked him up and held him tightly, telling him it would be all right, much as Servalen had tried to tell him. But then his father had set him back down in the crib, handed him a half-drunk bottle filled with a greyish protein mixture that was supposed to make babies strong and, most likely, quiet and pliable.

As this old memory flashed through Jeren's mind, he saw something in his father's eyes. They changed from anger, sadness and resignation to something else; something new. Jeren knew now that the new look in his father's eyes was something he had never seen before in that household and never saw again after that day: hope.

Then, his father had said something to him that Jeren remembered because he had heard it again moments before: 'Watch for your chance to act, and when it comes, take it.' After that, Jeren's father glanced into the kitchen quickly, and then left, never to return.

There were many lessons Jeren could take from that flash of memory. He could blame his father for not taking him with him when he left. He could rage at the man for saving himself with no thought as to how it would impact his son. Instead, Jeren decided to focus on the one piece of advice his father had ever given him.

Except, Jeren didn't have to watch for his chance and react when it happened. He could see it coming and prepare. As D'onne and Servalen continued to argue, Jeren inched away from them, slowly, across the rough ground. Just a bit. Not enough to be noticeable at a glance. He then stretched out, putting his head as far from Servalen as he could get, and waited for his headache to reappear.

CHAPTER 26

FATAL INTERLUDES

Kordon Brann was desperate. He hadn't heard from Wicker Crag and reports coming out of Down Town were not optimistic. It sounded like a war had erupted down there. And here he was, a respectable businessman caught in the middle and about to lose everything because of some petty squabble between the haves and the have-nots.

'It's always the middle caste that gets the squeeze,' he mumbled, remembering his father's last words, uttered right before he'd left the office to go jump off the top of the Abyss after an unnaturally bad run of luck had bankrupted him. Luckily, Kordon had bet against his father during those last days and ended up with a tidy sum of credits, which he'd used to start his own business.

Now, it seemed his own luck had run out. But Kordon had no intention of offing himself and making some other poor schmuck rich. No. He still had one play to make; a way to salvage at least some of the good credits he'd thrown after all the bad.

'Hello?' he said into the vox connection on his terminal. 'Karga? It's your old pal, Kordon.'

'What do you want, Brann?' replied the Goliath bar owner, bluntly. *'Kinda busy here.'*

'I'll bet you are,' replied Kordon, still trying to strike a cordial and casual tone. 'Nothing like a good riot to make gangers thirsty.'

'Get to the point, Brann, before I close the link.'

'Right,' said Brann. 'Always straight to the point with you. Fine. I have a favour to ask.'

'No.'

'Hear me out. This will be profitable for you.'

'No!'

Brann sighed. 'I have reason to believe my scummers are dead,' he said, deciding to lay it all out there. 'And I happen to know they have a large sum of credits stored with the Guild of Coin. You have the best contacts in Hive Bottom. If you can free up those credits, I'll cut you in for a ten per cent finder's fee. I have their ownership codes and can transmit them immediately.'

'Fifty per cent,' Karga replied, adding, *'or I terminate this call, find the codes myself, and keep it all.'*

Kordon was desperate. He might be able to survive a trip to Down Town to meet with the local Gelt Guilder, but he hated that place. It was dangerous and he had no protectors any longer. Plus, now that Karga knew about it, he'd never make it to the guilder's office alive. 'Fine,' he said finally. 'Give me a sec to pull up those codes.'

Kordon opened another interface on his terminal and began tapping away. He might have lied about having the codes already.

'Kordon Brann?'

'We're closed, mate,' replied Kordon without looking over his shoulder. 'And this is a private office. Shove off.'

'Are you Kordon Brann?' repeated the voice. It was deep, with a mechanical edge, as if it were being spoken through a respirator.

'Yeah,' replied Kordon. 'Yes, I am. Now leave. I'm busy.'

'I am here for you, Kordon Brann.'

Kordon whipped around in his chair, furious at the impertinence, but didn't have time to scream in horror before he was slammed against the far wall of his office. His head cracked back against the wall, and his vision swam, but he stayed conscious. He staggered towards the door to his balcony, hoping to escape from whatever had attacked him.

'Where can I find Morn Dawingen, Drey Stummey and Nardan Keld?'

'Who?' asked Brann, hoping against hope that if he could remember those names and give them up, he might be allowed to survive.

'Morn Dawingen, Drey Stummey and Nardan Keld,' repeated the annoying, booming voice, which seemed to echo inside Kordon's brain as well as across the room. 'Cawdor sludge workers in your employ.'

Brann's head throbbed and his mind felt like it had been scrambled, but he remembered the names. He'd talked to them recently about the Jerenson kid. 'In the sludge pits,' he replied without worrying about their fate, or the fate of anyone unlucky enough to be working with them today; only that giving them up might save his life.

'Thank you,' replied the intruder. It held out a skeletal appendage and Brann went flying. The last thing Kordon Brann ever heard was Karga's voice through the vox connection.

'Goodbye, Brann. Your time is up,' she said as he crashed through the door and sailed over the balcony. When Kordon hit the street, his already concussed head struck the rock-crete ground hard and cracked open like an over-ripe melon.

Wicker Crag trudged along the shore of the sump with Dani, Brak and Hawk; they were all that remained of his gang of hive scum after that bloody riot. Wicker was already preparing the version of events he'd tell in Down Town, where he had led ten gangs on one hell of a chase, and gave as good as they got in a run-and-gun battle through the depths.

A heroic battle pitting scummers against gangs of all six houses was sure to play better than the truth. The only reason the four of them had survived was they had hightailed it away while the gangers fought over the mare's eyes.

Even Krotos Hark, Wicker's hired gun, had abandoned them over those damn spider eyes. Wicker didn't know where the bounty hunter was now, but hoped he'd got the lion's share. That might keep the armoured Goliath from blaming him for this fiasco of a mission. Wicker knew better. This was all Kordon Brann's fault. Once he got back to his hideout, Wicker planned to use the rest of that guilder's credits to gear up and hunt him down. If there was any money left after that, Wicker planned to drink himself into a long stupor.

'What's next?' asked Dani, clearly mirroring his thoughts. 'More recruiting? Anything left in the gang's coffers? Nothing like a good scrap to get the blood up, right, Brak?'

'Sump yeah!' yelled Brak. 'Nothing makes you feel more alive than surviving a big battle.'

Wicker felt himself tensing, and a day's worth of frustration bubbling up. He'd lost friends today, but worse than that, he'd lost an opportunity. For a moment there, he'd had hope. He'd already mentally spent the take they'd get from giving the kid over to Brann, but then Mad D'onne had to get involved... Hawk put a hand on his shoulder. He looked at her and she shook her head.

Wicker sighed. As always, his sniper played the long game. He turned back to Dani and Brak, ready to lie so he could keep them on long enough to get his revenge against Kordon.

'I've got big plans,' he said. 'We have a sizeable amount of creds stored away, and I have a new target in mind that should provide a suitable payback, er, pay-off.'

Dani smiled, causing the wrinkles around her eyes to smooth out as the skin on her cheeks tightened. *She seems pleased, at least,* thought Wicker. Brak's response was different, though. His eyes widened and his mouth opened into a large circle, as if he was taking a deep breath before screaming.

As Wicker realised that Brak was staring at something behind him, the old ganger flew through the air as if a huge gust of wind had picked him up and tossed him like a leaf. Brak's blunderbuss clattered to the ground as he soared over the edge of the sump and dropped into the lake, which seethed and hissed as it devoured his body.

Brak never did scream, but Dani began shrieking the moment her partner's body left her side. A moment after Brak hit the sump, Dani raised her hand flamer and fired. The gout of fire nearly scorched Wicker's face as he dived to the ground to avoid the flames. Hawk wasn't so lucky, though. The flames engulfed her slight body, turning her flesh to ash and igniting the long mohawk that ran down her back like the wick of a candle.

'What the sump?' Wicker yelled from his prone position. In response, Dani pointed with her free hand before advancing on an unseen target behind the immolated sniper. He rolled over to see what was attacking, but only saw Dani fly over his head towards the sump to join her partner. Her screams doubled in intensity for a split second after the splash but were silenced by an explosion as her fuel tank erupted.

Wicker tried to draw his heavy stubber using his one hand while lying prone on the ground, but only flailed about helplessly. As he struggled to get back to his feet, the hive scum leader felt something enter his mind and command him to stop moving. He had no choice but to obey. He couldn't move his head to look at his attacker.

'You coward!' he yelled, realising what he must be up against. 'Fight like a human, you psyker scum!'

A moment later, cold, rigid claws grabbed Wicker by the arm and leg and lifted him off the ground. As he dangled there, unable to move and held aloft like a sack full of rats, all Wicker could see were rolls of pink flesh and the occasional flash of plasteel tubing. After a moment, searing pain wracked his entire body as the claws yanked his limbs apart. In an instant that seemed to stretch into eternity, Wicker's bones broke and his organs ripped apart as his entire body was torn asunder.

Enforcer Barker had returned to guard duty after replacing the gear D'onne had stolen and setting a splint on his ankle. As long as he didn't have to fight or save anyone's life, he'd be fine until Nox and the squad returned, and he could finally stand down from this mission.

It had been hours since D'onne had left him bound in the silo. He hadn't heard from the sarge in that time either, so was simply following his last orders: patrol and report any activity to Proctor Bauhein.

So far, he'd made two reports. The first was a slightly

altered account of his encounter with D'onne, wherein he saw her leaving Dust Falls and heading towards the Abyss, with no mention of his time held as her captive. His lost gear and injury took some fast-talking, but he wasn't the first enforcer to lose his footing while patrolling the Abyss gates.

The second was hours later when a transport landed on the barren plains outside the wall to the city and four psi-hounds emerged. This report was more accurate, if no more useful to the proctor who, it turned out, already knew the psi-hounds were coming.

Since then, nothing out of the ordinary had happened inside or outside Dust Falls. The transport had made a huge racket when it landed and yet no gangers nor any of the vermin living in the tunnels beneath the Dust Falls plains had ventured forth to check it out or attempt to snatch it. Even the normal level of bar fights and street violence inside Dust Falls had almost completely ground to a halt. Nearly everyone seemed to be staying indoors. The big, bustling town was eerily quiet.

As Barker looked down into the Abyss, it felt to him like the hive was waiting for a heavy shoe to drop down there, at the bottom of the world. Perhaps everyone was waiting to see which way the underhive would twist in the aftermath of whatever was happening in Down Town before making their next moves.

As comforting as it was to have a quiet time on guard duty, Barker knew the tension building in the air would soon snap and anyone caught in the wrong place at the wrong time would lose more than an arm and some gear.

Barker took one last look down into the fading light of the Abyss before heading back towards the warehouse district. When he turned towards the silos, he saw the silhouette of a misshapen figure seemingly floating in the air before him. As the figure moved forward, Barker felt himself rooted to the spot. He could still feel his limbs but could not make them obey his mental commands to move.

As the figure floated in front of Barker, its grotesque body and multiple faces were illuminated by a light from one of the nearby gates. The enforcer wanted to turn away to avoid looking at the monstrosity but couldn't move his head or his eyes.

'You are Barker of squad HC-51086,' the face in the middle of the creature's torso said. It was a statement, not a question. 'Are there others?'

Barker tried to answer, tried to shake his head, but couldn't. It didn't seem to matter. From the itchy feeling inside his head, the enforcer was certain the information had been scraped from his brain.

'Good,' said the same mouth. 'Did any of HC-51086 talk to anyone inside these walls?'

Again, Barker's brain itched as the psi-hound searched for the answer to its question. Barker would have told the truth, and not just because he had no idea who his superiors might have talked with, but because he was a terrible liar, especially when terrified. But he was not allowed the option.

'Not good,' said the small mouth, which was surrounded by rolls of flabby pink flesh. 'We must find information elsewhere.'

Barker hoped that was that. He had no useful information and the enforcers and psi-hounds were on the same side, so it should release him now, right?

'Time to go,' said the mouth on the main face, which had multiple tubes feeding into it from a large piece of tech attached to the back of its head. Barker felt the hold on his mind release and took a step back, waiting for the psi-hound to leave so he could move forward.

Instead, an invisible force slammed into the enforcer's chest, flinging him back twenty metres, which put Barker five metres past the edge of the Abyss – and falling into the kilometres-deep twilight.

CHAPTER 27

BOTTOM OF THE FOOD CHAIN

Sergeant Vessa felt pretty good about herself. From the argument she'd overheard between Mad D'onne and Scrutinator Servalen, the sergeant felt certain the two women had reverted to hating one another. At the very least, it didn't look like they would actively work together, which would make her job easier.

Of course, she didn't believe Servalen had gone rogue down here at the bottom of the hive. Things happened in the field and sometimes strange alliances were formed in the heat of battle. As long as all the perpetrators ended up on a slab or in custody – including those used as a means to an end – there was no harm.

As far as Vessa knew, Scrutinator Servalen was a dedicated servant to the Spire, which is what made her rise to power all the more aggravating. She made everyone around her look bad. But it was all a trick. She didn't have to work for her successes like a normal person. All she had to do was stare at people until they gave her what she wanted: information, cult locations, contraband smuggling routes, gang hideouts, and on and on and on.

Her success rate disgusted Vessa. It was about time someone took her down, even if it was on some trumped-up charges. Helmawr wanted it and so it would be. The top of the palanite ladder would be easier to attain without Scrutinator Servalen in her way.

The other thing that had put a smile on the sergeant's face was how they had trussed up the two female prisoners for transport. Getting them both to the lift platform had been of some concern to Vessa's squad. She didn't want them walking, not with their ankles cuffed, but no one wanted to get close enough to carry either woman.

Ortruum 8-8 had been no help either. Talking to the psihound was worse than having a conversation with the pariah. He barely even bothered to acknowledge her presence, let alone regard her as worth engaging with on an equal footing. Ortruum commanded and all humans listened and obeyed.

Jankins came to Vessa's rescue, though, when Ortruum ordered the sergeant to prepare to move out after his repairs were complete. Vessa thought she would have no choice but to untruss the two women and take her chances on a forced march with less than a full squad.

The engineer had cut two long lengths of plasteel pipe from the nearby cliff wall. A slight rearrangement of the force cuffs binding the women's wrists to their ankles allowed Jankins to hang them from the poles so two enforcers could haul each prisoner with relative ease.

Vessa placed the rest of the squad on guard duty, with the young psyker leashed to the last pair of enforcers by the chains the kid was still wearing. Vessa had paid little attention to Jeren Jerenson since they had recaptured him. The kid seemed broken already. He said little and looked no one in the eyes. He had started complaining about some damned headache, though, which was irritating as hell.

That couldn't ruin Vessa's good mood, however. Sometime after passing the remains of the dead Goliaths they had chased off the hill earlier, their bullet-riddled carcasses already attracting rats, she caught sight of the lift platform. Once there, Vessa could turn the psyker and the traitorous pariah over to Ortruum 8-8 and the rest of his pack of psi-hounds, and those damn abhumans would no longer be her problem.

As they approached the platform, Vessa noticed the bloody remains of the riot had been almost completely cleaned. It made sense. Like all waste in the hive, bodies were valuable and someone had made a tidy profit today selling remains to the Corpse Guild.

Vessa almost smiled at the thought that her job of killing scum in the underhive actively helped the local economies, but at that moment she realised the lift platform was completely empty. Yes, the bodies had been removed, which was a good thing. The stench from that many decaying corpses would have made waiting for the lift unbearable. However, there was a decided lack of psi-hounds gathered on the platform waiting to take custody of her prisoners.

Vessa stormed up beside Ortruum 8-8, whose immense bulk glided along on the repaired repulsors ahead of the squad.

'Where are they?' she demanded. When the grotesque, fleshy psi-hound didn't answer, Vessa continued. 'I was told four of you lot were being dispatched from the Spire. Where are the other three?'

Ortruum 8-8 stopped and rotated slowly to face Vessa, although she found it nearly impossible to tell front from side or back on this monstrosity. Once the psi-hound's eyes locked onto Vessa face, however, the sergeant knew she'd overstepped.

The sergeant could no longer move and could barely force herself to breathe. The psi-hound had taken control of Vessa's mind seemingly without effort. Anger seethed inside the sergeant, at her stupidity but also at the abhuman's unnatural abilities, which gave him an otherworldly advantage over humans.

'Cohorts dealing with matters of import elsewhere,' said Ortruum 8-8, his voice seeming to pound straight through Vessa's skull into her brain. 'All will meet at transport once orders executed.'

Vessa became uneasy by the impact given to the word 'executed' when Ortruum drilled it into her head. She knew she needed to apologise for her insubordination, but she couldn't make her lips move to form words.

'Enforcers do two jobs,' continued Ortruum, twisting slightly in the air to maintain eye contact. 'Deliver prisoners. Ask no questions.'

After what seemed an eternity of being stared at by this gruesome parody of a human, Vessa felt the clamps removed from her mind and she could speak again. 'I apologise,' she said through gasps of air. 'I meant... no disrespect.'

If Ortruum had heard the apology, it was not evident from the psi-hound's next statement. 'Once prisoners delivered to transport, enforcers released from duty,' he said. 'Now is time to ascend.'

Vessa wasn't sure what to make of that last statement, but she knew enough not to argue any further with the psi-hound.

The sergeant turned and barked orders at the squad, taking her suddenly sour mood out on her subordinates.

D'onne ached all over. It had been a long scavving day of fighting battles, climbing pipes, cliffs, walls and scaffolds, followed by more battles and, finally, being hog-tied and carried on a spit. Her dislocated shoulder rolled around in the socket with every bump as the enforcers carried her to the lift platform, each step sending piercing streaks of pain through her pectoral and lateral muscles, which tightened into knots as hard as plasteel.

Even so, along the way, the mad noble watched for an opening. One of her guards stumbling, another attack by the remains of those idiotic scummers, anything that might distract the enforcers long enough for her to act. When that nasty sergeant and the psi-hound argued at the base of the platform, she had hoped it would turn into a proper row, but no such luck.

After the sergeant caved in to Ortruum like a crumbling tunnel during a hivequake, the enforcers trudged onto the platform and deposited the prisoners in a heap on the lift. D'onne lay there, winded and barely able to move her aching limbs. Nevertheless, she persisted in testing the strength of her shackles and running through escape scenarios in her head.

She might have a chance by rolling off the lift as it ascended the Abyss, but only after resting her arms and legs a bit. She could hardly move, let alone hold her own body weight or fight. Even so, she would need some sort of distraction to have any chance at all.

It would be easier if she could count on the scrutinator for help, but that door seemed closed. *Perhaps the kid*, she thought. *Maybe he could distract a few guards by revealing the locations of their long-lost pet rats.* But when Jeren and Servalen dropped to the floor almost on top of D'onne, she realised that option was not available either.

Proximity to Servalen seemed to shut down the young psyker's powers. *Shame,* she thought. She could use one of Jeren's premonitions right now. At least Servalen's presence had Ortruum keeping his distance. *If I see an opportunity,* D'onne thought, *the first thing I should do is toss Servalen at the psi-hound. Make the scrutinator help despite her little hissy fit.*

'The dogs will attack,' whispered Jeren, interrupting her train of thought. 'Their howls will open the window.'

The enforcer who had tossed the kid to the ground between D'onne and Servalen turned around and kicked Jeren in the stomach. 'No talking!' he growled.

D'onne turned to ask Jeren what he'd meant, but the kid seemed to have fallen into some sort of trance. His eyes were closed, but D'onne could see his eyes randomly darting around beneath the lids and his breathing came in short, shallow gasps. Worse yet, he didn't respond when the enforcer kicked him.

It was like the guard had kicked a corpse – something D'onne had done on more than one occasion. It was amazing how annoying people could be by being dead when she needed them alive. Whatever the kid had meant, D'onne hoped the dogs howled before they got to that transport and she had three more psi-hounds to contend with.

CHAPTER 28

PROPHECY OR LUNACY

Servalen spent most of her time on the lift to the top of the Abyss devising and rejecting various plans for escape. Overpowering the enforcers was out. Vessa had them too well trained. The scrutinator could handle the psi-hound if she got close enough, but Ortruum 8-8 was using the enforcers as a buffer between her and him.

Rolling off the lift seemed suicidal – more the type of idea Mad D'onne might devise. The scrutinator didn't want to trust her life to her upper body strength. Besides, she couldn't leave Jeren behind. Especially not now. He'd lapsed back into a trance, much like she'd found him in on the altar at the Deep Pyre, but this one seemed much worse.

Jeren's abstruse prophecy about the dogs had given Servalen hope. If it had ended there, she might have let herself believe KB-88 had somehow survived and was coming to rescue her. But then, shortly after the enforcers moved them all to the third lift, the young psyker started groaning more incomprehensible nonsense, despite being close enough to her that she thought she'd be breaking whatever connection his wyrd abilities were trying to make.

'Trust the madness,' he murmured, curled tight into a ball.

Enforcer Mauch came over and kicked Jeren in the back. 'Shut up, kid,' he yelled. 'You're picking away at my last nerve.'

This only made Jeren repeat the phrase louder still as Mauch kicked him repeatedly.

'Leave him be!' Servalen yelled. 'Can't you see he's sick?'

'Sick in the head,' replied Geoffers, before kicking Servalen. 'Both of you, shut up!'

As Mauch strode away, and Geoffers concentrated on Servalen, Jeren quieted down, but the nonsense didn't stop. 'The only way through is down. The only way through IS down. The ONLY way through is DOWN!'

This earned him renewed beatings, and a visit from Ortruum 8-8, who jetted closer, perhaps wanting to hear his ramblings. Servalen hoped he would venture too close, but the psi-hound knew the boundaries of the pariah well. Perhaps he had been coached before coming on this mission.

At a word from Ortruum 8-8, Vessa ordered the guards to cease beating the young psyker. 'Record everything he says,' Vessa ordered Geoffers, 'but otherwise leave the kid alone.'

By this point, it was time to move to the next lift platform. The enforcers trundled Servalen and Mad D'onne onto their plasteel rods, but Mauch had to toss Jeren over his shoulder like a sack of worm-meal. The poor kid's trance had only worsened. His eyes had rolled back into his head, giving him the creepy, white-eyed stare of a true psyker – or someone drugged out of his mind.

After Mauch dropped Jeren onto the final lift, the kid began chanting again. 'Death is the doorway to fulfilment,' he said, repeating the phrase at least a dozen times, before, 'Bearing witness is a death curse.'

Strangely, the first time the trancing psyker uttered that last phrase, Servalen was almost certain she saw the crumpled and broken form of a body fall from an outcropping of rockcrete far off to the side of the lift. It went by too fast to be sure, but for an instant she thought the body was clad in enforcer armour and missing an arm.

When they reached the top of the Abyss, Jeren stopped chanting. She looked at him, curled into a ball, hugging his knees to his chest, and rocking back and forth slowly as he whimpered lightly. His eyes had closed, mercifully, but every once in a while, his body shook violently.

Servalen had no idea what had come over Jeren during the trip to the top of the Abyss. Perhaps prolonged exposure to her null field had mucked up his psychic wiring, made him weaker when he was outside of it again. He was broken. One thing was certain; she couldn't leave Jeren to his fate.

If all else failed, she would find some way to take Jeren's life. That would be preferable. He wouldn't face the Psykanarium to be twisted into another Ortruum. Whatever D'onne was looking for, she wouldn't find. But the same was true for Helmawr – Jeren wouldn't be pulling secrets from recidivist skulls.

Two enforcers came over and lifted Servalen onto their shoulders for the trip to the Spire transport. They placed her facing backwards, which allowed her to keep an eye on Jeren. Mauch once again grabbed the psyker's chains and tossed the young man's thin, shuddering body over his shoulder. He draped the chains over his other shoulder and drew a laspistol with his free hand.

As the enforcers marched off the lift though, Servalen

once again caught something out of the corner of her eye. In between fits of shuddering on Mauch's back, Jeren calmed down for a brief instant. He made eye contact with her, and winked.

Immediately after, Jeren began whimpering and shaking again, with such severity and sincerity that Servalen almost doubted what she'd seen. But she couldn't shake the feeling that this naïve man, this ultra-powerful but raw and untrained psyker who had started the day as a passive prisoner on his way to being sacrificed, was pulling the wool over the eyes of an entire squad of enforcers and one of the most dangerous psi-hounds in the underhive.

As the column of enforcers made their way through the eerily vacant and silent streets of Dust Falls, Servalen mulled over Jeren's ramblings and searched for hidden meanings. It was all a jumble, but she couldn't shake the feeling that taken together, his incoherent lunacy might be prophecy. In case it was, Servalen scanned the ravaged plains and the walls encircling Dust Falls for any sign of her returning mastiff.

Mad D'onne swayed beneath the plasteel pole as it bounced and jostled on the shoulders of two enforcers assigned to carry her to the transport. After leaving Dust Falls, the single-file column of enforcers followed Ortruum 8-8 into the battle-ravaged plains outside the walls of the fortified city.

Dust Falls had become one of the wealthiest underhive settlements in recent decades due to its access to the Abyss, making it the central hub for the distribution of archeotech recovered from the lost hive layers and raw materials harvested from the sump.

The prosperity of Dust Falls made it a target, though. Construction on the walls around the settlement began after the first attacks, a relatively weak (in the grand scheme of things) series of attacks by gangs of various houses hoping for easy scores.

The various guilds banded together to finance the fortifications and take control of Dust Falls. As one of its first decrees, the Council of Dust refused entry to any house involved in an attack on the settlement. That alone helped the town prosper for years.

Then came more monstrous attackers. The hidden tunnels, barely accessible to 'civilised' folk, were prime real estate for abhumans and other vicious creatures. So, in addition to hidden treasures, the compressed levels running kilometres deep beneath Dust Falls were filthy with muties, ratlings, beastmen and plague zombies, as well as giant rats, milliasaurs and spider mares.

To combat the constant invasions, a tax was levied on all goods entering Dust Falls via the Abyss, which the Council used to pay for repairs on the walls, hire additional guards and construct a series of defences across the plains surrounding the walled city. Bulwarks, ramparts, fences and trenches crisscrossed the plains, designed to slow down advancing enemies so they could be picked off by sharpshooters on the walls.

It was around and through these battlements that the enforcer column now trudged. It was slow going. Much of the barbed wire once coiled around the fences had found its way into the trenches, where it lay half-buried in the dust along with the skeletal remains of long-dead attackers and the rotting flesh left behind by recent battles.

D'onne had tried to keep quiet and passive during most of the trip from Down Town, hoping to lull her captors into a false sense of security. It was natural. The longer you do a menial task without any outside interference, the easier it becomes to ignore the task. You lose concentration. This is what she hoped her two enforcers were experiencing.

As they made their way through the battlements, however, D'onne had to grab the force cuffs to pull her head and body out of the dust to avoid colliding with skulls, rib cages, half-eaten limbs and bloody entrails, not to mention the rusty barbs of half-buried wire coils that tore at her hair, clothes and flesh.

Twice during the procession, the guard holding the pole near her feet smacked her with his shock baton and yelled at her to release the cuffs. D'onne fumed each time, vowing to kill him first. She had no doubt this day would end badly for the enforcers. She had no weapons and no idea how she would remove the force cuffs, but her underhive intuition was screaming at her as they tramped through the dust and debris.

It wasn't the kid's lunatic ramblings that had her on edge, though. None of this felt right. Vessa now had five of her squad devoted to carrying prisoners. Vaundon, the squad's medic, was overburdened by all the confiscated weapons, making her useless if she should need to respond quickly in an emergency.

The clincher came when D'onne overheard an enforcer named Gillians report some news to the sergeant.

'Sarge, I've been monitoring enforcer reports,' said Gillians, who seemed to be the squad's sharpshooter as well as taking care of communications. She had a long-las strapped to her back under the vox-caster. 'It appears someone or something assaulted Proctor Bauhein within the past hour.'

'What, in the Spire?' exclaimed Sergeant Vessa from the head of the enforcer column. She dropped back to speak with her comms trooper as the rest of the squad, including D'onne's carriers, passed by. 'Report. What do we know so far?'

'Nothing solid. Bauhein's still alive, but a lot of his team aren't. He's with the docs,' continued Gillians. 'There have been similar incidents, however. Something attacked Sludge Town and the sludge pits, claiming the lives of a Promethium Guilder and several workers. There was another attack outside Down Town. The details are fuzzy and no one seems able to identify the attackers or weapons used. They thought it might be D'onne, but we have her right here.'

The conversation grew quieter as D'onne's haulers carried her out of hearing range. Strange attacks inside every community D'onne had visited in the past day? Even if she believed in coincidences, this would be hard to swallow.

She knew what it looked like when someone was removing witnesses. It didn't take a lunatic psychic to realise that everyone – prisoner and captor alike – in this little parade through the death fields outside Dust Falls was in grave danger.

CHAPTER 29

TRAPS AND ESCAPES

Servalen had come to the conclusion that Vessa was marching them straight into a trap. She looked to D'onne, desperate to know what was going on in her head, but she was quietly seething. Servalen was on her own.

The enforcers climbed out of a long winding trench, revealing what must have been the psi-hounds' transport. It was sleek and white, Spire tech. Even the recent dusting of waste ash and Dust Falls rain hadn't diminished the ship's shine, which gleamed in the bright lights of the dome.

Servalen recognised the design: the flattened fuselage, short, tapered wings and long, bifurcated tail section made the ship look like the twin-bladed head of some xenos craft that Servalen had seen in an off-world report. The small transport was perfect for infiltrating the underhive because it could fly through the sump tunnel and other narrow points of entry.

The seal emblazoned on the ship's hatch caught Servalen's attention after her guards dropped her to the ground. It was the same seal she carried, which had once opened all doors and locks within the hive: Lord Helmawr's official seal. One of his personal transports.

With twin thumps, Mad D'onne and Jeren were dumped nearly on top of Servalen. She glanced at D'onne, but the hunter's scowl and glare had not changed, so Servalen studied Jeren instead. The young psyker still whimpered and occasionally mumbled incomprehensible words. Servalen was beginning to think her earlier hope that the boy was up to something might have been wishful thinking.

'All right, Ortruum,' she heard Vessa say, a bit overly loud, as if she had something to prove. 'We got your prisoners here as promised. They're all yours.'

'Await further orders,' replied Ortruum 8-8. 'Squad HC-81365 not dismissed.'

'Yes, sir,' replied Vessa, clipping both words hard as if forcing herself not to continue past those two syllables.

Servalen could see the heat radiating up from the sergeant's neck. She'd seen the same ire in her own subordinates enough times to know how Vessa felt about being put in her place by beings she deemed beneath human.

'Circle and face captives,' continued the psi-hound. 'Maintain visual contact until mission termination.'

It was an odd request that Servalen would have questioned. The plains around Dust Falls were notoriously dangerous, as evidenced by all the defences. But Vessa had been repeatedly rebuked by Ortruum and acquiesced grudgingly.

'You heard the order,' she called, still clipping her words. 'Surround the prisoners and keep a watchful eye on them until further orders.'

Beside Servalen, Jeren took a break from his whimpering to mumble another single word. The first word she heard was 'overdone'. This time, he said: 'oversaw.' He'd stopped making sense hours ago.

After Jeren uttered the next word – 'beside' – Servalen understood. The number of letters lessened by one each time.

'He's counting down,' she whispered to D'onne beside her. 'Be ready.'

Servalen glanced at the noblewoman to see if she had heard and understood, but D'onne's expression had not changed – her scowl and glare were intact. It was like staring at a cold, stone face.

By the time Jeren said 'under', Servalen heard a low whir-ring noise she instantly recognised coming from several directions at once. It was small repulsor engines running at full speed. A moment later, the engine on the transport ship roared to life behind them, masking the weaker sounds.

'Over.'

'What was that?' asked Vessa. The sergeant had obviously heard the small engines as well.

'No concern,' replied Ortruum. 'Comrades return from missions.'

At that point, the sound of the three repulsor engines could be heard by everyone as they closed on the transport, the prisoners and the circle of enforcers.

'All!'

'Permission to order enforcers to face incoming personnel, sir,' said Sergeant Vessa in her most official voice.

'Permission denied,' replied Ortruum. 'Maintain prisoner monitor order.'

'ON!'

'Shut up, kid,' screamed Mauch, finally losing it as the words had got progressively louder and more insistent over the last minute. The enforcer moved forward, probably to kick Jeren again.

The whirring of the three distinct repulsor engines had become dull roars combined with the skittering sound of dust flying up from the ground.

'I!' Jeren called out loud. He then grunted as Mauch kicked him in the gut.

'Screw this!' said Vessa. Servalen heard the sergeant's force baton hum to life. 'Enforcers, about face! Ready arms!'

As one, the enforcers twirled around as weapons slapped into gloves and charged.

At the same time, the hatch of the transport slid open and a small ramp descended to the ground. In the doorway stood a man dressed in a military flight suit holding a lasgun.

'Now!' called Jeren.

Numerous events occurred simultaneously as bedlam engulfed the gathering beside Helmawr's transport: Vessa screamed. Three enforcers flew into the air. The screeching howl of a cyber-mastiff echoed off the transport. The pilot fired. The ground erupted beneath one of the surrounding trenches. And, perhaps most importantly for Servalen, D'onne and Jeren, the magnacles binding them disengaged at once.

'Time to act,' said D'onne as she scrambled to a crouch beside Servalen.

'As the kid said,' replied Servalen as she glanced at Jeren. The young psyker smiled and opened his hand to show her the cuff release mechanism, palmed from the enforcer who had been carrying him.

Mauch, who hadn't moved from Jeren's side after kicking him in the stomach, reached for the young psyker's wrist. Before he could grab the kid, though, he was flattened by

Vaundon. The medic fell from the sky after being flung into the air in that chaotic first instant, bearing the crouching Mauch to the ground beneath her.

D'onne dived towards the tangled enforcers, several pairs of force cuffs in hand, as Jeren scrambled away from the hapless duo. D'onne's hands, moving almost too fast to follow, connected one of Mauch's wrists to Vaundon's ankle.

'Stay down and keep quiet, and you might live through this,' she hissed at the prone and bound enforcers. With the battle already raging around her, D'onne liberated her weapons and gear from the medic.

Fully equipped and unrestrained, D'onne stood and took the time to rearrange her wig and corset as she surveyed the scene. Three enforcers – Vessa, Gillians and Geoffers – all stood still, apparently locked inside their own minds as D'onne had been during the previous battle. The rest of the squad had been surrounded by Ortruum 8-8 and his three comrades from the Psykanarium.

The new psi-hounds took turns tossing enforcers into one another or up into the air with some sort of telekinetic blast, while Ortruum advanced on the sergeant, weaving back and forth in the air on his repulsor jets to perfectly dodge bullets and las-shots aimed at him from the remaining enforcers.

Out of the corner of her eye, D'onne saw the immense bulk of Dog emerge from a trench and run towards a psi-hound to her right at full bore. She grinned. The monstrous creature was as big as her ogryn, but didn't look at all humanoid. He was more like snakes of human flesh fused into a floating ouroboros. Dog's attack wasn't going to succeed, but if the ogryn could keep the serpentine psi-hound's mind occupied, it might provide D'onne with an opening.

'Time to even the odds,' said D'onne. She turned to Servalen, who had retrieved her autopistol from the medic but remained crouched next to Jeren. 'Sorry about this!' D'onne added as she grabbed the lanky scrutinator by the waist and lifted her to a standing position.

D'onne rushed several long strides to the left, pushing Servalen towards a psi-hound with multiple mouths sunk into rolls of pink fat around an immense, morbidly obese body. With a mighty heave, D'onne half pushed and half threw the scrutinator at the psi-hound.

She figured the pariah's presence would nullify the monstrosity's psychic abilities, or at least provide a half-decent distraction. As soon as D'onne released Servalen, she drew Countless. A warm feeling of satisfaction enveloped the hunter as the familiar weight of the weapon rested in her hands again.

The scrutinator hit the ground with both feet but nearly fell in the cloud of dust blown into the air by her impact. She stayed on her feet, though and, apparently understanding her part in D'onne's little manoeuvre, charged towards the multi-mouthed monster, before crouching in front of its floating bulk, perhaps to give D'onne a clear shot. D'onne had other ideas, though. She closed the distance and leapt onto the crouching scrutinator, kicking off the woman's back to gain more height.

At the apex of D'onne's leap, she raised her chainsword overhead, triggered the spinning blades, and swung it two-handed in a downward arc, adding her considerable strength to the force of gravity as she fell.

Countless sliced through the psi-hound's rotund body as if it were a huge mound of pink butter. The blade snagged for a moment on the monstrosity's neural crown, but with a hard twist of her wrist, D'onne slid it past the obstruction and down through the creature's several faces, all of which screamed as she ripped them in two.

D'onne landed next to the bifurcated psi-hound, straddling the now prone scrutinator who had been shoved to the ground by the force of D'onne's leap. A pool of blood flowed towards Servalen, who scrambled to get out from under D'onne.

'Why didn't you shoot him?' Servalen yelled as she struggled to her feet.

D'onne didn't have time to deal with the scrutinator now. She'd served her purpose and needed to get out of the way. 'Help Vessa,' she said as light-pink blood sprayed from Countless' blade, 'if you want her to live.'

With that, D'onne sheathed her chainsword, took two steps to the side to get a better angle and drew Pig. It had half a charge after she'd used it to burn through the Goliath brothers' cover. She hoped it would be enough.

Servalen protested beside her for a moment before moving off towards the main battle. D'onne ignored her and concentrated on getting her timing and aim perfect. Dog had reached the serpentine psi-hound somehow and tackled its greyish-green body to the ground. If it had truly been a snake, it might have constricted around Dog to squeeze the life out of him.

Having watched Ortruum's fighting style a bit over the past day, D'onne waited for the inevitable counter-attack. The Psykanarium fiend didn't disappoint. A moment later, Dog went flying straight up into the air, which was D'onne's cue.

She squeezed the trigger on the plasma pistol, shooting a swirling purple beam of super-heated plasma through the air towards the prone psi-hound. With its attention focused on Dog, the serpentine psi-hound did not anticipate the attack. The beam burned into its thick, khaki-coloured skin below its repulsor jets.

D'onne continued pressing the trigger, pouring more of Pig's charge into beams as she slowly rotated the barrel to carve a deep gash from its green tail up through its middle snake head. The psi-hound's neural crown sparked and ignited as the beam cut through wires, tubes and plasteel housing.

A moment later, the neural crown exploded, destroying what was left of all three of the serpentine psi-hound's heads.

With the odds evened a bit, D'onne turned her attention to the next most pressing matter: escaping with her prize. She ran towards Jeren as she waited for Dog to plummet back to ground where he could be useful again.

Even after D'onne had used her as a shield to cut down one of the psi-hounds, the situation looked dire for the squad from Servalen's vantage point. The initial ambush had left most of the enforcers flying through the air or rooted to the ground and unable to move as the psi-hounds had jetted forward to take advantage of the chaos.

On top of that, the transport pilot, whose flight suit bore an Imperial Guard insignia, had been concentrating his lasrifle fire on Gillians, the squad's sniper, keeping her pinned down and unable to use her skills to aid her sergeant.

The Spire has done its homework, thought Servalen as she rushed forward. The psi-hounds had tossed the medic into the air during their initial attack and then targeted the squad's leader and sniper, while two other veterans remained motionless, waiting for someone to finish them off.

The biggest issue was Vessa, though. The squad needed

its leader. Servalen used her long legs to sprint across the battlefield, dodging falling bodies and stray weapons fire as Ortruum 8-8 jetted towards the sergeant on his repulsors, easily floating over obstacles and casually dodging incoming bullets and laser fire.

Servalen raised and fired her autopistol, hoping to slow down the psi-hound so she could get within range to disable his psychic abilities and free the hold he had on the sergeant's mind. Unfortunately, her first two shots sliced into rolls of fat on what would have been the chest and stomach on any other humanoid. Ortruum was one mass of flesh so thick that the chance of Servalen's bullets reaching vital organs was slim.

At that point, Servalen knew she wouldn't reach Vessa before Ortruum got to her. But the enforcer sergeant had the strongest armour in the underhive. Only the Imperial Guard deployed to war zones had better among human forces. There was still hope. She needed to change tactics.

'Hey, Ortruum,' she called. 'Your prisoners are escaping!' She pumped her legs across the dusty ground. She needed the psi-hound to hesitate for a second so she could get close enough to break his mental hold and free Vessa to fight.

Ortruum ignored her taunt, though. Hovering before the frozen sergeant, Ortruum reached out and grabbed Vessa with a mechanical arm. The fingers of the plasteel hand closed around the sergeant's neck and the arm lifted her off the ground as if she weighed little more than a long-las. Ortruum swung the sergeant's stiff body around and caught one of her legs with his other mechanical hand.

The servos that attached each arm apparatus to the psi-hound's bulbous stomach whirred to life and spun in opposite directions as the articulated arms lengthened to their full extensions and turned rigid. In an instant, the sergeant's armoured body was stretched to breaking point. After an abrupt series of bone-jarring cracks, Vessa's head and leg ripped away from her torso, spewing blood, bone and cartilage into the air. The rest of her body fell to the ground, the impact spraying a cloud of dust into the bloody mist and turning the air pink around Ortruum 8-8.

Rage and frustration boiled over inside Servalen. She had never wanted any of this. Vessa may have represented the most brutal aspects of enforcer justice, but she didn't deserve to be torn apart to serve the political purposes of the Spire.

Servalen rushed straight at Ortruum 8-8, unloading her autopistol. Each step narrowed her shots. Round after round sheared off chunks of skin and fat, but something was interfering with the bullets. Nothing penetrated deep enough to do any real damage. The acrid smell of Vessa's pooling blood filled Servalen's nostrils, and she felt her training kick in.

It was too late, though. Servalen's mad rush had brought her within grasping distance of the psi-hound's mechanical arms. Ortruum dropped the sergeant's head and leg and reached for Servalen as she tried to skid to a stop.

As the battle raged around Jeren, he scooted back through the dust towards the cuffed enforcers. Mauch, the guard who'd carried – and beaten – him trembled in fear, his eyes widening as the young psyker reached for a weapon that Vaundon had dropped when she fell to ground.

'I'm not going to hurt you,' Jeren said in as soothing a voice as he could conjure, considering his experience with kind words was low. 'If you do as I say, you both will live. I've seen it.'

'Why should we trust you, freak?' spat Mauch. 'All of this is your fault!'

'Trust me or not,' replied Jeren, his voice calm and steady. He would gain nothing from yelling.

He laid the weapon aside for the moment and showed his open palms to the two enforcers. 'The choice is yours,' he continued. 'My way leads to life, the other to a painful death.'

'What do we do?' asked Vaundon. Mauch opened his mouth to continue arguing, but the medic kicked him.

'Don't move until Gillians fires three times,' Jeren said. 'I'm going to release your cuffs now, and then I have to go. I don't have any choice. Do not follow me if you want to live!'

'To hell with that,' hissed Mauch.

Jeren shook his head, but he'd done all he could – except for this. 'One last thing, Mauch. The vid-log you once carried, with scenes of your brother. Sergeant Vessa confiscated it. You will find it in her bunk locker. Vaundon can help you retrieve it after her promotion.'

'What the–' started both enforcers, but Jeren cut them off.

'And Vaundon,' continued Jeren quickly. He had precious little time left. 'Enforcer Barker's body lies on a U-shaped buttress jutting out from the Abyss below the second lift landing. His mother and sister deserve to see him laid to rest properly.'

Vaundon nodded, confusion warring with opportunity on her face. 'Thank you,' she whispered.

Jeren grabbed the web pistol from the dusty ground and then pressed the remote release for the force cuffs. As he stood and swung the chains still attached to his wrists in a slow arc around his body, the young psyker hoped Mauch would stay in the dust. He didn't want to see D'onne cut him in half; not again. Seeing it once had been more than enough.

D'onne sprinted past Jeren, grabbed the chains out of the air, and kept running towards the transport without missing a stride. Jeren pumped his legs as fast as he could to keep up. Ahead of them, D'onne's ogryn bodyguard slammed his way through the hatch, flinging the surprised pilot into the far wall with a thud.

As Jeren half ran and was half dragged through the debris of the battlefield, he concentrated on the memory of this scene in his mind to avoid tripping on any errant detritus or severed body parts. He had one last thing to do, and Jeren knew he would miss his chance if he fell. He had seen what happened if he did.

CHAPTER 30

HOLLOW VICTORY

Because Servalen was a null, Ortruum 8-8's mind control didn't work on her. His powers couldn't get a grip on her, and separated, like oil on water. And yet, she still felt helpless – unable to react – as she slid towards the behemoth who had ripped a fellow enforcer into pieces. The scrutinator swung her arms in a desperate attempt to stop, but the dust in the plains was so light that the ground was nearly frictionless.

The servos operating the psi-hound's mechanical limbs hummed and whirred, and time seemed to slow to a crawl as his articulated plasteel arms snaked out towards Servalen's face. A sharp bark, like metal grating against metal, and a blur of motion behind Ortruum broke Servalen out of the torpor that had sapped the strength from her body. She dropped to the ground as Ortruum's hands closed with a mechanical snap above her head.

A moment later, the blur behind the psi-hound resolved into a metallic mastiff in mid-leap. KB-88, Servalen's loyal cyber-hound, landed on Ortruum's back and dug its plas-teel claws deep into his fleshy body, eliciting screams of pain from the normally stoic creature.

The extra weight of the cyber-mastiff atop the massive bulk of the obese psi-hound proved to be too much for Ortruum's repulsor engines, which whined louder under the strain before igniting and belching out thick clouds of black smoke.

Servalen rolled from beneath Ortruum 8-8 before his repulsors gave out completely. KB-88 held on as Ortruum dropped, riding the massive psi-hound into the ground. Once they landed, the cyber-mastiff leapt onto his neural crown, driving the psi-hound's huge, fat face deep into the dust.

Servalen scrambled to a crouch as her loyal mastiff leapt off the half-buried psi-hound into her waiting arms. 'Good boy,' said Servalen, surprised at the emotion in her voice.

The cold, unfeeling metallic dog, controlled by circuitry and programming, rubbed up against its master, doing a remarkably convincing imitation of responding to the praise. The reunion was cut short, however, when both heard servos whining back to life in the dust next to them.

Ortruum 8-8 still had some life in him and was attempting to use his mechanical arms to push himself into an upright position. Even without his repulsors, the psi-hound could still do a great deal of damage to the enforcers with his psychic abilities once he could see his targets again. Servalen couldn't leave his side to find a weapon and KB-88, as strong as it was, couldn't claw its way through that bulk.

They needed a long-term solution.

Servalen glanced around for anything or anyone near enough to deal a final blow to the leader of the psi-hound team. Gillians was now rooted to the ground and Geoffers had fallen to the pilot's rifle before the man strangely disappeared.

Then, from behind Servalen, she heard a sound she recognised. A web pistol. She turned to see Jeren being dragged through the battlefield towards the transport by D'onne, web pistol roughly aimed at Ortruum.

Jeren's aim was erratic, given the circumstances. Servalen dived to the ground and called KB-88 to her side to avoid getting webbed. The large, immobile, grounded Ortruum wasn't so lucky. As the webbing spread across the psi-hound's massive body, it solidified and tightened, pulling the Psykanarium monster back down into the dust.

Servalen scrambled to her feet and ran towards the hatch, calling, 'D'onne! Halt! Do not do this! Mad D'onne!'

The hatch closed as Servalen arrived and the engines roared to life. The scrutinator could do nothing but watch as the ship lifted into the air. A roar of hot wind blasted Servalen back and filled the chaotic battlefield in a thick layer of dust.

D'onne has won... for now, thought Servalen as the dust swirled around her, *but I still have work to do*.

Before the dust settled, Servalen marched across the plains towards the lone standing psi-hound. It would be blinded by the dust as well, but the scrutinator knew exactly where the creature had been – as well as the locations of every enforcer on the field of battle. She walked unerringly to the psychic monstrosity.

When the dust settled, Servalen stood just outside arm's length of the last psi-hound. The swirling dust had clogged its repulsors, grounding it. The monster wasn't going anywhere and Servalen's presence had incapacitated its psychic abilities, which meant all enforcers were in control of their bodies once again.

'Gillians,' called the scrutinator, without a single shred of emotion in her voice. 'Finish this. That is a direct order!'

Servalen picked one of the psi-hound's many eyes and stared daggers into it as the squad's sniper picked off the rest, one by one, with precise shots from her long-las rifle. After the third shot, the creature fell backwards into the dust.

'Right there!' D'onne said. She pointed through the cockpit window at a dark spot at the base of the Abyss where the kilometres-high cliff met the Sump Lake.

'You want me to land at the edge of the sump?' asked the pilot. 'In a field of rockcrete and plasteel rubble? It'll shear the bottom off this transport. Even with two good eyes and both my hands, that's a tough landing.'

To emphasise his point, the Spire pilot raised his black and swollen right hand to point his two unbroken fingers at his cloudy right eye, which had a huge slash running through it from his forehead to his cheek. The eye hadn't swollen shut yet, but behind the cloudy lens, D'onne could see swirls of red completely surrounding the black pupil.

D'onne shrugged. 'I thought you Imperial flyboys were made of tougher stuff,' she said. 'You're lucky Dog didn't rip your arms off or bash your head in. It's been a while since I ordered him *not* to kill someone. Don't make me regret that decision.'

The pilot shrank away from D'onne in his seat as she glared at him, before rallying enough to speak again. 'Look... all I'm saying, lady... is–' he started, his voice weak and wobbly.

'Do I look like a lady to you?' D'onne screamed. She shoved her plasma pistol into the pilot's reddened cheek right below the scar he'd got when Dog scratched his face. 'I'm Mad D'onne. You know that name, right? So shut up and fly before I vaporise your head and take my chances jumping. Won't even be the craziest thing I've done today!'

The terror in the pilot's good eye helped soothe the fever flaring inside D'onne. Pig didn't have any charge left. Of course, the pilot didn't know that. She let his fear fester for a bit as the transport descended towards the sump. The black spot she had pointed at grew into a cavern opening ahead of them.

'If you're done pissing and moaning,' said D'onne, 'manoeuvre us into that cavern and land at the back. I promise the floor is smooth and clear of debris.' Of course, she didn't tell him the other issue with the cavern – the one that ensured no one ever ventured inside for long.

The pilot nodded without saying a word, probably afraid to face D'onne's wrath again. He began flipping switches and adjusting levers. The transport slowed as the engines rotated to keep them aloft.

The mouth of the cavern was barely wide enough to accommodate the transport's swept-back wings. The pilot began sweating as he gripped the yoke with his left hand to guide the nose through the opening while modifying engine thrust and angle using only the forefinger and thumb of his injured right hand.

The transport swerved to the side and tilted at a forty-five-degree angle as it slipped through the hole in the wall. For a moment, it seemed he had performed the complicated manoeuvre perfectly, but as the pilot brought the transport level again, a horrible screech reverberated through the cavern as the left wing scraped against rockcrete.

The cockpit shuddered from the impact, tossing D'onne from the co-pilot seat and dumping her on the floor. Something heavy landed on her. At first she thought a piece of bulkhead or a bank of controls had torn loose and pinned her to the floor, but then she felt fingers close around her neck and a knee press into her injured shoulder. The pilot had found his bravery.

'I wasn't sure I had the time to kill you,' quipped D'onne in an attempt to mask the pain that shot through her shoulder as the pilot pressed his advantage. She could barely see him above her through the powdered strands of wig hair and the blur of pain. 'But I'm starting to change my mind!'

'You're not giving the orders any more, crazy lady!' spat the pilot, emphasising the last word, probably to get under D'onne's skin. He then pressed his knee further into her shoulder and wrenched the plasma pistol from her weakening grasp with his injured hand.

'You don't want to do that,' D'onne said as she saw the barrel of Pig inches from her face.

'Your bounty is the same dead or alive,' said the pilot. 'And there's nothing critical under this floor.'

'And no charge in that weapon,' replied D'onne.

The click of the trigger was audible. The silence that followed was deafening… for about two seconds before D'onne slammed her head forward to smash the pilot in the face, flattening his nose across his cheeks. Blood gushed across D'onne's face as the pilot toppled to the floor beside her, grasping his bloody face in his good hand as he curled up into the foetal position.

D'onne stood, drawing Countless from its scabbard. 'My chainsword, on the other hand, has plenty of power.' She keyed it to life to prove her point. 'By the way,' she asked, suddenly curious, 'who's flying this bucket?'

'Servitor,' hissed the pilot as he groaned and rolled on the floor.

'Huh,' replied D'onne. 'Nice trick. I mean it. That whole manoeuvre took some balls. You should be proud of yourself.

You almost pulled it off. Now get your arse back in that seat and get us on the ground.'

'What do we do about that... thing?' Vaundon asked, pointing at the webbed form of Ortruum 8-8.

'Leave him to the scavengers,' replied Servalen.

The scrutinator had been directing the post-battle clean-up effort from beside the trapped psi-hound to keep his psychic abilities nullified.

They'd have to knock him out before they left the area, but she couldn't bring herself to kill him herself – Ortruum was feted as one of the greatest examples the Psykanarium had ever produced. The number of bounties he'd brought in was astronomical. He could be a valuable tool in the enforcement of Helmawr's Peace. If her superiors found that she'd actively killed him...

'He's not going anywhere,' she added. 'The Psykanarium will send handlers to recover him as soon as they realise he's not responding. If we're lucky, he's going to be stuck here for a while. Maybe some muties'll find him and try to see if he's edible.'

Vaundon smiled and chuckled, but the unease behind her eyes was evident. Fear at the sight of the monster they had left alive, certainly, but the medic and field-promoted sergeant had that haunted look everyone got around Servalen, especially those who had to deal with her on a somewhat equal footing. Yet another reason Servalen had been directing things from the side.

'And if we're not lucky?' asked Vaundon, the smile still plastered on her face.

'Then we'll be coming back here to purge a mutie cult worshipping some blubber god.'

They both laughed, and it almost felt like two women sharing a joke, but Servalen knew it wouldn't last. *It was what it was*, thought Servalen. For now, they needed to survive the next twenty-four hours and there was a lot of work to be done to ensure that.

'Are we all set?' asked Servalen, switching the conversation back to business to keep both women's minds off the uncomfortable psychic elephant in the room.

'With the cyber-mastiff's help, we were able to move and dump the remains of the dead psi-hounds in the three closest trenches,' said Vaundon. 'At least one of those seems to have been breached by an underground tunnel, so it shouldn't take long for scavengers to notice.'

'And our own fallen?' asked Servalen.

'Mauch and Jankins constructed a makeshift litter to hold the bodies of Sergeant Vessa and the others,' replied Vaundon. 'I think the two of them can manage carrying it back to town.'

Servalen shook her head. 'No. Rig the litter so KB-88 can drag it. I want all enforcers ready for battle at all times until we reach Precinct 1313 inside Dust Falls.'

'Yes, ma'am,' replied Vaundon with a salute. She turned sharply and took a few steps towards the squad.

'Sergeant?' called Servalen. 'One last thing.'

Vaundon hesitated a moment before turning back again. 'Sorry, ma'am. Not used to responding to that rank.'

Servalen stepped as far away from the webbed form of Ortruum 8-8 as she safely could and beckoned Vaundon to come close. 'When we get into town, I need you to coordinate specific matters with the squad,' Servalen said in a low voice only she and the medic could hear.

'Ma'am?'

'All records of the young psyker any member of the squad

has logged must be purged,' replied Servalen. 'In addition, no official report can mention any contact with the boy. The long-term safety of the entire squad depends on everyone forgetting they ever met Jeren Jerenson.'

'I understand, ma'am,' said Vaundon. 'As far as we know, he died at the hands of the Cawdor.'

'Good,' said Servalen. 'Good.'

'What about Mad D'onne?'

'Leave her to me,' replied Servalen. 'I know where she went. I won't risk the lives of any more enforcers on her capture. She is my problem now.'

CHAPTER 31

APPROACHING STORM

Jeren stared at the cockpit door. In a minute or two D'onne would usher the pilot into the main cabin. He'd seen it happen. But Jeren knew most people didn't like to be reminded that he knew things he shouldn't, so he bowed his head and rehearsed a normal reaction.

His psychic powers had increased since he was captured by the Cawdor. A few days ago, he could only locate lost objects. The visions came with piercing pain that felt like needles behind his eyes.

Now it seemed he could follow those lost items through their owners' lives and see their importance to them. He could, in essence, see important intersections in time between a person and their most prized possessions.

When D'onne finally threw open the plasteel cockpit door, the hatch clanged against the wall. The noise reverberated down through the fuselage, startling the ogryn bodyguard awake. Jeren remembered to look startled.

D'onne grabbed the pilot and shoved him through the hatch one-handed, her other hand holding her chainsword, which hummed and spun and jumped in her single-handed grasp. The pilot stumbled a bit and instinctively reached out to steady himself but ended up screaming in pain and falling to the floor after jamming his black-and-blue fingers into the wall.

Jeren could have saved the pilot that pain – as well as the future loss of the fingers – but he needed a calm and jovial Mad D'onne for what came next. If not, things would go badly for Jeren.

Seeing how everything connected in a person's life, like how the pain the pilot endured made D'onne happy, was dizzying and almost intoxicating. If not for the splitting headaches, Jeren could see becoming addicted to this power. He almost welcomed the headaches as a reminder to temper himself.

Through that haze, Jeren watched as D'onne grabbed the pilot again and half pushed, half dragged him to one of the seats in the main cabin. 'Strap yourself in,' she said. 'I may need you later, so don't try anything that will make Dog kill you.'

D'onne looked at the ogryn bodyguard, who somehow had fallen back to sleep, his bulk spread across two seats. Jeren might have wondered how the ogryn could rest in such a precarious position, but he'd seen enough of the intersections between Dog and D'onne to know that sleep was a blessing the ogryn could never pass up. It did, however, lead to other moments.

The mighty kick D'onne inflicted on her bodyguard's inner thigh would have felled a normal man for many long and painful minutes. The ogryn grunted awake, a sheepish and apologetic look on his face as he stared at his master with open, loyal eyes.

'Watch the pilot, Dog,' she stated, pointing at the injured man trying in vain to snap the buckles of his harness around his chest with one hand. 'He's a tricky one who could outwit you in his sleep,' she continued, 'so I will make this simple: if he gets out of that chair, sit on him!'

The ogryn nodded his head vigorously, his mouth open and slack like an actual dog's when trying to please its master. Satisfied, D'onne turned to Jeren.

'You and I are going to have that talk now,' she said. 'Come on. We're going outside. This information is for my ears only.'

A day ago, Jeren wouldn't have thought twice about giving Mad D'onne the information she sought. Even though he was certain she would kill him as soon as she got what she wanted. At the time, he longed for that release from the power that had consumed his life, and it seemed the most expedient path to that end.

Today, he had doubts. He had seen intersections between D'onne and the item she had sought since leaving the Spire that truly frightened him. Jeren almost longed for the blissful ignorance of yesterday, before the surges of adrenaline of the past day had made him more receptive to the deviations inherent in the warp.

Still, he unstrapped and followed D'onne to the hatch. He trusted people to make the right decisions. It was, after all, their life to live, not his. Yes, there were bad people; most humans had the capacity for evil locked away inside them, but they also could choose to do something good. Even with all the chaos D'onne had created and could create in the future, it had to be her choice, not Jeren's.

Yet it still made sense for Jeren to do what he could to help keep D'onne centred as she navigated the next few decisions in a life that had been a nexus of important, far-reaching intersections.

These next few hours would be critical to the safety of everyone in the hive.

Proctor Bauhein felt the scrutinator's presence before Servalen knocked on his office door. No, that wasn't quite right. He felt the lack of Servalen's presence on the opposite side of the door. It felt like, at that moment, nothing existed beyond his office door, as if a void had opened in the universe and sucked everything outside the walls out of existence.

That was how it felt to be in the presence of Scrutinator Servalen, like you were an island floating in an endless void sea. In that moment, nothing you believed and nobody you ever knew currently existed, had ever existed, or would ever exist again. You were lost, standing at the edge of eternity. To call contact with Servalen unpleasant was like saying that the death of the universe was a bad day.

After what seemed like an eternity, Servalen knocked on Bauhein's door. The proctor of Precinct 1313 reached under the top of his desk and pressed a switch, releasing two large plasteel clamps and sliding three long bars into the wall to unlock the security door.

'Enter,' called the proctor. 'Leave your metal dog outside,' he added after a moment.

Servalen pushed open the heavy door and, after wagging her finger at a dark shape prowling around the outer office, strode into the room. Immediately, the distress Bauhein had been feeling intensified, heightened by the stench coming from the antechamber.

'Close it, please,' Bauhein uttered as he covered his mouth

and nose to block out the metallic odour wafting through the door.

Once the door had closed, the proctor pressed the switch again to re-engage the locks. The plasteel bars ground out of their recesses in the wall and the thick door, which had several large dents and a definite bow to its open edge, shuddered from the security measures clanging into place despite being bent after recent events.

'What in the Spire happened out there,' Servalen asked, 'and to your door?' The scrutinator ran her hand along the visible gap between the bowed metal door and the rockcrete wall.

'I think you probably already know the answer to that,' replied Bauhein. 'We were attacked.'

'By a psi-hound,' said Servalen flatly.

'Is that what it was?' asked Bauhein. 'I locked myself in here, but it flung me against the back wall before the door shut.' The proctor wiped sweat beading above the bandage on his head. 'One second later and the cleaning crews would be wiping my guts off the walls, too.'

'Why remain here amidst the carnage?' asked Servalen. She had not moved from the door, a small gesture that Bauhein appreciated. After his close encounter with the psi-hound, he needed a break from the otherworldly.

'The people of Dust Falls, and the Council, need to be reassured that the city remains under palanite protection,' said the proctor. Of course, that was only half the truth. His office was more of a fortress than most Trader vaults, and still that... psi-hound... had nearly made it inside. If the thing hadn't left unexpectedly, Bauhein had no doubt he wouldn't be having this conversation.

'I assume this all has to do with that unholy psyker kid?' asked Bauhein, although he already knew the answer.

Servalen nodded her head. 'Powerful people want that young man,' she said.

'I do know who controls the psi-hounds,' said the proctor. He shivered as the sweat on his brow grew cold and clammy. 'So, you brought death to my door. Thank you. There's no stopping the Spire once the nobles set their sights on something of value in the underhive. This town will be destroyed, and over what? Some kid?'

'That won't happen,' said Servalen.

Despite his cold sweat and the deafening sound of blood pumping through his ears, Proctor Bauhein could still read Servalen. He had watched her rise through the ranks before becoming proctor and probably knew the scrutinator better than any other enforcer. Servalen was being as sincere as she could be. She at least believed what she was saying.

'We can still control this,' continued Servalen. 'The psi-hounds won't be making any reports, and after all the carnage they wrought you can bet the Spire will wash their hands of this mess.'

'So, we pretend it never happened?' asked the proctor. 'I write off the death of my assistant and six Precinct 1313 enforcers and go back to business as usual?'

Servalen nodded. 'Just like they do in the Spire.'

'Wouldn't it be easier to give the old man what he wants? Why go to all this trouble for one psychic kid?'

'Do you want to give Helmawr the ability to look inside your head?' asked Servalen. 'Are you sure he would like what he found there?'

Servalen took several steps forward and leaned over Bauhein's desk to make her point. It took all of the proctor's will not to push his chair back against the wall.

'They don't just want this kid,' continued Servalen. 'They

want all memory of him removed – human and electronic – so he no longer exists.'

She paced back to the door and ran her hands along the dents before turning to face Bauhein again. 'So, that's my plan,' she said. 'Wipe all data pertaining to the psyker from all records and make sure everyone who ever knew about him knows it is in their best interests to forget all about him. This psyker needs to have never existed.'

'I suppose you'll take care of that point,' surmised Bauhein. 'What about Mad D'onne, though? She's not known for forgetting – or forgiving – the transgressions of the Spire.'

'That is the other reason I came to see you,' replied Servalen.

Bauhein sighed. 'What do you need?'

'I have a small window to deal with Mad D'onne,' said Servalen, 'and I don't know how long my inside... man... can stall her. I need transportation. Now.'

D'onne sheathed Countless and opened the hatch. She stepped to the side to let Jeren go first. They'd been through a lot over the past twenty-four hours, but she still didn't trust the kid. Not completely. He'd cosied up to the pariah pretty quickly, which was weird. She'd heard the two of them whispering right before the psi-hound ambush.

No one could stand being so close to a full-blown null that long without turning to jelly. Your insides felt wrong near them, like all of your organs had been turned into a puddle of half-digested corpse-starch. D'onne could tolerate the presence of a pariah for a while. She felt empty inside all the time. But even she had her limits. If she never saw that null witch again, she'd be fine with that.

The kid was special, though, there was no denying it. He seemed almost at home next to Servalen. Well, now it was time for him to be special for her. She'd earned that much for saving everyone's ass multiple times.

'What the sump is taking you so long?' D'onne asked in exasperation. She turned to look at the kid, wondering how long she'd been standing there waiting for him. Somehow, he'd got the entire harness tied in knots and was desperately fumbling with the latches, trying to free himself. He shrugged and gave her a 'please don't hurt me, I'm harmless' look.

'How can so much power be contained in such a ridiculous person?' she asked. The kid, true to form, opened his mouth to answer her rhetorical question, but she waved him off.

'Don't talk,' D'onne said as she strode to his seat. 'And don't move!'

Mad D'onne drew Countless from its sheath, activated the chainsword, and raised it over her head all in one smooth motion. Jeren closed his eyes and scrunched his face as D'onne revved the blade. She then reached forward with her free hand and jabbed two fingers into the main release button above the kid's head.

D'onne's roaring laughter filled the cabin alongside the whirring of the chainsword. Jeren opened his eyes and his mouth went slack when he saw the harness falling away from his body.

'You should have seen your face, kid,' D'onne said, still laughing. 'Priceless. Now, let's go, no more dawdling.'

With that, D'onne re-sheathed her sword and stepped through the hatch, jumping down from the transport onto the sloped surface of the cavern, which was as smooth as glass and black as night. She scanned the shadowy cavern using her cybernetic eye to make sure nothing moved in the shadows.

Not that it was likely. No creature used this cavern as a lair;

at least none that lived long enough to become a problem. That's what made it a perfect place for impromptu clandestine meetings.

Assured they were alone, D'onne turned back to the transport. The kid was standing in the hatchway, apparently uncertain how to cross the metre-high distance between transport and ground.

'Weren't there stairs here before?' he asked.

D'onne answered with an angry sigh. 'Jump down,' she said.

'Sorry,' he said. 'Sorry.'

Jeren's face contorted. It started sheepish, with a slight smirk and forward tilt of his chin. Typical disarming stuff used by kids to stay alive after destroying some important bauble in their parents' house. D'onne had used it all the time growing up.

But, for a moment after the sheepish look disappeared – and for a split second before his normal, semi-blank, 'uneducated kid from a backwater town' look returned – something else crossed the kid's face. His eyes softened and drooped a fraction. His eyebrows furrowed and went slightly askew, and his lips stretched to a thin, slightly curled-down line.

The look happened so fast it might have been D'onne's imagination. But it wasn't. She'd seen it, and she knew it – only too well. Before she left the Spire, D'onne Ulanti had learned the art of body language. It was critical to political survival up there. After leaving her noble life behind, Mad D'onne had perfected the art; it was critical to survival in the underhive.

That look was deep sorrow. D'onne knew that. Sure, there was a lot of sorrow in the underhive, and there was more of it in the Spire than most underhivers realised – or that most Spireborn were willing to admit. But true, deep sorrow, the type that eats away at your heart over years, only comes from love and death.

D'onne had felt it before, and now Jeren was feeling it. Perhaps deeper and stronger than D'onne had experienced.

The mad noble grimaced, and refocused. There was no time for maudlin thoughts. It didn't matter. Nothing mattered except finding the location of the treasure she sought.

'Time for that talk, kid,' she said. D'onne grabbed Jeren by the elbow and pulled him out of the transport. He stumbled when his feet hit the black, glassy ground, but D'onne held him up with her iron grip.

'Over here,' she said, leading him to the back wall of the cavern. 'This is between us. No one else ever needs to know, okay?'

Jeren nodded his head, the sheepish look plastered on his face again.

'I'm not going to kill you!' D'onne practically yelled at him. 'Unless you tell anyone else what you reveal to me here. If you do, I will hunt you down.'

Jeren gulped, the sheepish grin wiped from his face by the threat. 'I understand,' he said.

D'onne released his elbow. 'I trust that you do,' she said.

'My only fear, D'onne Astride Ge'Sylvanus of House Ulanti,' he said, his voice low and mournful, 'is that what you seek could destroy you. It might be best if it stayed buried. Are you certain you want to know?'

D'onne had never been more certain about anything in her life. Everything she had done after leaving the Spire had built to this day. Every decision, every battle, every death-defying risk she had ever taken had been to get to this point. This was her revenge, her redemption. This was her plan, the only plan that mattered.

'I am certain,' she said. 'Tell me what I want to know.'
'What is it you want to know, D'onne?' asked Servalen.

CHAPTER 32

ENEMY MINE

Servalen had burned into the cavern a few moments earlier on a personal transport she'd borrowed from Precinct 1313.

'How the scav did you find me?' yelled D'onne. She glared at Jeren. 'Did this little snitch rat me out?' The hunter grabbed the young psyker and held her chainsword across his neck. 'I knew I shouldn't trust you.'

'No! No, no, no!' pleaded Jeren. 'I didn't say a word.'

'That's good advice,' called Servalen. 'Don't say a word to *her* either! She's the one who can't be trusted.'

KB-88, who had howled during the entire flight down the Abyss from Dust Falls, leant forward, ready to rush D'onne down, but Servalen held up a hand. She wanted to maintain some distance between her and D'onne, but also knew this cavern and needed to keep her exit strategy from becoming compromised.

Servalen told KB-88 to heel and placed her hand as casually

as possible on her holster. 'Look,' she started. 'Let the kid go and we can talk. He didn't tell me anything.'

D'onne tightened her grip on Jeren's arm and pulled him close, her chainsword never wavering at his neck. 'Then how did you find me? No one comes here.'

'I know that,' Servalen replied. She tried to smile. 'But it was a fairly easy deduction considering the direction you took us after the Goliath battle.'

D'onne tightened her hold on Jeren and triggered the chain, which began spinning around, the blades a few centimetres from the young psyker's neck.

It seemed D'onne didn't believe her.

'Honestly, D'onne, I can find you any time I want,' continued Servalen. 'I've been a step ahead of you since Sludge Town. You're not that hard to predict any more. Wherever you take the kid, I will follow.'

Servalen tried to inch closer to D'onne so the uneasiness of her null presence would help convince the mad woman, but as soon as she moved, D'onne revved the chainsword. Servalen backed up a step.

'I offer a compromise,' Servalen started again, trying a different tack. 'Give Jeren to me and walk away. No tricks. No argument. No chasing you with an enforcer squad. I didn't bring them with me.'

As soon as Servalen said it, she knew she'd made a mistake. D'onne didn't answer. Instead she pushed Jeren to the side and pointed her chainsword at Servalen.

'Just you and your dog, huh? I'll take those odds,' D'onne said as she began striding forward in a battle-ready stance.

'Wait!' demanded Servalen. She raised her hands in front of her to show she didn't want to fight. D'onne stopped moving forward but kept her chainsword at the ready.

'I know the information you want from Jeren is dangerous. It's the only reason Helmawr would send psi-hounds down here,' Servalen continued. 'He doesn't need another psyker. He's afraid – of you, of Jeren, of what the Mad Ulanti noble could do with the information locked in that kid's brain.'

'I just want to bury my sister!' yelled D'onne. 'And not you, your enforcers, Helmawr, or the goddamn Emperor will stop me.'

Servalen was taken aback by the revelation. D'onne seemed... sincere.

'Your sister's body?' asked Servalen, hoping to get a second read on the truthfulness of D'onne's statement. 'You want Jeren to divulge the location of your sister's body? That's all?'

D'onne switched off her chainsword and let the tip drop to the ground next to her. A look of true emotion crossed her face as she worked to form the words. 'My youngest sister,' she said. 'There were a lot of us. All spares. She died a long time ago, before I came downhive. I have nothing of hers.'

'Your sister,' said Servalen again, not believing what she was hearing, but D'onne's sorrow seemed genuine and Servalen was certain the mad woman believed that what she was saying was the truth. Servalen turned to Jeren, who didn't want to look her in the eyes.

'Is that true, Jeren?' she asked, the force of her question making the boy raise his head and lock eyes with her.

Jeren didn't speak, though. Instead he nodded his head.

'All D'onne wants to know is the location of her dead sister?' Servalen asked again. She watched the kid fidget with his hands and look back and forth between her and D'onne. 'Answer the question, Jeren.'

He nodded again, but then spoke a moment later. 'I know

where to find her dead sister's body,' he said. 'D'onne wants me to give her the location.'

D'onne might be able to lie to Servalen without her detecting it, but not the psyker. As far as Servalen could tell, what Jeren had said was true, but the scrutinator was certain neither of them was telling the entire truth. None of that mattered, however. None of it changed the bigger problem.

'It doesn't matter what you're after, though, does it?' she said. 'Helmawr wants what's inside Jeren's head, and he wants everyone who knows about the psyker dead. That's why we need to erase him from the hive's memory.'

'You'll kill him over my corpse!' yelled D'onne. 'Dog! Get your sorry ass out here. We've got company.'

Servalen sighed. That's not what she meant, but it was no use arguing with the mad woman once the blood-rage flared behind her eyes. Seeing D'onne's ogryn bodyguard emerge from the transport, Servalen called to her own pet. 'Eighty-eight!' she commanded. 'Attack!'

The cyber-mastiff loped off towards the giant, lumbering bodyguard as D'onne bore down on Servalen, swinging her massive chainsword in crossing arcs in front of her corseted chest as her ridiculous powdered wig bounced on top of her head.

Servalen backed away quickly, using her long legs to stay out of the reach of D'onne's deadly sword. She continued trying to reason with D'onne as she backpedalled. 'I don't want to kill Jeren,' she said, but the mad woman had stopped listening.

Jeren ran after D'onne, waving his arms. 'Please!' he wailed. 'Don't do this. It doesn't have to end this way!'

'Listen to him,' Servalen called out. She then turned and ran as D'onne charged. She sprinted along the curved cavern wall, which took her towards the rising tide of the sump. They didn't have long before it cut off the exit.

To Servalen's right, she saw KB-88 and the ogryn come together. D'onne's pet swung his meaty hands in long arcs towards the cyber-mastiff. Everywhere his fists hit, he cracked the glassy surface, sending huge chunks of rockcrete spraying into the air.

But KB-88 was too fast. The ogryn's metal-crunching punches landed too late. The mastiff was already inside the ogryn's reach, snapping and clawing at the bodyguard's legs. It was a standoff. KB-88's sharpened claws and fangs couldn't puncture the metal plates that served as the brute's armour.

The scrutinator glanced at D'onne. She had altered course to cut Servalen off. Jeren had fallen behind and finally stopped and doubled over, breathing hard from running and screaming.

Servalen turned to go behind the transport, hoping to use it as a barrier between her and the blood-crazed mad woman. The pilot appeared at the hatch and lowered the boarding ladder. He glanced at all the confusion and apparently decided this was his best chance to escape. He leapt to the ground and sprinted towards the cavern entrance, which was slowly being enveloped by the sump.

'Damnit,' muttered Servalen as she turned and chased after the pilot.

D'onne was tiring of this infuriating battle already. Servalen's long legs gave her a distinct advantage in a chase, but D'onne's Pig had no charge, leaving her the chainsword as her only viable weapon. She could throw it. She'd done it before, but the sump was rising quickly and even D'onne wasn't crazy enough to chance tossing her only weapon into a toxic lake. Waiting for the sump to narrow Servalen's choices wasn't an option either because it would swamp the transport and strand D'onne in a rapidly filling cavern.

Seeing the battle raging by the transport gave D'onne another idea, though. Dog, bleeding from a dozen gashes on bare patches of his calves and thighs, had stopped trying to pound the mastiff into the ground and begun kicking at the metal beast. The ogryn was big and strong, but dumb as a lump of rockcrete and couldn't handle the mastiff's speed and reflexes.

D'onne could change that, though, and turning the tables on that fight would give her an advantage against Servalen, who seemed to care about her metal mutt. D'onne turned and headed towards the dog fight, revving her chainsword as she approached. When she glanced back to see if she had got the scrutinator's attention, though, she saw Servalen chasing the imperial pilot.

Servalen never called out to the man, who was so intent on making it through the narrowing cavern entrance that he hadn't noticed the enforcer closing in behind him. A few strides later, at point-blank range, Servalen raised her auto-pistol and fired into the back of the pilot's head.

The man's forehead burst open in a spray of blood and brains as the shot exploded out of the front of his skull. His momentum sent him sprawling forward onto the glassy rockcrete floor where he bounced and slid towards the rising sump. Servalen stopped and fired two more shots into the pilot's back between the shoulder blades.

D'onne stopped dead in her tracks. 'What the sump, Servalen?' she called.

The hunter had not expected such a cold-blooded execution from the scrutinator. Sure, she was a pariah, but D'onne didn't put much stock in 'souls' anyway. People with souls did evil deeds all the time. Look at her, her father – or Lord Helmawr, for that matter.

'Why did he have to die?' she asked as Servalen turned away from the body. 'If you think that strands me here, think again. I'll fly your transport out of here after I kill you.'

Servalen began walking slowly, purposefully, towards D'onne. 'He had to die,' she said as she holstered her weapon. 'Don't you see that? If Helmawr ever finds out we talked to Jeren, he will stop at nothing to eliminate us.'

'I've been on the run my entire life,' D'onne replied. 'What do I care who's doing the chasing?'

Next to D'onne, the dog fight had come to a standstill. The two pets were locked together, with the ogryn lying on his back holding KB-88 in a bear hug as the mastiff dug its claws into the bodyguard's chest and stomach. Both pets stopped attacking during their masters' conversation, but didn't release the other. They simply cocked their heads to the side as they waited for their next orders.

'What about Jeren?' asked Servalen, still walking forward, a point not lost on D'onne. 'He won't survive Helmawr's wrath or, worse, he'll end up in the Psykanarium.'

D'onne glanced at the kid, who stood to the side about halfway between the two women. His eyes had become unfocused and he'd begun whimpering and mumbling again, like he had during the lift trips up the Abyss.

'It's coming,' he mumbled. 'No time.'

'His life is a hellscape no matter what we do,' said D'onne. She took a step to her side. 'Maybe you're right. Killing him may actually be a mercy.'

'I never said that!' said Servalen through clenched teeth. 'What is wrong with you? Stop letting your fake madness dictate your real-life action!'

Time – and the hive itself – seemed to come to a halt around the two women as they stood motionless in the middle of the cavern, faced off, as the sump rose higher and higher into the cavern.

'Watch out! It's here!' Jeren screamed, breaking the tension of the moment before crumpling to the ground.

Two things occurred simultaneously to D'onne: first, a foul, heavy odour had invaded the cavern, even overtaking the stench of the sump. Second, she could no longer move a muscle.

CHAPTER 33

PARALYSIS

Servalen felt the presence, the ripple in the fabric of the warp, at the same instant that Jeren screamed. She turned around to see Ortruum 8-8 glide over the sump-covered cavern opening followed by more than a dozen armed muties that leapt, several at a time, across the widening pool of foetid, caustic liquid.

Ortruum was covered in the tattered remains of the gooey webbing, but his mechanical limbs and head moved freely. The muties' hands and weapons were also covered in shreds of webbing, but from the scowls on their faces, it didn't seem it would impede their attacks.

The last two muties didn't make the jump, and struck the sump. Their screams of pain sounded like banshee screeches and echoed around the chamber, ending abruptly as the muties fell backwards into the rising sump, which bubbled and frothed as it dissolved their scrawny, scar-ridden bodies.

The air in the cavern filled with the acrid smell of acid-baked flesh. The rest of the muties turned to watch the spectacle, hooting and hollering and jumping around as the two bodies liquified. At a command from Ortruum 8-8, however, they stopped, turned and fanned out in front of the psi-hound.

Servalen needed to get close to the psi-hound to impede his psychic abilities, but the muties, which had begun advancing towards her, made that impossible. She needed help.

'Dog!' called Servalen, doing her best to imitate the disdain in D'onne's voice when she ordered her bodyguard around, 'Protect D'onne. Release KB-88 and attack!'

Servalen didn't wait to see if the order got through the thick skull of the ogryn. She drew and fired at the nearest mutie, clipping its scabby head and removing an ear. Blood soaked its face and neck, but the shot didn't slow the mutie down.

Giving up on reaching Ortruum for the moment, Servalen retreated towards Jeren as she continued firing. If Dog and KB-88 didn't enter the battle, she would have to rouse the kid and make a run for the transport. She hit the bleeding mutie again, taking it down with a shot to its chest. That left ten more.

'Stand down. Give psyker. Survive beyond today,' said Ortruum as he moved further into the cavern behind his wall of muties. The psi-hound's voice was raspy and hoarse, like fingernails dragged across rockcrete, and lacked a bit of its former power.

'We'll die first!' sniped Servalen, knowing full well that the psi-hound wouldn't spare anyone once he got what he'd come for. Fight or not, they would all die here if Ortruum won. She straddled Jeren's foetal body and fired again, her autopistol shot ripping a chunk of flesh from the shoulder of another mutie.

The rest of the muties were closing on D'onne, who hadn't

moved since Jeren had screamed. Dog, still lying on his back and holding onto the mastiff, seemed confused about what was going on. The cyber-mastiff stared at the incoming muties and howled its dismay at being unable to attack and help its master.

'As you wish!' Ortruum rasped.

He raised one mechanical hand and gestured towards Dog and KB-88. For a moment, the cyber-mastiff lifted into the air out of the ogryn's grasp, but KB-88 dug its claws in deeper, making the bodyguard yelp. Dog then flung out a hand to grab the mastiff around its metal neck.

Without releasing its grip on KB-88, the ogryn stood and roared. The bodyguard pulled KB-88 away from its body, ripping the mastiff's bloody claws from its chest, and threw it towards the oncoming army of muties.

KB-88 rotated its body and legs around in the air to land on its feet in the middle of the scarred and filthy muties. It leapt at the first enemy that advanced, snapping its jaws around the mutie's neck and ripping it out. Blood sprayed across the mastiff's snout as it spat scabby skin onto the floor of the cavern and turned to find more prey.

Before Ortruum could react, Dog entered the fray as well. The ogryn barrelled into the muties and soon had four of them attacking its legs and torso with sharpened pieces of metal and rusty knives. Dog grabbed two muties by their necks in his meaty hands and yanked them off him.

With two mighty heaves, the ogryn launched the muties out past the transport into the rising sump. The two splashes were followed by a froth of churning sump acid that quickly turned the bodies into blood and spinning bones.

Servalen felt a twinge of hope after seeing Dog and KB-88 make quick work of three of Ortruum's muties, and two more shots from her autopistol increased the death count by one more.

Then Ortruum retaliated. Servalen felt the ogryn was too big of a target for the psi-hound's telekinetic push, but he pointed a mechanical arm at the ogryn and sent the bodyguard flying up and over the transport.

Servalen kept firing at the muties left behind after Dog's unexpected exit. Only six remained between her and Ortruum 8-8, but they had another problem: the rising sump had reached the landing gear of the transport. It was an Imperial craft made to withstand harsh conditions, but the struts would corrode eventually. Worse, though, the corrosive tide would soon rise above the lip of the hatch and swamp the cabin. They were running out of time.

Mad D'onne had become a prisoner, trapped inside her own body. She could see the battle raging around her but couldn't move a muscle to help. She ordered her legs and arms to move, but they refused to obey. The utter feeling of helplessness infuriated her. She screamed inside her head, but the only sound that escaped her lips was a whimper.

She began to spiral into the darkness that always waited for her down within the shadowy recesses of her mind. It was a creature that roamed her subconscious, looking for any crack through which it could surface and wreak horror upon her life. It had been a constant companion to her all these years in the underhive, howling and snapping at her whenever she was made to feel powerless.

When it surfaced, D'onne reverted to that timid little girl who hid while her older sisters played their cruel tricks and soul-crushing mind games on the younger ones. D'onne had been too small, too weak to stand against their bullying, and that helplessness ate away at her; made her feel small, worthless, hopeless.

When D'onne had left the Spire, she had vowed she would never again be made to feel like that lost little girl. She lived her life as if every action might be her last, because in the underhive it truly might be. Anytime she was threatened by the possibility of imprisonment, Mad D'onne took chances that no sane person would consider, because insanity and death were preferable to capture.

And it all stemmed from that one fateful night when her sisters had pushed her little sister off a balcony as part of a game while D'onne had watched from behind a potted plant. The game had been played a thousand times before and the forcefield should have caught her, but it didn't. A lightning storm outside had made it glitch.

Seeing her faithful ogryn companion flung over the transport towards the certain death of the sump brought it all back to D'onne in a mad rush, that fateful night when her sister had plummeted towards the Ash Wastes.

That rage returned to Mad D'onne now, banishing the creature that tormented her into the dark shadows of its mind-cage. Adrenaline surged through D'onne's muscles, breaking the chains of the psi-hound's mental hold on her body.

D'onne was free.

'Die, you psychic mongrel,' D'onne cried as she rushed towards Ortruum 8-8.

She swung Countless in a vicious arc that sliced through one of the muties attacking the cyber-mastiff. Before the chainsword bit into the glassy rockcrete floor, D'onne flicked her wrists to change the angle of the blade and reared back on the pommel to swing the blade into another of Ortruum's muties.

Countless exploded through the spine of D'onne's second victim sending bone shards flying into the air along with a gout of blood and viscera. Beside her, she saw a third mutie fall to the floor, riddled with autopistol shots, while KB-88 turned its full attention to the last mutie attacking it.

Ortruum's wall of filth had been nearly obliterated, but before D'onne could rush forward to attack the psi-hound, his rolls of fat jiggled as he raised his mechanical arm towards D'onne and the last two muties charged her – one holding a relatively pristine fighting knife that D'onne recognised.

D'onne cut the first down as it charged, slicing its filthy, web-covered head clean in half and leaving a small section of its brain to fall out of the back half as it crumpled to the floor. The other mutie, the leader that D'onne had left alive in the utility tunnel, made it through D'onne's blade barrier, and swung the large knife that D'onne had given her, which dug into her leather corset and drew blood. A moment later, D'onne felt the return of the now familiar numbness of Ortruum's mind control.

D'onne couldn't move, couldn't defend herself from the filthy mutie leader she should have killed when she had a chance. She was helpless again. Her scream was cut off as her muscles seized up and locked her inside her own body, again.

For one brief, incredible moment, Servalen thought they might actually win this battle before the sump swallowed them all. Even as Ortruum 8-8 locked down D'onne's mind again, the scrutinator thought they had a chance if she could get to the psi-hound before the mutie cut the helpless D'onne in half. The scrutinator moved forward, trying to get an angle to shoot without firing through D'onne.

Next to that battle, KB-88 leapt up and slammed its forelegs into the chest of the last mutie attacking it, driving the barely humanoid creature over backwards. As it fell, KB-88 landed on the filthy creature's chest, driving its head into the glassy floor. From its perch, KB-88 chomped down on the mutie's neck and ripped out skin, muscle and a chunk of spine with its vice-like plasteel jaws.

Servalen took a step towards the psi-hound, hoping to break his mental lock over D'onne, but before she could close the distance, Ortruum pointed his mechanical arm at KB-88 and sent Servalen's cyber-mastiff flying over the transport towards the sump in a nearly identical arc to D'onne's Dog.

'You'll pay for that, monster!' said Servalen through clenched teeth as she charged.

'I doubt that,' replied Ortruum calmly. The psi-hound fired his repulsors to back away from Servalen as the final mutie raised its fighting knife high over her head to bring it down through D'onne's powdered wig.

Time was running out. The sump had swamped the bottom rung of the transport ladder. D'onne had moments left before her skull was cut in half, and Servalen could either sprint towards Ortruum or move around D'onne to get a clear shot at the mutie. She couldn't do both.

In desperation, Servalen decided to try something reckless – a dangerous and crazy move worthy of, and inspired by, Mad D'onne.

Servalen raced towards Ortruum, whose repulsors couldn't outdistance her at full speed. As the scrutinator sprinted across the blood-slickened glassy floor of the cavern, she twisted her body, raised her autopistol and fired directly at the top of D'onne's head.

The shot flew through the mad woman's ridiculously tall powdered wig and slammed into the mutie's fighting knife as it slashed down towards D'onne's skull. With a loud clang that echoed through the chamber, the knife went flying from the mutie's hands. It clattered across the smooth rockcrete floor and slipped into the sump.

As the sump ate the mutie's only weapon, Servalen turned her weapon on Ortruum and unloaded a shot into his pink gut. She continued firing as she ran at the psi-hound, who was frantically trying to turn and increase his repulsor power to escape the oncoming pariah.

'You're too late!' said Servalen. Behind her, the scrutinator heard the revving whine of D'onne's chainsword followed by a howling shriek. She closed the distance between her and Ortruum, ensuring the psi-hound wouldn't be able use his psychic powers on D'onne again.

Unfortunately, she misjudged Ortruum's objective. His retreat had been a feint.

'You will be the last one,' said the psi-hound as he turned and grabbed Servalen by the neck with one mechanical hand. His plasteel fingers clamped down on her throat with a vice-like grip, threatening to crush her larynx.

With visions of Sergeant Vessa being ripped in two, Servalen flailed her legs as Ortruum's other mechanical arm waved around trying to get a grip on her. It was only a matter of time, though, before he crushed her throat or Servalen suffocated.

As Servalen began blacking out, her legs getting heavier and heavier, Ortruum turned and floated towards the unconscious Jeren. 'No,' rasped Servalen as she fired round after round into the psi-hound's prodigious gut, but it didn't slow him down.

Before the darkness overtook Servalen, a familiar sound invaded her cloudy mind – a tinny, buzzing sound that grew louder and louder as if a swarm of giant insects was approaching. In a flash so fast Servalen was unsure it had even happened, D'onne's whirring chainsword spun past the scrutinator's face and sliced through the psi-hound's mechanical arm.

Servalen dropped to the ground, gasping, as the psi-hound flew over her. She raised her autopistol one last time, aimed and fired. The shot flew straight and true, right up Ortruum's repulsor tube, where it blew out the rotund psi-hound's engine. The psychic monstrosity fell to the ground in a fleshy, flabby heap.

Servalen pulled the dead mechanical arm off her neck and stood up. 'Get Jeren on the transport,' she called over her shoulder. 'Quickly.'

D'onne didn't hesitate, despite being ordered around by an enforcer. Servalen turned to watch her sprint to the side of the young psyker, grabbing her chainsword along the way, and hoist him over her shoulder before running back to the transport where she vaulted on board.

'Get out of sight,' Servalen called.

As soon as D'onne had hauled Jeren into the cabin, Servalen turned and raced towards the transport. The sump had cleared the second step. It would be close. From several yards away, Servalen dived for the hatch. She landed inside, with her feet dangling over the edge. As she began to slip back towards the sump, two sets of hands grabbed her wrists and pulled her inside.

'Can you fly this bucket of bolts?' asked D'onne after slamming the hatch shut and locking it down.

'Well enough,' replied Servalen.

D'onne followed Servalen to the cockpit, where the scrutinator sat and began flipping levers and pushing buttons in what seemed to be a purposeful order. From outside the fuselage, they heard a dull banging sound.

'Sooner would be better!' said D'onne.

'Working on it,' replied Servalen.

The engines roared to life and Servalen yanked a large double lever down, increasing the throttle and lifting them off the ground. As they flew towards the narrowed cavern opening, D'onne feared they would crash into the sides and end up back in the sump.

They cleared the exit with centimetres to spare, but outside the banging continued and seemed to get more persistent. D'onne went to investigate.

'Bring us down!' she yelled towards the cockpit. 'As soon as you can!'

'This terrain will rip the ship apart!' replied Servalen.

'I know!' yelled D'onne. 'Do it anyway! Now!'

'Strap in!'

A few moments later, the transport landed hard on the rocky mound outside the cavern, tossing D'onne about like a rag doll, and then heaved to the side as the landing struts, already weakened from sitting in the sump, snapped, dropping the transport another metre. The fuselage creaked as it fell onto the jagged rockcrete and plasteel below.

Servalen emerged from the cockpit. 'What in the Spire was the emergency?' she asked.

D'onne unsnapped her harness and jumped up to open the hatch. 'We had stowaways!' she replied as she climbed down onto the uneven ground.

A moment later, Servalen joined her and looked up towards the top of the transport where D'onne pointed. Dog scrambled to his feet, gripping the now severely bent tail of the transport.

The big ogryn smiled and held up his other hand, in which he held KB-88.

'Huh!' said Servalen. 'What do you know about that?'

D'onne could tell Servalen was trying to maintain her serious composure, but there was a sparkle in the scrutinator's eyes, and the corners of her lips had curled up into what D'onne assumed passed for a smile.

'So, what do we do now?' D'onne asked.

The two women looked at each other in silence for several long moments. Their lives had followed different paths, but both had found themselves isolated and fighting lonely battles against their separate daemons. Despite what they'd just been through, both knew that they'd take up weapons against one another again.

'I might have an idea,' Jeren said, softly.

EPILOGUE

OF PSYKERS AND SECRETS

Two figures trudged through the Ash Wastes outside Hive Primus. One was dressed in standard if ill-fitting nomad clothing: thick leather breeches, jerkin and gloves, a heavy, woollen cloak covering the head and a rebreather plus hard-soled boots on the feet. A mishmash of metal tape, leather straps and strips of burlap had been tied around the travel-ler's neck, wrists, ankles and waist – anywhere the toxic ash might penetrate the outer layer.

Yet, with all the various ties and tape, the clothes still sagged in some places and pulled too tight in others – espe-cially across the chest – showing even the least observant viewer that these clothes had not originally belonged to this traveller. A closer inspection would have shown bloodstained holes covered by more metal tape, possibly indicating that the original owner had not given up the outfit freely to the current wearer.

None of this was an oddity in the Ash Wastes. The second

figure, however, would have given pause to the most hard-ened nomad and the Waste's most fearsome monsters. Firstly, it was huge. Some might call it a giant. Secondly, it was almost completely naked except for a loincloth and metal plates bolted to its limbs, yet the giant figure seemed to be completely unaffected by the toxins in the air, the driving ash-laden winds or the biting cold.

The giant forged through the storm ahead of the nomad, shielding its companion from the worst of the wind. The two were connected by a tether, which was another odd-ity. Most nomads would never tether themselves together. That was a good way for one person's mistake to kill every-one. Between deep ash pockets that could swallow a man whole to bubbling pools of acid and rivers of sludge that could pull a body beneath the surface in seconds and dis-solve it in minutes, the Ash Wastes had more ways to kill a man than the lord of Hive Primus had to torture prisoners.

If anyone alive inside or outside Hive Primus had been watching this unlikely pair trudge across the Ash Wastes, they might have seen them approach a long, curving ridge carved into the bedrock long ago by a now dried-up river of sludge. The duo followed the course of that dead river into a gorge half-filled with ash.

The two figures stopped at the end of the gorge and, with wind-cracked ridges rising around them, began to dig with their hands through the loose ash. Again, any unlikely observer might have been surprised to see them hit solid rockcrete less than a metre below the otherwise featureless surface, and would have been utterly astounded when the giant opened a large plasteel hatch through which the two figures dropped.

The only creatures to notice any of this were a pair of giant beetles atop the ridge that decided to scuttle down into the gorge and investigate the pair as a possible food source.

Servalen sat at her desk staring at the final report on the case of Mad D'onne's brutal rampage. It was fiction, hung on the barest trappings of truth. It made no mention of the psi-hound team and hung the deaths of Sergeants Nox and Vessa, as well as the majority of two squads of enforcers square on Mad D'onne's neck. The report made no mention of Jeren Jerenson. As far as anyone knew, the last time he'd been seen was entering the Cawdor house in Sludge Town.

D'onne's bounty would triple after this, but there had been no other way. The whole truth would have seen them all dead. In the end, though, while truth had been subverted, the scrutinator believed justice had, ultimately, prevailed. And for her, that was what mattered.

She flipped to the last page of the report and reread her account of the battle in the slowly filling cavern at the edge of the Sump Lake. She worried no one would ever believe she could have driven off Mad D'onne, let alone survive to tell the tale.

With no witnesses alive or willing to refute her version of the story, though, this report would stand as the truth of the matter. Yet, after all they'd been through together, Servalen didn't trust Mad D'onne. She trusted Jeren, though, and this arrangement had been his idea. He had seen a future where the intersections of their paths kept everyone safe and protected from the powers above them.

Servalen had decided not to ask if the powers above would be safe from Mad D'onne. She still didn't believe the crazy noble was only searching for her dead sister. 'People should be able to choose their own path,' Jeren had said to her at the end. She had to hope D'onne's path didn't intersect her own again.

'Vaundon,' she called. The sergeant poked her head through the door. 'I'm heading out to meet with an informant who has intel about that doomsday cult making noise down near Perdition.'

'Naming your town "Perdition" seems like an open invitation to all doomsday cults, if you ask me,' said Vaundon with a smile.

'I'll mention that to whoever named the place,' replied Servalen. 'I'll be out for the rest of the day. The meeting is in some backwater.'

'You need back-up?' asked Vaundon. 'I can have the squad prepped and ready in five.'

Servalen waved the sergeant off. 'No need,' she said. 'I'll take KB-88 with me.'

Once inside the ash-entombed building, Mad D'onne pulled the heavy, rubber rebreather off her face and let it dangle from a long tube that snaked under her leather coat to a filter unit strapped to her side. She took a deep breath, but immediately regretted that decision. The stale air inside the building reeked of death and decay. And yet, it was still preferable to breathing air from her own armpit.

'How the sump do nomads live out here?' she asked. 'Two hours trekking through this crap-land and my sweat smells worse than the sludge pits and the sump combined.'

Dog shrugged in response. Somehow the Ash Wastes had made the ogryn's skin and metal plates shine as if he'd just bathed. D'onne knew her bodyguard was nearly indestructible but being sandblasted by toxic ash couldn't be good for him.

'Make yourself useful,' she said, handing him a light before turning on her own.

D'onne scanned the room they had dropped into. It looked like it might once have been some sort of control centre. Banks of consoles lined the outer walls, which seemed to be made of transparent plasteel.

What had Jeren said? D'onne thought. 'Seek the watchful tower under the river of dust.' *Why did he have to give directions in metaphor?*

'It seems the little freak's info was right,' she said. 'Glad I got him to draw a map, though. That kid sure can be scavving cryptic. Now we need to find a tiny tomb in a crypt of steel, whatever that means.'

In one corner of the room, between two banks of consoles, D'onne spied a staircase that led down into the buried tower. As she strode towards the stairs, though, she heard the scrabbling of feet and the rustling of dust behind her. D'onne turned in time to see the second of two giant beetles drop through the hatch and land on the floor.

They were huge, filling half the room. Their bulbous carapaces fitted through the two-metre opening and, when the beetles stretched out their chitinous limbs, their backs banged into the ceiling, sending more ash cascading into the room.

The beetles scuttled forward, their pincers snapping together with an almost metallic *snikt* as if they were giant plasteel shears. Behind the pincers, their mouths gaped open like giant toothy caves. They roared in unison.

Without a word from D'onne, Dog rushed them. One turned towards the ogryn giant to bring its pincers to bear. That was a mistake. Dog grabbed a pincer in each of his meaty hands and began prying them apart. The beetle's roar turned to a scream as they broke off at their base. Now Dog had weapons.

D'onne debated whether to draw Countless from its scabbard and really enjoy this battle or to use Pig and get on with what had brought her out to this Spire-forsaken place. As she dithered, the second beetle advanced on her. Fun won out in the end and she whipped out her chainsword in time to clang it into the beetle's front legs. It reared and tried to bear her to the ground.

Encumbered by the nomad trappings, D'onne still managed to spin to the side of the giant bug as it came crashing to the floor. After finishing her clumsy pirouette, D'onne flicked on her weapon's spinning blades and swung it in an arc back at the beetle. With the added power of D'onne's spin, Countless' razor-sharp teeth sliced easily through the thick carapace and dug deep into the beetle's thorax. It screamed, and D'onne felt certain this one's scream was much louder than the one Dog was fighting.

After yanking her blade free from the beetle's side with an explosion of chitin and flesh, D'onne climbed onto its back, using the wide gash in its carapace as a step. From atop the beetle, D'onne thrust Countless down towards its head, plunging the spinning blade through its skull and driving the beast's pincers and mouth into the floor.

As D'onne rolled off the dead beetle she glanced at Dog, confident she had finished her bug first. She was mildly disappointed to see the second beetle's pincers protruding from its dead eyes as Dog feasted on the bug's flesh from a hole he'd ripped open in its carapace.

Servalen landed the transport at the back of the cavern, and KB-88 bounded out immediately.

She had been pleasantly surprised to find the transport mostly intact the first time she'd returned to the cavern to meet her informant. The sump hadn't completely filled the space that day, and since she'd already declared the transport lost, Servalen got a new vehicle for her clandestine meetings. It did worry her that perhaps other things had survived the rising tide.

'What do you have for me today?' Servalen asked her informant as he walked out of the shadows to greet her. 'Do we need to worry about this new cult?'

KB-88 padded over to sniff at Jeren. Always the protector, it didn't trust its visual databanks when determining friend or foe. When the cyber-mastiff returned to Servalen's side and sat, it confirmed what Servalen already knew from the tingling sensation inside her head: this was, in fact, Jeren Jerenson. She reached down and scratched between KB-88's metal ears. 'Good dog,' she said.

As Jeren walked closer, the stress in his face drained away. He smiled, although he clenched his stomach in one hand at the same time. Servalen knew Jeren wasn't glad to see her so much as that his constant headaches ceased while they were together. She'd keep him close at all times if she could, but to the world at large Jeren Jerenson was dead. Besides, no headaches also meant no powers. And his psychic abilities made Jeren an incredibly useful informant.

'You don't have to worry about that cult,' Jeren replied. 'They're all talk and bluster. I see no destructive acts intersecting their current futures. They're just a bunch of sad kids who couldn't make it as gang juves and banded together to share in each other's misery.'

'So, pretty difficult to infiltrate then?' asked Servalen, the barb escaping her lips before she thought about it. Perhaps D'onne had some effect on her after all.

Jeren smiled, taking it in stride, as he always did. 'Yeah. It was tough,' he quipped. 'I'm gonna need some combat pay.'

At the mention of payment, Servalen grew concerned. 'Do you need credits?' she asked. 'I can free up some funds.'

'Nah, I'm good,' he replied. 'After you stashed me in that hive scum gang's vacant bolt hole, I located a large stash of credits they'd lost. Once that runs out, I'm sure I can find more. It seems like people are always losing things.'

After the beetle battle, D'onne and Dog made their way down the stairs to the next level of the tower, where they found the remnants of a dead nomad's hideout along with the remains of the dead nomad.

The corpse lay on top of a burlap mattress stuffed with shredded paper, which the nomad must have pulled from the cabinets lining the room. Whatever the room above had controlled in the buried building's heyday, this room stored its records before they had been ripped apart to make batting for a nomad's bed.

D'onne began yanking open drawers and doors on the cabinets, hoping one of them was the 'steel tomb' Jeren had seen in his vision. Some cabinets still contained files the nomad hadn't yet torn up for his bedding, but most were filled with junk.

The dead nomad, it seemed, had been a collector of sorts. In cabinet after cabinet, D'onne found broken cogs, shards of chitin, ash-pitted tools, rusted and ruined weapons, and other junk salvaged from what looked like a lifetime of roaming the Ash Wastes.

Yet, although it was all junk, every piece had been laid carefully in its final resting place. The dust accumulated around the junk showed none of it had moved in years, maybe decades. The entire room was one lonely man's museum of lost and forgotten objects – detritus flung from the Spire into the sea of Ash over centuries.

D'onne's hope flared as she realised what 'treasures' the room held, how this lone nomad must have spent his life. When she opened the second-to-last cabinet, D'onne found it: a latched plasteel footlocker – the tiny tomb!

She pulled the metal box out from the floor of the cabinet where, from the accumulation of dust, it looked like it had lain for decades, and knelt beside it. D'onne's hands trembled as she worked the latch, and she took a deep breath before throwing open the lid. Anything or nothing could be inside she reminded herself, trying to calm her fears and her hopes.

Inside, laid out with as much reverence and care as a priest might have taken with a devout adherent, D'onne found the desiccated body of a young girl draped in a frilly and flowery – if somewhat charred and torn – silk dress. The nomad had crossed the girl's arms over her tiny chest.

D'onne fought not to cry out. She had looked for this for more years than she could remember. The search had consumed every waking moment not devoted to staying alive in the underhive. And now, at last, here it was.

D'onne removed her gloves and reached out to grab hold of her long-lost sister, whose murder had long ago been covered up and forgotten about. She picked up her sister's small, frail, desiccated body and held it, almost lovingly, before her. She turned the body this way and that, stroking the delicate fabric as she stared into the mummified face. Then, after turning her sister around a couple of times, D'onne tossed her into a dark corner of the room.

'Where is it?' D'onne screamed. Her sister had been carrying something on the night she had been killed. It wasn't on her body or under her dress. Had it flown off on her way down the side of the Spire? Had the nomad not found it, or maybe used it and its contents as a pillow for his bed until it wore out?

D'onne willed her trembling hands to calm down. Her sister's body had been laid to rest with such loving care that she felt certain if the nomad had found it, it would be with the body. She reached back into the locker, grabbed the tiny burlap mattress and tossed it out.

She peered inside the locker with her lamp and there at the bottom was a parcel. Breathless, she tore it open. Inside was a large vellum envelope sealed with wax. The insignia on the seal didn't belong to any Spire noble family or any of the houses of Hive City. In fact, D'onne had only seen the sigil once before – on the night her sister stole the envelope off their father's desk, less than half an hour before she had plummeted to her death.

The envelope was the reason D'onne had witnessed the murder. She had followed her sister to see what the envelope might be. Now, decades later, she finally had it in her hands. The letter was addressed to her father and bore the stamp of customs certification.

Whatever it was, it had arrived from off-world, and the knowledge of its existence had cost her sister her life. That much alone made it valuable to D'onne. She had no doubts at all that the contents of the envelope would, at the very least, throw House Ulanti into chaos – if not the entire Spire. And that had been and always would be Mad D'onne's main goal in life.

The arid Ash Wastes air had dried out the wax seal, and it crumbled away as D'onne opened the envelope. Her hands trembling from excitement, she pulled out a sheaf of vellum papers and unfolded them, breathing deeply to calm her nerves. The papers contained a coded report to her father from one of his spies.

Fury threatened to overwhelm D'onne as she realised she couldn't decipher it. It was an old code, or at least one she hadn't been trained in. Her hands tightened, bending paper, when she noticed a word that reoccurred. One that wasn't gibberish. A name.

Aranthus.

The fury D'onne felt waned, fading beneath a tide of relief. This was not the end. This was a trail, one that she would follow until Hive Primus was a smoking ruin, and only she was left standing.

ABOUT THE AUTHOR

Will McDermott is a fantasy and science fiction writer who has written three Necromunda novels for Black Library featuring the bounty hunter Kal Jerico: *Cardinal Crimson*, *Lasgun Wedding* and *Blood Royal*, co-written with Gordon Rennie. He lives and works in Bothell, Washington with his family.

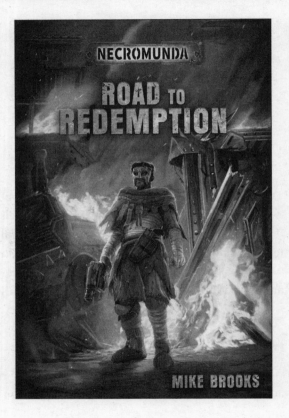

ROAD TO REDEMPTION
by Mike Brooks

Zeke of House Cawdor is on a crusade of vengeance. His entire world has been burned down, and he'll stop at nothing to find those responsible – even if it means facing his own troubled past.